JACKIE WARREN TATUM

UNSPEAKABLE
THINGS *a novel*

JACKIE WARREN TATUM

UNSPEAKABLE THINGS *a novel*

Mill City Press, Minneapolis, MN

Mill City Press, Inc.
2301 Lucien Way #415
Maitland, FL 32751
407.339.4217
www.millcitypublishing.com

ISBN-13: 978-1-63505-359-3
LCCN: 2016915532

Author Photograph Back Cover by James Patterson

Printed in the United States of America

To the memory of

James Luther Warren Jr.
"Jimmy"
(July 28, 1939–August 14, 1967)

A faithful and devoted husband,
and loving Father to our sons,
Jim and Walt

Thank you, family and friends,
for your encouragement and guidance in support of
Unspeakable Things: A Novel.

PART ONE

*Throbbing, Neon-Sign,
Soap-Opera
Passion*

1.

INTENSIVE CARE UNIT

Samone would not return. My life had left me.
And Grandmother Tracy, who was over there, comatose, on life support, behind those swinging doors—she would be leaving, too.

The aloneness hit me all at once, zipping off my lungs. I could not breathe. I will die if I cannot breathe; I cannot die and leave Janie alone, I scolded myself. So, I closed the *Cosmopolitan* and twisted around in my seat in the intensive care unit waiting area, trying to get a full, deep, satisfying breath. It would not come. Frantic, the impulse to run side winded me. I had to get some air.

A person not breathing will die, Renee, I warned myself silently. So, run. Run. Get out of here. It is the only way to stay alive. You must run and get some air. You must stay alive.

Then, the stupidity of running *out* of a hospital to save myself from dying hit me. Ashamed and afraid, I stood, gasping for breath. But I could not break through. I stretched my chest up and out. Only shallow, fake breaths came. I bent over and grabbed my knees.

A fortysomething woman across from me, wearing a royal blue knit sheath and big gold bracelets, reached out a perfectly manicured hand and touched my arm. She asked, "You okay?"

I nodded, "Yes. I'm just nervous. Thank you." I sat down. That was it. I was just nervous. Renee, you are just having another panic attack; you are not dying; try to think about something else, I argued with myself.

The woman in blue walked to the water cooler, drew a cone shaped cup of water, brought it back, and handed it to me.

"Thank you," I said. As I swallowed a sip, praying I could stay alive, a tight-muscled redhead, about my age—in his early thirties—entered the room, scanned it, and sauntered directly over to me in the corner, despite vacant seats all around. He flipped back a stray lock of red hair from his left eye.

I didn't want anybody near me, not while I was fighting for my life, so I did not look at him. But he paid no attention to my not noticing him.

"May I sit there?" he asked, pointing to the seat to my left.

"Sure, fine," I replied, not making eye contact. I had something important going on here. I did not need to be interrupted in the middle of trying to stay alive.

The redhead positioned himself in the chair to my left, bringing with him a clean scent of Ivory soap.

I stretched again, trying to suck enough air deep inside me, but it stopped up in the top of my chest. I felt dizzy.

Then the redhead said, "Excuse me," and pointed to a *Sports Illustrated* on the table to my right. "Would you please hand me that magazine there on top?"

I did, annoyed at being distracted from trying to breathe.

However, he appeared to be insistent upon continuing the distraction: he reached the most beautiful forearms I'd ever seen in my life across me to take the *Sports Illustrated*; his forearms were covered in soft red fuzz. I don't know what helped me forget about dying, his forearms or his whole body, for he was in such good shape. It could have been my concentration on that scent of Ivory soap or all of it together. Whatever it was, I became distracted. I forgot to think about needing air. So, as if on cue, a full stream of life-giving breath flowed deep down inside me, spreading out, freeing me.

I wanted to stand up and shout: "I am not dying!" Of course, that was not what I did. Instead, for some unexplainable reason, my nostrils that had zeroed in on the scent of the Ivory soap enticed me to stretch out just a wee bit over the left arm of my chair to get a stronger whiff of him. All the while I was wondering why Janie never smelled like that when I bathed her in Ivory soap.

Suddenly, I realized what I was doing, so I sat back quickly. A nice woman just doesn't do that sort of thing—sniff a six-foot stranger like a starved stray puppy would sniff a juicy bone—in an intensive care unit waiting area.

Regardless, right in the moment that I retreated, the redhead flipped back that stray lock of red hair again and the red fuzz on his forearms swayed, fanning the faint odor of the Ivory soap around. He had come in here and invaded the place. I couldn't have concentrated on the *Cosmopolitan* in my lap if I'd been told a hundred-dollar bill was tucked somewhere inside it. He flipped that lock of hair. I shifted in my chair to better smell him. He flipped. I shifted.

I dropped my *Cosmopolitan* on the floor between his right leg and my left leg and bent over to pick it up, accidentally brushing his right leg as I rose. That part—the leg brushing—was an accident, pure and simple. But it was just not like me to deliberately drop a magazine; I still can't understand that at all. I guess I was just flustered. So I placed the *Cosmopolitan* squarely on my lap with some ado, patting it down as though it were a very important document.

He noticed. I saw him notice.

I opened the *Cosmo* and focused on it, to ignore him and his noticing, which should certainly have been doable, my having only uttered two words in my entire life to this nameless person, nonexistent until a few minutes ago. But as I concentrated on not thinking about him, I was actually thinking about him harder.

The stranger reset his legs further apart, deliberately—I'm quite sure it was deliberate—and looked over at me. "Gotta read my *Sports Illustrated*, keep up with the latest goin' on. You know how that is," he said, tilting his head toward me as if we were old friends, his chin down, his right ear waiting on my response.

I just sat there, speechless, like an excited ticket holder who'd won she-didn't-know-what and couldn't speak up after hearing her winning ticket announced.

The redhead cleared his throat, like it was a big deal. He appeared to be focusing intently on the *Sports Illustrated*, though he batted his eyelids fast and kept glancing over.

I noticed that the magazine issue was over a year old, but mostly I noticed how the thin red fuzz on his arms fluttered ever so slightly when he turned the pages.

He looked over at me again, smiled, and said, "I hate these places."

I looked halfway up. "Me, too," I said.

"Got a family member in here?"

I didn't respond. He repeated the question.

"Oh, you're talkin' to me?" I pled innocent, barely looking up, embarrassed.

He turned his head toward me and said, "Yeah." Then he chuckled.

"I do," I said, realizing immediately that those words, "I do," suggested a realm of relationship that imposed discomfort. Quickly, I added, "Yes, I do have a family member in here." There, there, now.

He chuckled again.

Oh my God, he's laughing at me. Here we are in this serious place where death may be happening this very minute right behind those swinging doors, and he's reading my mind about my wanting to touch the fuzz on his arms, and he is chuckling about it.

I felt giddy and totally confused, a very likable combination. However, I had not a clue as to what I liked about it any more than an illiterate, uneducated person would know what she liked about Newton's laws of attraction.

I wanted to grab my handbag and run. I chose, however, to sit very still and try to enjoy the wardrobes of the disheveled women in *Cosmo*.

He continued, as if I'd suggested he explain. "I'm here with my aunt. She's only in her forties, not that much older than me. She's had a stroke. Doesn't look too good for her. She's been here for weeks. She's my favorite person in the whole world." His voice was smooth, his mouth alive with saliva when he spoke.

"I'm sorry about your aunt," I said. "My grandmother has had a stroke, too."

He grinned a satisfied grin and dropped his head in success. He lifted his eyebrows knowingly and began twisting a tidbit of fuzz on his right blue jean leg.

Almost as an afterthought, I said, "I hope your aunt improves."

"Your grandmother, also. She has a beautiful granddaughter."

"Thank you," I said. My neck flushed red. Suddenly, I became very uncomfortable with this intimacy with a man who had just shown up with those arms in a freshly pressed short sleeve shirt. And sat next to me. And began ice-picking the wall around me . . . that Samone built . . . when he did what he did . . . Samone, my husband.

6

He was gone now. I never even got to try to argue Samone out of going. Of course, I didn't know that was what he was thinking about, but even if I had known, I don't think that arguing would have made any difference. Once Samone made up his mind, it was made up. He was a kind soul in hiking boots who said very little and always meant what he said, but he left so much silence between his words that the air could get very empty, and if a person weren't careful, she could get lost in the emptiness and think everything better was somewhere else, which happened to me with Samone.

I used to stand there, sometimes, chopping onions for soup, crying from the fumes, imagining that cheerful, interesting people somewhere were gathering in some place having fun, and I wasn't there with them and I wanted to be. Those imaginary people, to my way of thinking, didn't chop onions or have any worries. But I certainly did.

I wish I had a nickel for every time I used to say to him, "Samone, you never say that you love me anymore."

His face would drop. He'd look helpless, and say, "Renee, you know I love you; surely I don't have to say 'I love you' every day for you to know it."

I'd think, You just don't get it, Samone: I'm listening for words about you loving me, and when they don't come I feel outside us, not included with you. Separate. Alone.

It just seemed to me that my and Samone's love oughta be a throbbing, neon-sign, soap-opera passion. But it wasn't. Though, I must be honest, being broke for a long time and trying to pay bills might have messed up my and Samone's chances for throbbing, neon-sign, soap-opera passion. And got us into fighting. It is real hard to fight a person into throbbing, neon-sign, soap-opera passion.

One day, after one of our "you never tell me you love me anymore" spats, Samone, who'd been pruning lantana in a flowerbed at the end of the house, kicked and accidentally hit the rock edge around the flowerbed. I know it must have hurt him badly, but when he cursed, it was more at me than the foot. "Goddamn it, Renee. Goddamn it!" he shouted.

Plus, I guess the reason I have remembered this is that Samone hardly ever shouted. And he sure didn't curse. And he sure didn't curse at me.

Then he just stood straight up, like a man suddenly rising to his feet in a boat in the middle of a wide lake, shaking his head at the misfortune of having dropped the most important piece of the broken-down boat motor into the water, which left him, therefore, stranded, alone, without any hope of ever getting back to shore. He didn't speak to me for the rest of the day. Which wasn't really too different.

I reasoned that I was the one who should be mad, not Samone, because he just wasn't catching on to needing to make me feel loved. I had to admit, though, that he was not like my daddy, who could rage at the drop of a hat and was actually called to his face the best curser on Green Mountain. I think some of Daddy's cursing might have been because of Mother. Once I heard a person say Mother could manipulate a screw out of a hole without a screwdriver, which sounded like a compliment when I first heard it. As I grew up, I wondered exactly what it meant. She always could get her way. Still does. But I've gotten off track. Back to Samone, the real story.

That day that he cursed and kicked the brick edging around the lantana, after he got over his pouting he walked into the bedroom where I was changing clothes. I didn't feel him come up behind me until he encircled my bare midriff with his arms. He said, "I try to be good to you, Renee."

I admit it startled me, both his arms around my midriff and his words. I said, "Samone, lots of times I just don't feel like you love me."

He pulled his hands from my waist, lifted them like he was about to pray, and buried his head into them, pondering something deep. He didn't speak another word.

I figured that he was coming to terms with what he needed to do to make me happy. So I just left him alone.

*****

But, in this intensive care unit waiting area, Samone's memory scaled those old walls of silence and inattention, pushing back against the redhead with the *Sports Illustrated*, while I held on for dear life to the *Cosmopolitan*. Then, to make everything even crazier, the memory of Samone's voice spoke in my heart with the words he used to say when

Janie was a toddler and I'd get cabin fever: "Why don't you get out of the house this afternoon, Renee; do something for yourself."

One afternoon I looked up from washing dishes in the kitchen sink and said back to him, "But I thought you were going fishing, Samone."

And he smiled at me with a sweetness that to this day I can still taste in my mouth and said, "I will, tomorrow. They're not biting today anyway. I'd bet my life on it."

His smile. I remember his smile. And how I said back, "Okay, let me go get dressed."

So I went to get out of my house clothes and put on some clean slacks, and when I came back into the living room to pick up the keys, he said, "Enjoy yourself, Renee; Janie and I'll go down to the duck pond and play for an hour or so. If you go to the mall, window shop *only*, now!"

I laughed.

He grinned, winked, reached over and mussed up my long blonde curls, rough but gentle, kissed me hard on the mouth, and walked out with Janie in his arms, a domesticated John Wayne who couldn't remember not to let the screen door bang shut. Over its noise, he said, "Be careful."

*****

If I hadn't known better, I would've said Samone was jealous of the stranger next to me, but that couldn't have been it, because I didn't even know the stranger—we'd barely spoken. And, anyway, Samone was never jealous a day in his life, which always annoyed me, to no end.

2.

MAGAZINE MAN

Silver kept the pornography under his bed. Magazines mostly. Lots of old ones with key pages. He'd flip back a stray lock of red hair from over his left eye and turn down the corners of the pages he liked, to get to them easily. Which he did, often. They were a kind of stress reliever for him. Simple. Nothing more. Sensible. Nobody got hurt. He liked it.

But the girl with the blonde hair on page twenty-eight in the publication with the woman on the front wearing leather ignited his imagination past the moment and the page. He dreamed about her at night while he slept. The dream always went the same. He watched her from afar, trying to get to her, struggling, almost touching her and then falling short of making his skin touch hers, which made him yell and rave in the dream and chase her as her hair flowed behind her, and she turned while running swiftly like a fawn and smiled a seductive smile at him that caused him an erection fiercer than he'd ever known, that lured him toward the edge of the cliff where he caught her.

She'd turn—always counterclockwise—and point a handgun at him, scraping his face with the cold steel of it. He'd stand perfectly still, and then, just when she thought she had him under her control and he'd actually fallen to his knees groveling before her, she'd lay the gun aside and he'd rise, circling her neck with his hands. She'd smile up at him despite his deadly grasp and flick her eyes at him like lightning, and he'd press tighter—he had to; it was the only way—tighter and tighter, until she'd go limp and fall with a thud onto the deep, thick grass that was rhythmically waving at him. He'd roll her over and enter her body, still unable to feel if she were alive, praying she was still breathing, rushing toward climax, in hopes she was, for it was, after all, the life in her that intoxicated him so. As he came in wretched wave after wretched wave, he'd lose his footing, and the two of them, limp doll and he, would fall over the cliff; he'd scream in delight, aroused again, no less from the fall, still inside her, but she'd move off and he'd be unable to catch her now, the free fall overtaking them, both bodies swirling helplessly toward the nothingness of a bottomless ravine.

He'd wake, sweating, afraid but aroused, pull the magazine out, and live the scenes in his mind and his body again, from start to finish. Then, exhausted, he'd fall over, alone, spent, damaged, unsettled. He'd go naked and wet to the bathroom. There in the mirror was a man he did not know.

3.

FOUND

Samone and I grew up together, but he insisted that we "met" in the eighth grade on the school bus the day he pulled his and Charlie's bullfrog from the red shoebox and dropped it into my book bag.

"The reason I did it, Renee," he pled when he retold the episode, "was because your lips looked so plump. I needed to get your attention."

Nothing about that explanation ever made any sense to me, but he certainly succeeded in getting attention. Clem, the bullfrog, leapt up and out and over the school bus seat into Rowena's blouse.

She screamed, "Help! Something's attacking me! Help!" Out of her seat she came; up and down the bus aisle she ran, slapping at her breasts—which were already an important topic of conversation for the boys. As Clem plopped around inside her blouse, Rowena began unbuttoning it. With each unbuttoning of a button, more boys popped up out of their seats to gawk.

Not a soul was trying to help her, so I chased her down and reached in and grabbed the nasty bullfrog. Rowena collapsed in the aisle. Some of the girls lifted her up off the floor of the bus. I teeter-tottered down the swaying bus aisle back to Samone, and I slapped that bullfrog into his hands and said, "You rascal! Planting this stinky thing in Rowena's blouse to show her breasts to your friends. You'd better stay away from me and stay away from my friends. And I mean it!"

Samone grinned up at me. It was the wrong thing to do.

Over the years, when he retold the BUStcapade, he'd smile and blush and admit, "The whole thing made you so mad, Renee, that if you'd had something to hit me with, you'd have beaten me to death. It would actually have been worth it, for the BUStcapade turned me, the awkward book nerd, into the eighth grade hero. After Clem and the BUStcapade, the same boys who had ridiculed and excluded me now sauntered up, slapped me on the back, and grunted with admiration, 'How's it going, Boobs Samone? You're the frog guy, you know. Mr. B.S.' I'd just stand there, happily befuddled. But, mostly, Renee, the BUStcapade revealed to me that you were more than plump lips. I wanted to know you. I couldn't forget you.

So even though I did not plan the BUStcapade, your calling me a rascal in front of our schoolmates and accusing me of planning it triggered an 'aha': if you thought I had any 'rascal' in me and the pluck to plan such a thing, maybe I was more than I had ever realized. You changed my life that day, Renee. You changed how I saw myself. When a woman does that, she's unforgettable."

And, Samone insisted that the frog brought us together. He would sometimes get a faraway look in his eyes and reminisce, "Charlie spied that ugly frog, Renee, the day before the BUStcapade. It hopped right up into his hands; Charlie cuddled it and whispered to me, so as not to scare the frog, 'Sam, a premedicated universe has done sent us this frog for something important.'"

Of course, Charlie misused words; he did that all the time in school, trying to sound smart. But Charlie called Samone "Sam" with a good explanation: "Samone sounds too much like 'someone' to me; you are not 'someone,' Sam. We are blood brothers; done took the Indian pact in the third grade."

So, names being important to Charlie, he insisted they name the frog Clem. "We have to name this beauty Clem. After all, Sam, our favorite story is Huck Finn. So there it is."

"There what is, Charlie?" Samone asked him.

"The reason we have to name him Clem, Sam. Everybody knows that Samuel Clemens falsified his real name to Mark Twain to write about Huck Finn without getting caught. So, if we name our bullfrog Clem, it will honor Samuel Clemens: you, Sam, and Clem, together, are Mark Twain's real name, Samuel Clemens. Course, you ain't quite Samuel and Clem ain't quite Clemens, but it's close."

"Okay, works for me, Charlie," Samone agreed, shaking his head, reasoning it was just the way Charlie thought, being an artist and all.

Though Charlie resisted being an artist through years of unsuccessful studies of various other college subjects until, as he put it, "My parents felt pressured to stop paying my tuition." After the money ran out, Charlie finally accepted his life as an artist with the enthusiasm of a person with no loaf bread in the house who has to make a sandwich on crackers. He told Samone, "I was just left with it."

Over the years, I always believed that I understood what Charlie meant by being "just left with it," but I didn't, not until after Samone did what he did and I felt I, myself, had been "just left with it."

Oh, I know I am not innocent. I should have seen the signs. I should have stopped us back there. I don't know where. And I don't know what it was that I should have stopped. But I should have. For somewhere during our twelve years of marriage, Samone and I had lost our way, ended up on totally different buses. The spark died. Maybe we killed it. We tried to rekindle it. But, whenever we tried, we trampled on each other, like we were clumsy blind. So we just quit trying. We lived in the same house, separately. I cut him off. I guess Samone could not face our not being us. I guess he just gave up.

*****

I didn't want to remember the Samone who gave up back there.

I wanted to remember the Samone I "met" years after the BUStcapade, the night after the pep rally, when he parked his daddy's car in front of my house. As soon as the car stopped, I reached for the door latch. He laid his right hand on my left arm and said with kindness, "Hold up."

"What da'ya need, Samone?" I asked, turning toward him.

He leaned over me and placed his left hand on my right one. Firmly. I still felt that hand on me, though Samone was nowhere near the emergency room waiting area, except in my heart.

"I need to tell you something," Samone said to me, seriousness all over his face.

"Okay, what?" I asked.

"The homecoming game is next week," he said, as if he were telling me a secret.

15

Annoyed, I said, "I know; that's not news." And then I tried, again, to reach for the latch, but Samone held my hands. He held me in his gaze, too, light streaming in on us from the streetlamp, spreading a mellow ancientness over us.

"Well, in a way it is news, Renee," he said.

"What'ya mean it's news?" I asked, raising my voice an octave. Why did I raise my voice with Samone? How uncalled for.

"I've been thinking, Renee," Samone spoke, seemingly trying to convince himself. Then he abruptly stopped talking, took back his left hand, settled back into the driver's seat, placed his elbow on the steering wheel—his head in his hands—and sat there.

I swallowed so loudly that we both probably heard my swallowing.

Finally, he spoke again. "Charlie tells me I should take Sharon to the homecoming dance." Samone's embarrassment clung to every syllable.

Good Lord, I thought, that tramp: every guy in school has had his way with her. Why is he telling me that? I said with disgust, "Well, go for it." And then I reached back over for the door latch.

He turned again and placed his big wide palm over my right hand and gently squeezed it. He lowered his voice almost to a whisper to assure I heard him and said, "No, don't think so, Renee, Charlie's crazy."

This was the strangest conversation I'd ever had with Samone in all our years of growing up together.

I said, "Charlie's crazy all right, Samone, but I didn't think he was that crazy!"

"He's not as crazy as I am blind," Samone said. He sat back, and sighed deeply.

My heart raced. I was afraid. "Blind? What are you talking about?" I asked, seeming then not to know what to do with my own arms and hands.

Instead of answering with words, he moved his face directly in front of mine, as if he'd planned this, even down to how softly he touched my face, and in the blink of an eye he changed everything about us right there in his daddy's old car parked in front of my house with the television playing loud enough inside for me to hear the ten p.m. news out of the raised windows across the front porch. I froze and held my breath. And then he did something that I had not expected: he kissed me, slowly exploring everything about my heart. I tasted him and kissed back. He opened his lips, tenderly taking mine in so gently that I wanted to cry, though crying was never something I did very much. Suddenly, like daybreak, he slipped the sweet strength of his tongue into my mouth and I recognized him. We began breathing very fast. But he just pulled away and looked into my eyes. I let him look. We shuffled around in the front seat and straightened up. He sat there, silent, like he was thinking how to say what he had to say.

"The dance," he said, clearing his throat. "Will you go with me this year . . . as my date? I'd really like it if you would."

I did not know how to respond to him. So I looked out the window instead of at him. "As your date?" I sat very still, not wanting to move the air around us and break the spell.

He responded quickly, emphasizing each word on its own: "Yes. As. My. Date."

I remember being confused. "We don't date," I said, like I was reminding us of something important.

He countered, looking directly at me. "I want to date you, Renee."

I had to look back into his face. "What does that mean, Samone?"

He didn't answer. I remember the sound of the leaves falling off the oak tree in the front yard, and Mother yelling to my sister Ashley inside the house, "You need to pick up your clothes." Ashley was a pig and her room was always a pigsty.

I broke the silence. "What about Sharon?" I asked, knowing the minute I did that it sounded silly.

He laughed and I began to giggle, but I wanted to slap him, while at the very same time I wanted to grab his face in my hands and pull him onto me again.

"Sharon who?" he asked, as if I'd just pulled her name out of thin air. He twisted his neck, long like a giraffe's, and preened, feminine like, lowering his eyelids easy over his eyes, waiting for me to respond.

"Darn it, Samone, you're acting crazy now," I said.

He straightened up and got serious. "Please go with me to the dance, Renee." He held his eyes on mine until I answered. "Please" spread out comfortingly around me, taking up every bit of extra space in the front seat.

"I guess so," I said. I smiled at him.

As soon as I said, "I guess so," he breathed out and relaxed and grinned back at me. Then he reached over and pecked me on my forehead like he was putting a period at the end of the sentence.

Suddenly, unexpectedly, I felt afraid that Samone might leave me.

He got out and came around and opened my door and reached in with his hands and took both of mine and lifted me out with an air that everything in the entire world had just been settled. We walked to the front porch and there, amidst Daddy's words to Mother inside, "It's way past everyone's bedtime," I felt Samone smelling my hair and breathing it in, and I choked a bit and stood close in to him and waited on what to do next. I felt found.

It made perfect sense. We tied the knot that summer after we both graduated from high school.

4.

THUMBS & LIES

Yes, Samone found me in the front seat of his daddy's car and took me to the homecoming dance, but, just as unpredictably, he abandoned me. Left me gutted out, emptied.

If you didn't know better, you'd think I was inside my body back there when he did it. But I wasn't. I was nowhere, in no place, out in the wilderness, splayed out, helpless, disconnected, numb, unable to feel. Lost. I would not accept it, what Samone did, though. Any of it. Give me one good reason why I should have accepted it. What good would it have done? I couldn't even get my brain to want to think about it.

Some afternoons at six, even though he was gone, I would hear Samone's car pull up into the garage and hear him slam the car door and call my name. Almost always when this happened, I would get up from what I was doing—which wasn't much then—and go to the kitchen door and look out the door pane to see if Samone might have come back. He had not.

Just as, in my recollections, I was trying to accept that Samone would never again be in our car in our garage, the redhead invaded my space on the top step of what used to be my and Samone's garage and jolted me back into the reality in the intensive care unit waiting area with his words, "You seem somewhere very far away."

I thought, He's just not going to leave me alone, is he?

"Me?" I said too loudly, turning my torso toward the stranger. He was so close that if I caught on fire he would, too.

"Yeah, you," the redhead said, slinging his words out.

I blushed again. He saw it. He smiled like a man admiring a new car he'd found that he knew he was going to buy.

I thought, He has Native American cheekbones. Do Native Americans have red hair? And teeth that white?

I lied, only partly, and said, "I am thinking about dying—my grandmother—hoping she doesn't." Dying. The hollow meanness of that word. Dear God, how the noise of it hurt.

At that moment, a very wide nurse walked into the waiting room. She stood sentry to the right of the double doors, her hands crossed primly in front of her stomach. I swear there was not a wrinkle anywhere on her clothes. She bossed in staccato, like we were little kids: "Visiting time. You have fifteen minutes. One person at a time. Don't carry any items in with you."

I stood up. The redhead rose, too, turning toward me. He snatched my right hand in an awkward handshake, like a kid stealthily grabbing a piece of candy from a candy bowl, trying not to be caught. He held on to me and tucked his thumb between our hands. It flicked my palm. I jumped. I could feel his hand feeling mine, now, his thumb navigating, rolling around like a marble over my palm. Was that on purpose? Yes, it was on purpose. I couldn't be imagining that.

He threw back his shoulders and said, "I'm Silver."

I quivered and tripped over my own words as I said, "Silver." Even as I spoke his name, my mind raced around trying to clear this matter up, all of it: I had walked in this place, innocent, alone, abandoned. For all intents and purposes, I was dead inside. Dead. Dead. First, this Silver person flagged me down with unacceptably gorgeous forearms and red arm fuzz. Then he talked to me, while I very well was trying to read my Cosmopolitan and keep my mind on my grandmother, who was dying, for God's sake. Now, without any okay whatsoever, he had just reached out and touched me with a thumb. A thumb? Something wasn't right about that. But earthquakes above 8.0 on the Richter scale don't move things around as much as his thumb did.

Suddenly, I felt light-headed. I raised my left hand to my brow, reflex like, and wiped it, speaking words strung out on their own out of my reach: "Glad to meet you, Silver."

But we didn't look directly at each other. I really couldn't risk seeing him up close. It would have been too bold.

After a time, he moved back and took his thumb from my hand, though my hand stayed stretched out toward him. He turned and walked away and looked back over his shoulder and said, "Very nice to meet you, too; I hope I'll see you again." And then he stumbled, like he'd lost his footing. But he caught it. He walked right on out of the room.

"Yes, you, too," I said, flabbergasted. I didn't even know if he heard me. I realized something startling: I was wet between my legs. I thought, My God, I am actually still alive!

I left Grandmother Tracy's cubicle exactly fifteen minutes later, for which the wide nurse couldn't have been happier, I'm sure. But she didn't smile. To cut her some slack, though, I'd guess that she'd not ever practiced smiling all that much. She frowned and said, "Good-bye, dear," as if she were perfunctorily dismissing me from a classroom.

When I walked back through the waiting room, the redhead was nowhere to be seen. I felt relieved. And disappointed. And afraid of not being afraid of the rolling around of the redhead's thumb waking life in me. For, unbeknownst to me, after Samone left, I closed the curtain on living and light, even that in Janie's eyes some days. I couldn't stand seeing what was in the light; the dark was safer. So I began living in the dark, obsessed with whether or not Samone had known that I had loved him.

The question actually moved in with me and began sleeping in Samone's place in our bed. I thought about it day and night. I wandered across days and meals and people, seeking the answer to the question, stumbling around, drunken with the need to know. I badgered the universe: "Samone, did you really know that I loved you?" I would say, out loud sometimes, over and over, again and again, with not another soul around. "If only I could know that you knew that I loved you, I could live with this," I would scream.

It was all a lie, of course, though, a bald-faced lie. Nothing could ever help me live with this. Nothing. Nothing could help me feel acquitted. Acquitted? Isn't that what a criminal seeks? Acquittal. Had I committed a crime? Yes. A crime of not loving him. But maybe I wasn't guilty. Maybe. But how could I prove that I loved him? I couldn't prove it. I couldn't make sure the facts would bear out that I had loved him. They didn't. They flew in the face of it. But I tried. Oh, how I tried. I sat for hours rummaging around in every single detail I could uncover from our life that would prove it. Anything.

Then, I would pray, "God, give me a judge who can understand." But when I saw God staring at me with that look on His face, I would argue with God and call God names. And I would say, "You damned me, God, you knew you were damning me." Then I would know for sure that I was going to hell. But sometimes I would get the crazy notion that there could not be any hell anyplace that could surpass the hell of the place I was in. So I would announce it out loud, raise my arms up into the air, wide, and scream, "Goddamn it, God, I'm in hell. Where in the hell else could you send me any worse that this fuckin' place?"

Then, having attacked God and knowing for sure that I was now doomed, I would feel as desolate as a baby abandoned by her mother, lying in a trash bin alongside the stinkiness of everything not wanted, and I would, in my helplessness, quickly, frantically repent and say, "Please, God, please! Get me out of this hell. Damn it, now. Please. Please."

And I would be back in the front seat of his daddy's car with the word "Please," begging God to let my then tenderness count for something. "God, please go back there and look at it and hold it up to the light and let it mean something. Let Samone know that it meant something. Let him see my heart smiling at him."

And I would sit and sob. Alone. Sobbing is a one-person act.

And sometimes I'd say, "Dear Lord in heaven, how it hurts to remember. I simply can't. And it is my only way out." Then I would realize: I am never going to get out; I cannot bear the pain of it, getting anywhere close to the smells, the tastes, the touches, the laughter. So my remembering would turn into rote recollections of day after day, in black and white, distant, akin to an austere kneading of dough, churning of butter, cutting out of biscuits, hanging clothes on a line. I could never smell the sunshine and fresh air of it.

I began to believe I was tricking myself into not remembering in order to save myself from being split down the middle, which is cowardly, isn't it, cowardly, cowardly, to turn my back on the sunshine and the fresh air and the breeze and the sound of birds chirping back there. They were, you know—they were back there. I swear to God they were back there—they had to be.

Then, having closed the shutters to the fresh air and sunshine, I would cry and hear my heart flailing me, saying, "Renee, you were not a good wife. You could have made a million biscuits for Samone and buttered them and spread homemade jam on them from side to side and fed him by hand yourself, breaking the jammed biscuits into bite-sized pieces for his ease of chewing, but it simply wouldn't have made up for your refusing to smell the sunshine and fresh air 'back there' when you were actually with Samone. That was the crime."

No wonder God punished me. I stole life. I stole Samone's life.

Then a stray memory would drop into my mind, like a tiny thread that falls from a skirt hem onto the floor, alone, singular, and I would re-remember Samone in his workshop at the back of the garage, sitting on his red stool, bending over, sanding a piece of wood he'd found on a hunting trip, lifting its grain up and out and leaving its ego on the floor in tiny piles of sawdust.

It hurt so much to hear the loudness of the tap of the string in my mind and the crash of the sawdust falling rhythmically over it to make a mountain of memories best kept in the garage.

There, for a minute, I thought I caught a glimpse of Samone's back or the side of his face. Was it? No. No. No. No.

His back and the side of his face are gone.

5.

THE PREY

I stepped out of the hospital air conditioning and into the smothering heat. Thank goodness I'd parked my car along the street at the edge of the parking lot under a fat old pecan tree spreading shade every which way.

I sat down in the car. I sighed and inserted the key in the lock, thinking about Samone's back and how he had fooled me. Tears welled in my eyes and rolled down my cheeks, mixing with the sweat streaming down my face. I lowered the window on the driver's side. The tears stopped, fickle like Samone. They tricked me into thinking they were there, and then they fled about the time I could find the courage to even think about dealing with them.

I reached for a tissue to dry my face. "Darn it, I left the box in the back seat," I mumbled, twisting around to find it. There, standing on the passenger side of the car, was Silver. He'd squatted down to lower his six feet, and his face was eye level in the window.

I felt like a small bird sitting at the water's edge trying to quench her thirst that turns and sees the eyes of a large hawk aground peering at her.

"Hello," I said weakly, plopping the box of Kleenex on the floorboard under my legs.

Silver grinned a knowing grin, alive with expectancy.

I didn't move.

He motioned with his right hand for me to lower the right window.

My mind said, Renee, wave good-bye to this fellow and back the hell up and get out of here. But my dead body had liked the feeling of aliveness from his thumb rolling around in my hand, the titillation of it. The liking the feeling ruled. I rolled down the window.

He stuck his head inside it and said, "Hi, I told you my name. What's yours?"

I could smell the clean scent of him and I wondered how he'd kept clean in this heat. "Renee," I said, breathing out deep and hard with the word as if it were, in and of itself, a significant disclosure.

"Renee who?" Silver asked as he leaned back out of the window and squatted again, confident.

"Renee Sims."

He smiled as if he'd heard the words he wanted to hear. Then he said, "Can I sit down with you for a minute?"

"In this heat?" I asked.

Quickly, Silver said, "You're right. What about we go get a bite of lunch? In air conditioning? I'll treat." His face opened and he waited.

"Well, I dunno," I said.

He chuckled, an I-ought-to-just-give-up-cause-I-don't-need-this chuckle, but his eyes were steadfast. He asked, "Don't you eat?"

I replied, "Of course I eat. I just don't know. I don't know you."

"You already do know me, Renee Sims, you just don't know it," he said.

That didn't make any sense to me. I was hot and tired and disgusted, and I didn't want to banter back and forth with this stranger out here in this parking lot. I said, "I don't know you, that's the point, Silver."

He smiled as quickly as an actor in a movie might smile and said, almost like a child, "Well, how are you going to get to know me, Renee, if we don't talk?"

I bought it, but I begged with myself in front of him. "You don't understand," I said.

"It's you who doesn't understand, Renee. I want to get to know you better. You are an interesting woman," he said, like a man who was asking to be reintroduced to someone he wished that he'd met earlier and was desperate to know more about.

"Well, okay, but where would we go? There's not anyplace around here to eat," I said, thinking I was changing the subject. I placed my hands on the steering wheel and sat there.

"Tulley's," he replied, and, without an invitation, he opened the door and crawled into the front passenger seat before I could change my mind. The Ivory soap scent came in with him.

A red flag began flapping around inside my gut. I tried to heed it. I said, "I don't know this Tulley's. Tell me where to go. You take your car; I'll meet you there."

Possession is nine-tenths of the advantage. He knew it. He didn't move a peg. He said, "Well, we are already in the car together, Renee. It's just a couple of blocks over, pizza that will knock your socks off." He slowly brushed my right arm with his left forearm, akin to how his thumb had explored my palm. I felt it. He knew I felt it. He sat back in the passenger seat and inserted both his hands between his legs to caress his own thighs. I gasped. He sat there in silence, waiting on me to speak. I believe he would have waited until dawn.

After a time, I whispered, like it was a secret, "Tulley's. Okay. Tulley's."

A satisfied glow spread across his face. He sat up very straight and looked over at me and asked, "Are you married?"

"Married?" My God, I thought, would he just take off to Tulley's in broad daylight with a married woman?

"Yes, Renee, are you married?" He repeated his question like a detective who was interviewing me to work a case.

"No, not really," I replied, patting the steering wheel as if doing so were part of the answer.

"I don't think I've ever heard it put that way," he grimaced, pulling his hands out from between his legs and holding them both out in front of his chest, seemingly absorbed in looking at them, turning them palms down and then palms back up, several times. After a moment, he reached over and turned the key in the ignition and started the car. He brushed back that stray red wisp of hair with his left hand, rolled the passenger window up with his right, and settled back like he'd won the first round of a chess tournament.

"Are you?" I asked, as I reached to turn up the AC.

He looked at me quizzically and asked, "Am I what?"

"Married," I shot back, thinking, You know exactly what I am asking.

"Hell no!" he said. If he'd had a guitar, it would have sounded like he was singing a song.

My questioning him didn't please him. He retreated into silence. I began driving us toward the parking lot exit. He turned his attention to the radio and found a contemporary station. A love song was playing about trying to love someone. Silver began singing along. Suddenly, loneliness burst through my angst. A tear fell out of my right eye onto my cheek.

Silver must have noticed the tear. He stopped singing and turned toward me. "You have the most beautiful blonde hair I have ever seen." He could have been saying it to cheer me up, but he sounded as if he meant it.

Regardless, I blushed.

"Do you mind if I touch it?" he asked with the urgency of an alcoholic asking for a drink of whiskey.

The weight of his question seemed enormous. "Not here," I said.

"Later?" he asked.

I let it lie.

I was thinking that this felt like what I thought all those people were doing years ago while I was chopping onions and feeling left out. Parts of my body that had been stuck a long time moved around. As I pulled out into the street, Silver laid his hand on my shoulder. I let him. Then he moved his hand and put it near my neck. He acted like his hand had been there before. His hand was warm. I felt the warmness down inside me.

I thought, I am a nice girl, nothing like Sharon, whom everybody in school did, and here I am picking up a strange man and driving off with him to a restaurant I don't know and letting him touch my neck and getting all warm inside from it. I must be finally going crazy.

6.

COMMAS

Silver asked, "How long have you had this 1960 Chevy, Renee?"

"I dunno. Several years. Samone bought it. I left that kind of stuff to him," I replied, rolling up my window and adjusting the vent on the AC. "Feel free to turn this air on you, Silver, however you want," I said, pushing my hair back out of my eyes. Silver noticed my touching my hair. I noticed him noticing.

"Where is he? Samone?" he asked, settling back into the passenger seat, his hands now in his lap.

I didn't answer. I didn't turn in the direction of Tulley's, either. Neither of us mentioned it. Finally, I said, matter-of-factly, disregarding his question, "I've never just driven off with a total stranger." I twisted the dial to slow the AC fan: the temperature in the car was becoming bearable.

He lowered his voice, as if he were taking me into his confidence, and said, "I'm not a total stranger, Renee." Then he smiled a knowing smile.

I felt uncomfortable with the smile. I don't know why.

He continued, "You know some things about me. I know some things about you. I'd like to know more things about you."

I didn't respond. I was thinking that, truth be told, it didn't matter. Nobody ever knows anybody. I thought I had known Samone. I knew nothing, even after we had been in each other's lives since grade school and had waded through the mundane swamps of marriage together, even after I had labored up hill after hill of anger trying to be his wife. I'd kept my anger from Samone, though. He couldn't have known about it. I never said it in words. But Samone and I didn't use words very often.

Back there when Samone and I were together, I'd sit at the kitchen table paying bills from our dwindling savings account and shortening the grocery list, fantasizing about a world of pizzazz and color and laughter and frivolity, people dancing around in elegant costumes, popping corks, splashing champagne.

Janie would whine, "Mommy, I dropped Sweet Thing behind the sofa."

I'd look up from the bills strewn amongst elegant people popping corks and say, "Wait, Janie, I'll get it for you."

But Samone would yell from the backyard, "Renee, could ya' bring me that lug wrench from my red toolbox? I need it to tighten this outside water faucet."

The champagne would crawl back into the bottle. I would stand in the middle of the room fiddling with the pen. Janie would look up at me and raise her eyebrows and let her arms flop at her sides and pout. I would lay the pen down on the table and it would begin rolling off, as I would say to Samone, "Uh huh, give me just a minute . . ."

Janie would follow me out into the utility room to the red toolbox. I'd scrounge around inside it and yell at Samone, "These wrenches all look alike to me. Is it the one with the big black grip on it?"

"Yeah, that's it; just throw it out to me, Renee, okay?"

The music would fade away. The colors would mute. The people in elegant costumes would depart with a frown on their faces.

But the outside water faucet wouldn't drip anymore.

One day, long after the faucet was repaired, the phone rang. Samone answered it. "How, Mama?" he asked, turning white, reaching for the edge of the chair, then freezing midair, like a paused TV image. He finally plopped into the chair and began running his thumbnail back and forth on the kitchen table. Samone did that when he got nervous or upset.

I was stirring some black-eyed peas that had boiled down too low and needed more water. I stopped stirring. "What is it?" I asked, lifting the long phone cord and moving under it to face him.

"Daddy was in a car wreck a few minutes ago," he whispered to me with his right hand over the receiver. His face was wet.

His daddy died that night.

The Shoppe, his daddy's pride and joy, became Samone's, along with twelve and fifteen hour work days. He slept, sometimes four hours, and got back up and drank coffee and drove back downtown to The Shoppe.

Before The Shoppe, I had only not heard words from him. Now, also, I never saw him. I'd call him on the phone. "Samone, pot roast is on; it smells so good. When are you coming home?"

Offhandedly, without revealing any desire for pot roast or our table or coming home, he'd say, "When I get this inventory worked, Renee. Go ahead and eat; leave me a plate on the stove."

It became clear: The Shoppe and Samone were having a love affair. Even when Samone was home, he and his lover were inseparable. He pored over catalogs and accounts receivable and planned for the new building construction. Samone stopped laughing. We quit talking.

His longest sentence to me in the evenings was, "Renee, could ya' make me some more coffee?"

Yes, oh yes, I was relieved that we could stop living off our almost depleted savings, but a woman gets jealous of a man's love affair with a shop. And jealousy lashed out. "You are trying to find your Daddy in that damn shop," I said before I realized what I was saying.

Samone threw the bottle of shampoo he was carrying to the shower across the room and it shattered on the dresser and dented the wood in the shape of a comma.

"Can't please you, woman. Can't please you," he yelled as he whirled around.

I eventually heard the shower spraying. He must have dropped the soap: he kept saying, "Damn it. Damn it. Damn it."

Later that evening, I went in and inspected the dressing table and ran my index finger through the indentation again and again. Suddenly, like a bolt of lightning, I understood that Janie and I were now living behind the primary message of Samone's life, as its comma. I got the best furniture polish my budget would let me buy and I pressed it into the comma, over and over, and rubbed up a shine on it. I knew where I was. I could go see myself on the wood.

Samone came in late, night after night. He'd shower and tuck himself around me in the bed. Sometimes, he'd reach over and caress my breast. I'd contract, rigid, cold, and think how his cupping around me just pressed home the comma. "It's late, Samone," I'd say.

We'd lie alongside each other in the dark. Silent. Not touching. He was wanting to touch, I think, but afraid to risk another "no." A man can take only so many "no's," you know.

We'd go to sleep slowly, trying not to breathe loudly enough for the other to hear so we wouldn't have to acknowledge each other, so we wouldn't have to talk. We simply didn't know what words to say. Like Hansel and Gretel, deep in a mangled forest, we couldn't find our way back home; something had eaten the breadcrumbs we thought we'd dropped behind us to help find our way.

*****

Silver's voice interrupted the fairy tale. "What you thinking about, Renee?"

I didn't answer him. I was still back there in my mind pondering that comma on the dresser.

After a few minutes, Silver laughed and said, "Girl, you're entirely too sweet to be going back wherever you are going in that pretty little head. I know you well enough, already, to know that." If he'd been the Pied Piper piping a tune he couldn't have piped a better one.

Too, I hadn't heard a man laughing in so long. It held me. "You don't know whether I'm sweet or not," I said, and I laughed.

"You better watch out, Renee, you could catch laughing from me," Silver said.

"Catch laughing from you?" I laughed again. "That's funny!"

He pushed that stray lock of red hair back from over his left eye and said, "Yeah, and, if I have my way, you are gonna catch lots more than laughing."

I just kept driving.

7.

HUNGER

"I haven't laughed like that in a long time," I said, thinking it felt good. "See, I told you you'd catch laughing from me!" Silver preened. "Would I lie to you?" he asked. He placed his left hand, passionless, on my right knee, like it was the most ordinary thing in the world for a stranger to do to a woman driving him down an interstate toward no place in particular. "I like your legs," he said, looking at them as if they were objects he was viewing in a museum, his hand firmly on my right leg, holding me in place, "but you know where my hands need to be?"

"What do you mean where your hands need to be?" I asked.

He was silent.

I thought how Silver's hand on my knee had an ownership clasp.

Like Samone's hand had that night during our trip to his mother's that we took in an April snow—it never snows here in April, but it did.

Samone's mother called and said, "The weatherman said it's a wet snow, that traveling is okay, temps will stay around freezing and warm up tomorrow. Thank God. But please drive carefully."

"We will," Samone said. "Hitting the road in a few minutes. Don't cook supper, Mother; Renee is bringing a picnic basket: garlic stuffed pork loin with apricot jam and sweet potatoes. Chocolate pie, too."

We loaded the food and extra blankets in the car. Janie and I snuggled together in the front seat watching the swish of the windshield wipers swatting the fluffy snowflakes. About thirty minutes into the trip, Samone—the best driver I'd ever known—began wrestling the steering wheel up an icy incline, but the car skidded to the right, out of his control. It stopped about fifty feet from the edge of an embankment.

"Damn, that was close," he said. He held the steering wheel and dropped his head. We both sat there, our hearts racing, no words.

Janie whimpered. "Momma, what's happening?"

I pulled her in on me. "We just had to stop, sweetie. Everything is okay."

I saw it first, something green down in the white mush alongside the ditch we'd barely missed. "What is that, Samone?"

He wiped the moisture off the inside of the windshield with the back of his gloved hand and leaned in to look where I was pointing. "Somebody is stranded, I think, Renee," he said.

A forlorn elderly driver, wearing only a thin jacket, his arms crossed, was shaking with cold and moving around beside the green Ford sedan, occasionally stopping to pat his back and his thighs.

He saw us, lifted his hands to his mouth, and yelled, "I need help!"

Samone got out and tramped through the muddy snow toward the man, waving to him, yelling, "Hey, mister, you okay?"

"I am. My car just skidded off that road like nobody's business. I can't get it back on the highway. When I try, I get stuck worse."

"We'll get you out," Samone said. "Why don't you get inside the car? Try to stay warm; give me a few minutes."

"Sure, thank you, mister. Guess I'd freeze to death out here if you hadn't showed."

Samone said to me, "Sit still, Renee. Don't get out. Leave the car running." He walked back up to the road and waved down a pickup truck approaching the foot of the hill.

He motioned toward the green Ford and shouted, "Hey, can you men stop and help us get this guy out of the ditch?"

The pickup pulled in behind us. Two middle aged, overweight men got out. One blew into his fists to warm them and then rubbed his hands together. "Cold as a witch's teat out here tonight, fellas, in April," he said. Then he noticed Janie and me in the car. "Oh, I'm sorry ma'am; I didn't see you there."

I smiled. He nodded and began talking with Samone. The three of them turned their backs to walk toward the green Ford. Samone patted the back of the man who'd apologized. The other man reached across and shook Samone's hand. They walked together down the hill.

Another car pulled over. Then another. A string of travelers lined the highway to help, the flashing taillights of their cars reddening the side of the road. It took a dozen of them to lift the stranded car as the elderly man behind the steering wheel pressed the accelerator, spinning the car's wheels, splattering brown gunk up and into the air all over the Good Samaritans who dodged and spat, and, together, pushed until the tires gripped gravel and the green Ford zigged and zagged its way up the hill. As it topped the crest, the old man waved back over his shoulder, a smile in the wave.

The Good Samaritans, including Samone, got back into their vehicles.

Samone looked at me and said, "Damn, that man came close to buying the farm."

"Yeah, what if we hadn't seen him? That was a nice thing you did, Samone," I said.

I could see his smile in the low light. "Thank you, Renee," he said.

It occurred to me that the handful of words we'd just exchanged were the most we'd said to each other that was nice in a very long time without our ending up in a misunderstanding.

Samone slid and slipped us to the top of the hill, and we arrived at his mother's late, hugs waiting. She picked Janie up in her arms and hustled us inside. Samone showered to get the mud off, while his mother reheated the food. After supper, we sat in front of the fireplace sipping hot chocolate, his mother rocking Janie, Samone and I on the sofa watching The Rockford Files, one of our favorite shows.

Out of the blue, Samone said, "Rockford always takes chances, Renee."

"Well, yeah, I guess he does, Samone, he's a private detective," I said, thinking it was a strange thing for Samone to have said, but he didn't seem to hear my response or pay any attention to me.

He just continued thinking aloud, seemingly to himself. "He's not afraid to get in close enough to find the truth. I guess that's a trait a man ought to have if he is really a man."

"I guess," I replied, confused, shaking my head at him.

He got a look on his face that I'd seen a lot at that time, like he couldn't understand why I didn't think what he was saying was important.

It hurt my feelings—I don't know why. I turned away from him, ended the conversation, and went to the kitchen. I fumbled around in the fridge looking for a bottled drink. "Anybody else want a cola?" I asked.

"Thanks, sweetheart, I'm fine," his mother said. "Get whatever you want, Renee. There are cookies in the cookie jar, too. Get you both some of those."

Samone snapped, "No cola or cookies for me. I'm ready for bed."

His mother looked at Samone, compassion in her face. She had that way about her. I don't think I ever saw her mad. "You kids sleep in tomorrow, if you can, all day. Janie and I have cartoons to watch," she said.

"You'd let us do that, Mrs. Sims, not get up, stay in bed all day?" I asked, teasing her.

She laughed. "I surely would, dear. Just test me."

I hugged her. "Well, we might ought to take the test," I said, smiling. "Samone hasn't slept past five a.m. for so long, it'd be good for him."

Samone scorched me with his look, whipped around, and plodded down the hallway to the back wing of the house. I traipsed along behind him.

After I bathed, I laid down, turning my back to him. Surprisingly, he tapped me on the shoulder and asked me to turn over facing him. He said, "You smell nice, Renee."

In the softness of the light streaming in from the street lamp outside, akin to the one in my yard that night years ago after the pep rally, I watched Samone's brown eyes, unspoken questions swirling around in them. I softened. But we were different now. I felt afraid of the difference; I didn't understand it. Samone must have felt the fear, too; tears welled up in his eyes and he began to cry, silently. I'd never seen Samone cry except when his daddy died. Ever. I began to cry, too. I couldn't stop.

"What's happened to us, Renee?" he asked.

I did not speak. We lay together; he placed his wide, thick hand on my stomach and held it there, firmly, without passion, as if he were holding his place. It was a primordial ownership clasp. There was no sensuousness in the hold.

He coughed. I did not move.

We fell asleep with Samone's hand clasping my stomach.

*****

That's how Silver's hand was on my leg, like Samone's was on my stomach that night, in an ownership clasp, without passion.

I didn't understand that at all. That Silver person had no place in my life. I didn't even know his last name.

I broke the silence with Silver, repeating my question, "What do you mean where your hands need to be?"

"They need to be around your neck," he said matter-of-factly, looking far off out the passenger window, not at me.

"My neck?" I asked, shifting around so I could get a better view of the redhead.

He was still looking away from me out the window, a man, now, that I could never catch laughing from.

He turned a cold blank faced toward me and said, "Yes, you're too stressed. You need a neck rub."

"A neck rub? I've never had a neck rub in my life."

"Here, let me show you." Silver lifted his hand from my leg and placed it on my neck. It was a different hand on my neck than it had been on my leg. It was now filled with passion that made me shiver. He began kneading the top of my neck, first with that one hand that had clasped my leg but had come alive now, and then with both of his hands. I did not know how to resist.

He began to breathe heavily, stretching his fingers, waltz like, in and around my neck, with the seriousness of a masseuse—or how I thought a masseuse would move his hands, but I'd never had a massage at all, from a masseuse or anybody else, so I was only guessing.

But I liked it.

Everything about me began to melt away from any ownership clasp. My back dropped and spread out, loose. My neck became floppy. My eyes rested.

I purred like a kitten being stroked. "Oh, my, are you massaging my eyes, too, Silver? You are gonna put me to sleep."

He laughed, leaned back, and kept rubbing. He said, "Renee, you've caught laughing from me, I've rubbed your stress away, and now you want to go to sleep on me, baby. No way! I'm gonna put you somewhere, sweetheart, but it ain't gonna be asleep."

That shiver I'd had before came back, but deeper.

After about ten miles of my letting him rub my neck, I said, "I promise I'll try not to go to sleep driving, but I may have to rest some. I don't know if I have ever felt this relaxed."

He grinned and said, "You ain't seen nothing yet." He settled back into his seat with an authority on his face blended in with the same expectancy he'd shown when he first peered through the car window at me in the hospital parking lot.

He lowered his voice almost to a whisper and spoke into my ear, "Why don't you let your hair down?"

"Let my hair down? Really?" I responded, thinking he meant get wild. I didn't exactly know what a person who was driving down the interstate needed to do to get wild. I tightened my grip on the steering wheel. "I don't know how to do that—let my hair down."

He laughed at me and said patronizingly, "You don't know how to take your bobby pins out and let your hair fall down?"

"Oh, you mean really let my hair down?" Relief suddenly filled me, and with it came a childlike mischief. I said, "Silver, generally a woman doesn't unpin her hair while she's running down the interstate."

He said, "I don't do generally, Renee."

Then he snatched the word "running" and began repeating it over and over, like it was some kind of magic mantra, his eyes widening with every repeat, as if he weren't really in the car with me but in some other place he knew really well and longed to be.

How strange, I thought. Maybe "running" is a word that means something special that I don't know about, which could be the case. I'm not very worldly. I turned to look at him. His face was glowing. He was physically aroused. I quickly turned back. I could not look.

He knew I knew. He touched himself, again, maybe to prove to me that he knew I knew. I don't know. But he did it only briefly. I saw it out of the corner of my eye and pretended I didn't, believing if I pretended that I didn't see, he would stop.

"I'm sorry, sweetheart, you've just got me excited," he said and laughed.

I didn't know what to say.

He changed the subject back to the main one: "It's not such an odd request, Renee. After a good ole neck massage, you are too smart to leave that beautiful hair all bundled up in bobby pins on your pretty little head. It deserves a little fun, too, don't you think?"

A recklessness that I didn't know a thing about was all over us.

I laughed a nervous laugh, and said, "Well, I've never before today gotten a massage, never in my whole life, and surely not while driving, which goes without saying."

"Yeah?" he said, asking me, not agreeing with me.

"And it felt nice, Silver, so what the heck! I'll unpin my hair and let it loose." I really thought that might get his mind off everything. I reached up and pulled the pins out and held them in my mouth as my hair began to fall; he gently unwrapped it for me, like a child opening a Christmas package. It didn't get his mind off everything. And though I had very well dropped that Cosmopolitan between our legs in the waiting room to get his attention, I slung my head around now, not for that, but to loosen it and break the spell of the wildness on his face.

It didn't help.

He reached for the bobby pins, laid them in the glove compartment, and pulled my hair, fanning it out. He made that guttural sound a man makes when he throws doubles in a board game. "Let's roll down the windows," he said, "and drive some more before we go eat."

Good, I thought. That will do it. That will lighten this up.

My hair blew back and up in the car, a tangled mess, and he turned in his seat, wide-eyed, watching it, mesmerized. He began running his fingers through my hair, caressing the tangles like they were fine silk. Once, he even touched the index finger of his right hand to the pit in the front of my neck and ran his finger all the way around my neck in a circle.

I was, unintentionally, getting very aroused and having a hard time keeping my mind on driving. It suddenly dawned on me that as I drove down the interstate in broad daylight, I was being seduced by a strange man with electric red fuzz on his arms, the realization of which only intensified my own arousal and, apparently, his.

"Silver, don't you think we should stop?" I asked, breathing heavily.

At that very moment, an eighteen-wheeler passed and honked its horn; the passenger in the cab rolled down the window, stuck his hand out, and gave us a thumbs-up.

Oh my God. Thumbs. That man in the truck knows I'm being seduced. Which is what I was very sure Silver was doing. It had to be; this met every understanding I had of seduction from everything I'd ever read about it or seen on television. Of course, I'd never been seduced before, so I was limited in my knowledge of it. For as tender as Samone, my first and only lover, was, I don't remember him ever really seducing me. We just made love like we made dinner or read the paper, as part of regular life.

Right in the middle of my being seduced, the pain inside me vanished, like it does after a Vicodin begins to move through a toothache. The heavy emptiness that weighed me down all the time just floated off. Wild wonderful feelings overtook any pain. I was in the throes of throbbing, neon-sign, soap-opera passion.

8.

LOST IN COOPERATION

Which was not the case back there at Samone's mother's house that next morning. He and I lay on either side of the bed, past nine o'clock, alone, amidst a soft filtering in of Janie and her grandmother's laughter atop the screech of cartoon characters.

Samone looked at me with sad eyes, and said, "Renee, let's take Mother's advice and stay in bed all day and make love." He reached out for me, brusquely, a schoolboy wanting to hug me to him.

I pulled away and went to the bathroom and brushed my teeth.

He just lay there, deserted, his left arm bent up over his head, the palm of his left hand open like his thoughts, so loud that they badgered me as I freshened up behind the closed bathroom door.

"Are you coming back to bed, Renee?" he asked, little boyish.

I could hear him shifting around in the bed, waiting for an answer. I didn't say a word. I even caught myself holding my breath to hold myself in.

Then, he began bargaining. I hated it when he bargained. I always felt guilty, first that he had to bargain, and then that I didn't want to cooperate, which a wife is suppose to do, isn't she, cooperate?

Finally, he said, kindness and tenderness in his voice, "Please, come back, let me hold you, Renee."

"Please," the magic word rippled through me, flexing me, and I caught myself breathing easier, but I straightened up hard against relaxing into his invitation.

My mother always said that I was too serious, avoided having fun, like I was supposed to keep myself from it. "You're missing life, Renee," she'd say, and I never understood her, but maybe she was right. Maybe

I didn't know how to enjoy much of anything because I was too busy worrying about why I didn't.

Whatever was wrong with me, and God knows I'd have given my heart to know what was, so I could have stopped Samone from doing what he did, I eventually walked back to the bed, dropped my night-gown in a pile on the floor, and moved in under the covers.

I cooperated with Samone.

Cooperation is not making love.

Samone knew it and I knew it.

Afterwards, he lay away from me and silence came into the bed with us for a ménage à trois. As I lay there with the two of them, I real-ized that the three of us had been in this kinky relationship for a very long time.

9.

THE POINT OF NO RETURN

"D'ya carry stemware in The Shoppe?" a gentle voice asked. Sam looked up. There, standing in front of him, was Gloria, the middle-aged woman who'd walked into Mac's Coffee Shop a couple of weeks before, where he and Charlie were having their Wednesday coffee.

In the middle of Charlie's slurping his coffee, thick with sugar and cream, he had lifted the fuzzy awnings over his eyes and said to Sam, "Don't look now, but there's Bridges' ex: they say she took him for a cleaning."

Charlie finished his thought, "Josh, you know, was a wheeler dealer." His eyelids dropped. Charlie's next slurp dribbled coffee on his shirt; he'd never married anybody to teach him any manners. Been haunted with singleness all his life.

Sam kept stirring his coffee and worrying about juggling accounts payable, deciding whether or not to talk to the bank about using the accounts receivable to open another cash flow spigot, and trying to figure out how he and Renee had ended up having a knock-down, drag-out a while back in, of all places, the front flowerbed. They were living on two different planets; he was going crazy over all of it.

Sam replied, leaving one foot in the front flowerbed, "A wheeler dealer, Charlie? What da'ya mean?"

"A money-maker, Sam, makes it hand over fist, not much of a fellow a'tall, just looking at him, a crass stinky fellow, but he moves the money through. Or so I've heard." Charlie slurped again. Then he turned to the waitress and asked, "Jaleen, could I please have a piece of that lemon pie in the case?"

"You've got it, Charlie, coming right up," she said, smiling wide, flirting. He never noticed.

"Hmm, well, it's good to know, Charlie, that somebody's making money."

Charlie leaned in and began talking low and fast, which was his way of signaling Sam that what he was about to say needed to stay just between the two of them.

Charlie's eyebrows lifted again and dropped. He peered out from behind them. "Guys at the bank say he's in the Raleigh Mafia."

Annoyed at talk about crass men and mafias while his own life was falling apart in a plain lantana bed, Sam blurted out, "Who's in the Raleigh Mafia?" thinking how Renee had simply quit wanting to make love anymore, which had about done him in.

"Shh, she'll hear you," Charlie said as he moved around in his seat and put his left hand up to his face to shield his words.

Sam really didn't care who heard what, but he leaned toward Charlie to be polite and said, "There ain't no such thing as the Raleigh Mafia, and I don't give a flying fig what Bridges' wife did or did not get from him."

Sam was about as interested in Gloria Bridges or any woman walking in that door at Mac's Coffee Shop at that moment as he was in The Shoppe's accumulating more accounts payable. But as he tasted his coffee he looked up toward the front of the coffee shop, and at the exact moment that Sam looked up, Gloria looked up from over a tumbler of iced tea, and though neither one of them had a thing to do with it, their eyes met.

It was like stepping into a new place Sam had never been before and feeling totally at home and knowing that even when he turned around and left it'd be there, and, eventually, he'd have to return.

"What'dya say Bridges' ex-wife was named?"

Charlie took the last bite of the lemon pie, pushed his chair back, patted his stomach, and burped. "Excuse me—oh, Gloria, she's named Gloria."

"No problem," Sam said. "Wish I'd had some of that pie, myself. Thanks."

Charlie stood, stretched out his legs, pushed the chrome and red plastic dining chair back up under the table, reached over and grabbed a toothpick, and tucked it in the corner of his mouth. Same thing he did every Wednesday after he finished his meal.

He said, "See you here same time same place one week from today."
Same words he always said.

Sam got up and pushed his chair back. They walked out the front
door together.

As they passed the booth where Gloria was seated, Sam simply
refused to look at her. It was perfectly clear to him that she knew that
he was not looking at her. Sam could have sworn that he smelled pear
preserves.

He and Charlie walked outside into a strong sun. "Darn, it's hot,"
he said to Charlie, "but I'll be here next Wednesday, unless I'm not,"
his standard Wednesday departing words.

Charlie laughed and turned to go to his car.

Sam followed him, instead of going to his own car, and asked
Charlie, "D'ya smell pear preserves?"

"Pear preserves? Hell no. How am I gonna be smelling pear preserves? You're losing it, Sam. See ya."

Charlie could do that, sometimes, just not notice, but Sam never
knew if it was because he hadn't noticed, or had and didn't want to have
noticed just to be nice.

Charlie slid his baggy khakis into the seat of his five-year-old cream
colored Chevy sedan with a year-old dented fender. He backed it up
and screeched out onto the street, searching for a radio station with his
right hand while waving to Sam with his left, steering with his legs and
chewing on the toothpick, his eyes on the road.

Not a soul could have ever guessed from appearances how talented
or rich Charlie had become, his high school swirls and doodles starring
Clem having hit the big time as syndicated cartoons in major newspapers from L.A. to Manhattan.

*****

It was this woman whom Charlie had said was named Gloria who
was now standing before him in The Shoppe. She had the same eyes
he'd accidentally met at Mac's Coffee Shop.

"Yes, we carry stemware," he replied to her.

She was wearing jeans and a tucked in white blouse, the top button unbuttoned. She was built like Rowena on the bus. She still smelled like pear preserves.

Suddenly, a thought came to him: You know, I never saw anything about you below your eyes until just this minute. It seemed such a strange thought to have in the first place, and he felt uncomfortable, both with having such a thought, as well as with why he was even thinking about her eyes and what was or was not below them. Then he got confused at his discomfort. He laid down the ledger he'd been posting, which was useless to him now, and straightened his tie. It seemed like the right thing to do. He didn't know why.

He asked her, "What kinda stemware do you need, ma'am?"

Before she could answer, the bell rang over the entryway and two women from the church walked in. They stopped in unison just inside the door and stood perfectly still in the entryway, like they'd seen something. The tall one looked at the shorter one and the shorter one looked back.

Sam coughed and said, "Come in, ladies. Good to see you today." He stepped out from behind the counter. "Anything I can help you with?" he asked.

The taller of the two, who must've been seventy years old, was the leader. She stood very erect and held her left arm bent, rigid, at exactly 90 degrees across her torso. Neither her heavily made up face nor the frown of strictness it painted spoke of any flexibility or spontaneity. Clearly, she was deliberating carefully whether she should let him know why they were in the store.

Sam was amused, which was a blessing, for it temporarily distracted him from concentrating on Gloria and her white blouse with the top button unbuttoned.

Eventually, the taller woman made her decision and she said, emphatically, "Sally and I just want to browse some." It was clear she would have held that position against all the armies in the world.

The woman whose eyes had met Sam's, but whose name he was not supposed to know, held her position in front of him with the top button of her blouse still not buttoned.

He managed a weak response to the woman with the frown of strictness, "Okay, ladies, just let me know if you need anything."

At his words, the two older women giggled, as if on cue, and ambled toward the pottery he'd recently shelved on the far side of The Shoppe's front room. He felt he should be talking to them, so he said, "I've just stocked some interesting pottery over there in that section, ladies. In that first display." He coughed again. He didn't usually cough much at all.

Sally, the shorter of the two older women, wearing a tweed jacket, bent over the display and touched a round plate candleholder, oohing and aahing over it, "My, oh, my, how beautiful!" The two of them huddled, whispered back and forth their oohs and ahs, and began fondling the pottery.

Something about the way they touched the pottery, with Gloria standing in front of him with enormous brown eyes and a white blouse with the top button not buttoned, stimulated him. Startled at a sensation he had not had in a very long time, he coughed again, wondering if maybe he was in some kind of dream. But if the churchwomen were entranced with the pottery, Gloria was not. She began fidgeting with that top button on her blouse—did she realize what she was doing? And then she pouted and laid the index finger of her left hand on her bottom lip.

"Having my new neighbors over for supper next week. I so want to impress them. It's been a very long time since I've had anyone over for a meal. I'm a bit nervous. But, that's not the point. I didn't come here to tell you all that, now did I?" she spoke softly. Then she coughed, too, and said, "I need some new stemware."

Somehow, Sam felt relieved.

As if she'd forgotten the real thing she wanted to say and needed very much to rush into saying it, without taking a breath, she said, "I'm Gloria." And right behind it, she said, "Have we met before?"

Sam felt like a man walking a gangplank. He said, "Nice to meet you, Gloria, I'm Sam. Yeah, didn't I see you at Mac's Coffee Shop a couple of weeks ago?" His palms were getting sweaty.

"Yes. Yes, that's it." She dropped her eyes. She knew that she knew before she walked in the front door.

He left it alone and said, "Come with me, Gloria, to the back room; I'll show you what we've got." He realized that everything he had just said sounded suggestive.

Gloria smiled, avoiding his eyes, and said, "Thank you. I need some help with what's 'in.'"

"Oh, I'm good at that," he said, and then the way the conversation sounded hit him and must have also hit her. They both burst out laughing at their inside joke. Being with this woman was like a breath of fresh air. He walked ahead. She followed, saying not a word, recovering from her laughter. He could hear the click of her high heels. The click had a clean, clear ring to it.

Out of the corner of his eyes he could have sworn he saw the two churchwomen watching them. He didn't know why he felt like he was doing something wrong, but he did. He felt guilty, so he said to the women, "Now, let me know if there is any way I can help you, ladies."

They said together, as if on cue, "Oh, we will. Never you mind." Then one of them laughed.

As Sam and Gloria approached the area where the crystal was displayed, they stopped for him to explain to her what was what, and Gloria brushed up against the edge of one of the shelves. The smell of pear preserves floated around. It scared Sam how uncontrollably hungry he was. Maybe that was what was dumbfounding him, or maybe it was the top button being unbuttoned reminding him of Rowena on the bus and, also, therefore, Renee, which simply complicated everything. Round brown cat eyes. They looked at you. Looked at him. And, when they looked, it came to him, deep inside, how he and Renee had been going through a really rough patch.

Then Gloria reached over and picked up a wine glass and held it up into the light that was streaming in through the ceiling-high windows like it was trying to reach them before it was too late. It was too late. Gloria set the wine glass back on the shelf and brushed his arm. He felt it. She said, "Sam, this is the most beautiful shop. I do so love these wine glasses. Is there a possibility that you could deliver a dozen of these to me later this afternoon?"

He should have said, "We don't deliver."

She walked out of The Shoppe right past the two women in the pottery section; the tall one looked at the other, raised her eyebrows, and rolled her eyes over toward Gloria. They both backed away from the aisle down which Gloria was walking, like there was something about her that would infect them if they got close to her.

Sam wanted, then, more than before, to deliver the wine glasses. He delivered them that afternoon. Nothing happened. Everything happened.

As he pored over the books, restocked shelves, and tossed Janie in the air in the evenings, he smelled pear preserves. The scent would sift into his conversations with folks in The Shoppe.

He and Renee lived midst the pear preserves from then on out, neither one of them realizing it. He tried to convince himself that if Renee had ever actually stopped and looked at him, noticed him, Gloria might not have kept hanging around in his mind, even though her eyes simply would not leave. But Renee was infected with a free floating anger at everything, weighted down by it. It got in the way of her. It was bigger than them. Nothing about anything suited her, particularly not Sam. Boobs Samone was on life support. 'Til Gloria bought the wine glasses.

10.

GAZEBOED

The stronger the gusts of wind through the open window, the wilder Silver's hands became, moving hypnotically in the tangled strands of my hair and back to his crotch. I could see it throbbing.

"You're right, my lovely," he said, gasping for breath, "I do think we should stop. There's a roadside park at the next exit. Let's pull over so we can get out and stretch . . . everything that needs stretching, before it bursts." He laughed a haunting laugh, one hand holding a wad of my hair, the other groping himself.

"Okay," I said, knowing we were too far gone to return to the hospital parking lot. I flipped the blinker signal and turned the steering wheel, pulling into an area that was deserted except for one other car parked at the far end of the parking lot, a block away.

Silver touched my leg again as I pulled into a parking space; this time, though, his hand was alive, helping me press the brake pedal. The car came to a stop. Silver did not. He lifted my skirt over my right knee and bent his head forward, sniffing me, breathing me in as he kissed my thigh on the inside, midway up. I let him. It seemed exactly the right thing to do, although I was not thinking about what I was doing; my mind refused to get involved in it at all. It had seemingly left me. I had let it go.

"Yummm! Push your seat back a bit," he said.

I didn't resist.

He reached up under my skirt and inserted both his thumbs inside the front of my panties and removed them. Thumbs. I never knew until that day how highly I had underrated thumbs. I sat naked under my skirt. To my surprise, he did not seem to have much interest in that. Instead, he turned and folded my panties as carefully as if he were folding treasured linen and asked, "Can I put these in the glove compartment?"

I couldn't have cared less where he put my panties, but I answered, "Yes, of course."

Was this what people did with their underwear when they made love in a park?

"Let's get out of this car, dear Renee. Come on!" He reached for my hand and pulled me out of the passenger door. I left a streak on the front seat from sliding across it without my panties. An unexpected brush of wind blew my skirt up around my waist, leaving me exposed. Other than kissing my navel, he ignored my nakedness.

The car at the far end of the parking lot started and pulled out, moving away from us toward the entrance back onto the interstate.

Silver reached for my hands and pulled me toward him, fondling my neck again, as we walked down a pathway that meandered toward a thick grove of trees. Only a few steps down the pathway, he said, playfully, "Let's run." Then, like a kid on a vacant lot with a football in his hand to toss to me, he motioned me forward down the path and said, "You run ahead. I'll catch you."

I ran, fully aware of my pantiless-ness. I cannot recommend highly enough doing such a thing. When I looked back over my shoulder to make sure he was following me, it was as if I had flipped a switch that turned on a glow in him, and he began begging, "Run faster, Renee, run faster."

I picked up speed—maybe it was not having on underwear, I don't know, but I heard that guttural sound come from him again, just as a honeysuckle-covered gazebo popped into view at the end of the path, some fifteen yards ahead. I ran toward it and collapsed inside a natural canopy. As I turned, about to speak to him about how wonderful it had felt to run without any panties on and how tired I was and how I was so glad we had found a hideaway, he slapped his hand on my mouth. "Shh!" he said, flinging me on the floor, as if he were trying to stop me from running away. But where was I going to run? This was the only entrance to the gazebo.

He bit into my lips, deliberately, as he pressed in on me, roughing me up with his hands that moved from my neck to my hips, twisting them under him, scraping them on the concrete floor. I felt the little pebbles pointing up out of the concrete. I could not protest with his hand on my mouth.

After he had his way with me, I lay under him. My lips were bleeding. When I licked them, they tasted salty. He reached over and licked them, too. I was shaking. I tried to move. I was caught. He ripped the top button off my blouse and laid me bare. He covered my face, again, with his. I avoided his lips and began to push out from him, but he circled my neck with both his hands and squeezed.

"Ouch," I said. That one word seemed to wake him. He pushed himself back up on his hands.

"Does it hurt?" he asked.

"Yes, don't do that," I replied.

He sat back on his haunches and grinned, suddenly turning into a playful child who had accidentally hurt someone while innocently exploring how scissors worked and wanted to grin away the boo-boo. Startled and expended, I grinned back to try to hold onto that change in him. However, he took my grin as a green light to proceed and began, again, adoring my hair and my neck, wearing the hypnotic look that was on his face earlier in the car, and all of his adoration inspired him to begin another dance, this one tamer, that stretched us out together, horizontally. I held on, afraid for my life. He never noticed.

Afterwards, he rose and zipped himself up, as if he were finished with a task he had needed to accomplish. "Aren't you going to get up?" he mumbled, scowling. "I will drive us back."

I got up and pulled my shirt together. I did not speak. I moved behind him back out along the path, a shell-shocked child who had patted a gorgeous purring tiger, been mauled by it, and was still trying to survive. He did not look at me or hold my hand as we walked back to the car. For that I was grateful.

To anyone in the rest area, we could have been strangers who'd encountered each other in the gazebo and just happened to be departing it at the same time, unless they'd looked closely enough to see the blood on my lips or trickling down my hips or noticed that I was holding the top of my blouse together.

Neither of us spoke on the ride back to the hospital. He turned on the radio and the AC. I huddled in toward the passenger door.

Two blocks away from the hospital parking lot where Tulley's should have been there were no restaurants, only rows and rows of townhouses that spread for miles in either direction. I pretended not to notice.

He parked near where I'd had the car parked before, opened the driver's door, and stepped out. He stuck his head in the window and said, "Bye, Renee. Glad I found you today and made you laugh." He winked menacingly and ambled off across the hospital parking lot. As he turned the corner past which the hospital would hide us from each other's view, he waved back over his shoulder, like the freezing stranded man had waved back at Samone and me that night we had encountered him and helped him along on his journey.

I sat there speechless. For how long, I don't know. Eventually, I moved over into the driver's seat and drove home in a state of shock, oblivious to what streets I took or the time of day or the fact that blood was all over me. I just didn't know what else to do. I had asked for this.

11.

A Delivery

It just takes time for some things to sink in, things that startle you so much that you can't think about them except sideways, only to get a glimpse, not to inspect, heavens no, only to question if they really did happen, not to admit why, because their happening doesn't match anything in your life that makes any sense.

This was like that.

I was broken, sitting in the bathtub, letting water run over me, though I did not think there was enough water anywhere to help me. I held a plastic bag of ice against my bottom lip where he bit in deep. It was swollen to twice its size. When I licked my lips, I tasted him and got sick to my stomach. How could I have been that hungry?

All the while, the afternoon sun played over the clean white bathroom tile, an oblivious baton directing the birds to keep right on chirping outside the window, even though he dragged me across concrete and pounded my hips into it, over and over, as he ripped out a patch of my blonde hair from the back of my head. I had a bald spot there now.

The squirrels continued to bounce across the roof, apparently unaware of my shame or the deep red scratches on my neck. Is throbbing, neon-sign, soap-opera passion just empty violent lust? I didn't know what was what anymore.

I stepped out of the tub and pulled the plug. The water circled and gurgled its way down the drain and just went away. That's it, I thought. I'll let this just go away. I couldn't tell anyone. What would I say? I enticed a strange man who got in my car and I ran across a rest area along an interstate without any panties and ended up battered and bruised? I rationalized with myself that my neck would heal and my hair would grow back. I couldn't get pregnant: I was taking birth control pills to regulate my period. I'd never see him, ever again. I would let this just go away.

I combed my hair over the bald spot, pulled on a thin cotton turtleneck, and made my face. Yes, I felt better. My messed up-ness was not so obvious. I looked in the mirror and said to myself, "There, Renee, other than the lip, the damage is hidden." The house sounded so empty when it heard my words, like it knew that there is no disguise for what is inside us.

I heard Ashley's car easing up into the drive, bringing Janie home, so I pulled my turtleneck up as high as possible, trying to hide my neck. When I opened the front door, Janie bounced in, running toward me. She pulled back and frowned, her dark eyelashes blinking very fast, and asked, "Why is your lip so big, Momma?"

"I bit it, honey. Here, give your momma a big hug."

Before I could bend over to hug her, she hugged my legs, tight, looking up into my face, and said, "Momma, I'm gonna dress my new big girl doll, now, okay?"

"Sure, Janie. What did you and Grandma do today?"

"We played dolls. I got to go dress the baby doll in blue jeans 'cause Daddy'll wike that, Momma. He wore blue jeans."

"Yes, he wore blue jeans, sweetheart," I said. That part wasn't a lie.

Ashley stepped into the doorway and did a double take, both at Janie's words and my swollen lip.

Janie said, "Aunt Asht, Daddy'll wike the baby doll we dressed today, when he gets back, won't he wike it, Aunt Asht?"

Ashley gave me a what-am-I-going-to-say look and reached for Janie. "Come here. Sit on my knee and let's ask your momma how in the world she bit herself like that."

"Can't, Aunt Asht. Already done it. Gotta go dress my big girl doll," Janie said and scampered down the hall, dragging her doll behind her, thump, thump, thump . . .

"Did it at lunch. Can't chew straight," I said, attempting to laugh.

Ashley put her hands on her hips and looked at me, stone-faced.

"Have y'all eaten supper yet?" I asked to change the subject, hoping against hope that I wouldn't need to cook that night.

Ashley finally smiled and said, "Yeah, I fed Janie her favorite, fried chicken. And I brought you some, too. It's in the car. I'll go get it."

"Yum," I said, relieved. "Thanks, Ashley. I'm hungry." I realized for the first time that I had not eaten anything since breakfast.

After Ashley walked outside, I heard a car door slam, and then I heard her talking. Who in the world is in the front yard talking with Ashley? I sure don't want to see anybody tonight, feeling like I feel, I thought.

The voices were muffled, but I could make out Ashley's words, "Yes, she lives here. Sure, I'll take 'em in. Thanks."

I opened the front door. A floral delivery truck backed out of the drive as Ashley walked up the front steps, beaming all over. She carried a box of fried chicken and biscuits in one hand and a bouquet of roses in the other.

"What is this?" I questioned.

"You have a delivery!" Ashley said excitedly.

"A what?" I asked.

"Someone has sent you flowers. Aren't they gorgeous roses!"

Fear rose up in my stomach.

"My, my, Renee, isn't it sweet for people to keep thinking about you, nearly a year now after Samone?" she said, rambling on as she handed me the roses.

I didn't know how to hold the roses or what to do with them. I'd never in my life received long-stemmed red roses. "They are beautiful," I said.

"Is there somebody you aren't telling me about?" she asked teasingly, grinning like it would be the most far-fetched thing in the whole world for a man to send me flowers.

"Not telling you about?" I got defensive.

She hugged me and said lightheartedly, "I think it would be great if somebody special sent you magnificent long-stemmed red roses on a Tuesday. And darn, sis, you've got to tell Janie the truth about Samone."

"I will, Ashley, give me time; I've got to believe it before I can tell her. I just don't believe Samone did that."

The roses and guilt and pain all gripped me at the same time. I could barely listen to Ashley, but she kept talking. "I know, Renee, I know you are grappling with this. We all are. It's hard on you."

She set the box of chicken on the dining room table, went to the kitchen, and returned with a glass of milk and a plate for the chicken and biscuits and potatoes. She pulled out a dining chair to sit with me while I ate. I opened the envelope attached to the flowers. Ashley leaned in to try to read over my shoulder. I twisted in my seat to shield the card on which two words were written in longhand: "The gazebo!"

A slide show of Silver's face flashed across my mind: that expectant peer through my car window; the wildness in his eyes as he played with my hair; his tongue licking the blood off my lips; the menacing wink as he left me in my car in the hospital parking lot. I blinked to try to erase it.

"Are you okay, Renee?" Ashley asked, genuine concern showing on her face.

"Yes, I'm fine," I said. "Please, please, let's get you a plate, too; eat with me, Ash."

She pushed her chair back. "Thanks, sis, I've had all the chicken I can eat today. Janie and I did a number on it earlier."

I picked up a drumstick and bit into its crispness. Juice squirted out and rolled off onto my fingers. I grabbed for a paper napkin, dabbing myself, only halfway listening to her.

"But I need to ask a favor of you," Ashley continued.

"Okay, what?" I said, trying to decide if I wanted to pinch a piece of the white meat off the chicken breast next or finish the drumstick.

"Well, our receptionist who has been with us at the firm, from the beginning, is leaving to be with her daughter who is having a first baby; it'll be her first grandchild."

"How nice," I said, testing the creamed potatoes. They felt good going down. I was hungry.

"Truthfully, she's retiring; she is going to live there with her daughter up in the mountains."

"What does that have to do with me doing a favor for you, Ashley?" I wiped my hands, again, on the napkin.

"You'd be perfect for the job."

"For what job?"

"The receptionist job."

What a day, I thought. I've enticed a sexual pervert and gotten scratches on my butt that won't heal for weeks. My throat looks like it's been in a meat grinder. The man whose fingers have left me wearing a turtleneck in the summer, whose last name I do not know, has sent me long-stemmed red roses. Now, my sister wants me to go to work as a receptionist to solve her personnel problems, although I've never worked a day in my life outside my home.

I tried to be kind. "Ash, you know I appreciate your thinking about me, but I don't want to have to deal with a job right now. Samone left us okay for a time. I'm just not ready for a step like that."

"I know, Renee. I know," she said, crossing her legs and waving her top leg up and down. That was always a sign that Ashley was annoyed, had not gotten her way, and was not finished with her efforts. She just came right out with it: "Well, just to tell you the truth, Renee, it's time you got out of this house. That's what it boils down to. Mother and I have talked about it. Janie needs kindergarten and other kids to play with."

"You are right; I'm sure you are, sis. Other kids to play with are very important." I felt pushed.

"And, you need a life."

I gulped, but I didn't say a word. I bit into a biscuit and just looked at her, a woman who at twenty-eight was still living in the house with her mother and daddy.

Ashley got a second wind. "Renee, you are dying here in this house and over there at the hospital watching Grandmother die." She dropped her hands in disgust like I was a lost cause.

I dropped the biscuit, pushed back my plate, got up, and moved to the sofa in the living room. "Please don't keep using that word, 'die,' please, Ashley," I said.

"I'm sorry, Renee, how that came out, but it's been almost a year now; you have got to start living again." She followed me into the living room and sat down beside me. I felt cornered. I knew she meant well and I didn't want to argue, not today, when only a few hours ago I had behaved like Sharon, the girl in school whom Samone had said he was taking to the prom.

I just said, "I'm living, Ashley, really, I am—"

Before I could complete my thought, she countered with, "Renee, I mean actually living. Yes, you have the cleanest floors in six states. Yes, every towel is laundered and folded perfectly. Renee, I don't mean that. I mean being with people, socializing, doing things, laughing, talking."

This, I thought, from a sister who has never found it the least bit vulgar to leave her dirty underwear on the floor or sleep on sheets for six weeks. But I was exhausted. I didn't have the energy to deal with this. Nothing would have made me happier at that moment than to crawl under a rock and never come out ever again. I could not say that to Ashley; she never got tired, and the hardest thing she'd ever dealt with in life was trying to decide what to do with the money from the next raise she got. So I just said, "It's hard, sis, harder than you might think."

She didn't back up. "Okay, I understand. Just meet me next Monday at the office at 11:30. I'll introduce you to my boss and we'll take it from there. Mother will keep Janie for the interview." She sat back on the sofa, folded her beautifully manicured hands across her lap, and waited for my agreement.

"Interview? Gosh, Ashley, interview?" I nervously pulled on the turtleneck. I wanted her to leave. So I said, just to get her off the subject, "Okay, but I don't want a job."

"Good," she said. She'd won. She always won. I had the spine of a worm. She stood up and turned toward the front door. As an afterthought, she asked, "Are you gonna tell me who the roses are from?"

I went blank. Then, I misled her and said, "The church group I go to sometimes. They send flowers to members of the group on special occasions." That part was true.

"What is your special occasion?" Ashley shot back, not being ugly, just being Ashley, trying to relate, meaning no harm. She could staccato questions faster than a machine gun. I really didn't know why she didn't go on to law school.

"I'm not sure," I said, but I was thinking, I guess the occasion could be that I have actually survived today.

That clean, blank, I-don't-have-any-secrets-and-everything-in-my-life-is-out-in-the-open stare spread all over Ashley's face. She waited for me to say more. When I didn't, she got that serious look of struggling concern for me that she'd been giving for the last year, like she knew I was hurting and she wanted to connect with me and try to help me, but she hadn't a clue what to do or what to say or how to say what would need to be said, if she knew what it was. I just sat there. She hugged me and left.

I sat back down at the dining table, a woman fully feeling the weight of believing that she had killed the man she loved, had become horny enough to accidentally become Sharon, and had gotten long-stemmed red roses from a man with red fuzz on his arms who wouldn't even hold her hand after he attacked her. To call what we did "making love" would make a mockery of love, though God knows I didn't have a clue what love was supposed to be.

I sat there for a time looking at the roses—how they shot straight up into the air, reaching out. Something about that forced me to remember Samone's face reaching out, too, that night in his mother's bedroom, and my not knowing the face or even that it was reaching out or how to reach back to him. I'm not sure if I even wanted to reach back to him or let him reach me. Had we crossed a line in our hearts that we couldn't climb back over, or was I just sinful and arrogant and stupid, believing that life lasted a lifetime and, since I had forever, there was no rush to love?

Finally, I got up and found a vase big enough for the roses and set the bouquet in the center of the dining room table. Nothing about them looked right in my house. I checked on Janie; she was up to her eyeballs in dolls and doll clothes and didn't have much interest in talking with me. I sat down on the sofa and began mentally replaying the afternoon, trying to find the starting point, trying to understand the not understandable. Then a sheet of fear hit me. How on earth had Silver known where I lived? My phone was unlisted; he couldn't have found me in the directory, the thought of which had me pulling out the phone book to find the listing for Tulley's Restaurant. There was none. My hands trembled at the realization that no such restaurant existed. I don't know why. I already knew that place wasn't there, and his lying about that wouldn't come close to being worse than what he had done to me.

I reached for one of the roses. Smelled it. The scent was gentle, sweet. I took it with me to my bedroom and laid it on my bedside table, thinking that enjoying the roses could somehow salvage the day. I did not like the way I felt with the rose there. I threw it in the trash. I plumped up the pillows and leaned back against them. "Janie," I called.

"Yeah, Momma."

"You want to sleep with me tonight, sweetie?"

"Yes! Yippee!" In she came, dragging her big girl doll.

"No teeth brushing or face washing tonight," I said.

She grinned like I had awarded her a prize. She crawled in by me, laying her big girl doll between us. "Don't smush her, Momma, pease don't smush her," she said.

"I won't, sweetheart." I flipped off the light and hugged her to me and thought that quite enough smushing had happened already for one day.

She fell asleep immediately. I did not. I ran my finger across my swollen lip and listened to Janie breathing. Flashbacks from the afternoon seeped in. My mind was as bruised as my body. The one question for which I could not find an answer was, why would a man manipulate me and use such unnecessary brute force with me and then find out where I lived and send me roses? I got a cold chill inside. My pajamas irritated my buttocks. I couldn't get comfortable. For a very long time, I lay listening to the night sounds, the incessant calm of distant traffic, a neighbor's murmuring TV, and the gentle voices of some kids sitting under a carport nearby, talking low. I heard a train way off in the distance. I did not know where it was going, but I wanted to go there, leave this nightmare trap, but I felt I would never be able to. I was stuck in life, any way I looked at it.

I dreamed. In the dream, I was on a ship. A pirate attacked us. I couldn't see his face. He was wearing a hat made of honeysuckle. It clung to his face, hiding all of it except his brown eyes. The eyes looked familiar. They weren't the pirate's eyes. They were Samone's. But the eyes were the ocean, with tall waves. The man had a long, sharp sword. He flashed it at me and slashed my bra straps, ripping my skin. I bled and my bosoms fell out, large and ripe with milk. I tried to cover them and keep them safe, but when I tried, I bruised my hands. I knew that I was losing something important and I couldn't hold onto it.

I woke frightened, sweating. Janie stirred. I patted her. She fell back asleep. I got up, pulled on a bathrobe, went to the kitchen, and opened the refrigerator. I found the box of leftover fried chicken. I sat in the dark and ate it and listened to the summer cicada rub their legs together. Might be one of the loneliest sounds in the universe.

Tonight, the cicada's song reminded me that it had only been hours since my legs had rubbed against those of Silver, a man I didn't know who'd hurt me in ways I didn't understand and couldn't speak about. And I had let him, because I was so widow empty that I dropped that *Cosmopolitan* to get to touch his skin.

I paced the floor and finally fell asleep on the sofa. As morning came, I felt a tug on my sleeve. "Momma, why did you leave me?" Janie asked.

"I didn't leave you, sweetie. I just had to move around a bit," I said.

12.

Sandals and Saturdays

Happenstance and a conscious decision took Samone back to the wine glasses, though he did not have wine glasses on his mind when he walked into Janie's room that spring Saturday, hugged her, and asked, "How's my girl, Janie?"

She grinned up at him and ceased struggling to put on her sandals—the back strap on the right one was twisted and caught on her heel. She wiped her nose on the back of her hand and asked, "Where ya going, Daddy?"

"To The Shoppe, Janie."

Dangling her uncooperative sandal in front of him, she said, "Please fix it and let me go wif ya." She covered her face and whimpered to plead her case, peeking out occasionally as he untwisted the sandal strap.

The light of Samone's life, she knew how to work him. Amused, Samone sat on the edge of her bed. "Come here, Janie, crawl up on my knees," he said, motioning to her and patting his knee. She dropped her hands from her face and fell forward onto his knees, puffing out her lips.

"Yes, dear Janie, you can go with me—"

Renee burst into the room and interrupted him. "What's happening here, Janie?"

"Janie and I are getting our shoes on," Samone said and winked at Janie. She grinned.

Renee paid no attention to Samone. Without even a word to him, she grabbed Janie out of his lap, pulled the sandal from his hand, and whisked Janie off to the living room. She set her on the sofa, forced the sandal on her foot, set Janie back on the floor on her feet, patted her behind, and said, "Go play, Janie. Leave your daddy alone."

Samone followed them into the living room, a non-entity. He was confused. Dismayed.

The phone rang. Renee pushed herself around Samone to get to the phone. She picked up the receiver, listened, said into it, "Oh, hey, sis. Yeah, hold on."

She put her hand over the receiver and said to Samone, without looking at him, "It's Ashley. Where you going? Thought the store was closed."

He really had not decided until just that moment, but her disregard for him in front of Janie, positioning him to have to argue in front of Janie to take her with him to The Shoppe, was the last straw. "Got a delivery I need to make for a good customer. Be back in a little bit."

Even knowing where he was bound, he reached over to kiss Renee on the cheek; she kept chattering in the receiver, aware he was there but not responding to his affection. She shooed him away with the back of her left hand, like he was a fly, and said, "Okay, see you later." She resumed her phone conversation.

Samone walked to the van, lonely, feeling like he'd felt that morning in the bed with Renee at his mother's house when Renee's coldness moved on his skin and he'd realized that wide chasm between them, even when their legs were together. He was alone with Renee. A sudden breeze rushed through the weeping willow by the driveway, swinging it cruelly every which way, bending it up and down, sideways, then dropping it. No wonder a willow tree weeps, he thought. Damn, I know how it feels. He opened the door to the van and sat behind the wheel for a time before he started it. He backed out of the driveway and drove to 81110 Connie Street, where he had delivered the wine glasses.

Gloria answered the door dressed in white shorts and a black tee shirt. Her hair was mussed up and beads of sweat stood out on her crane-like throat, which was thin and brown; a tiny mole had taken up residence on the right side of it off near the edge of the shirt's neckline. It was the most beautiful mole he'd ever seen.

"Well, hello, Sam. Didn't expect to see you today. What an absolutely nice surprise," she beamed.

It felt damn good for somebody to be glad to see him. "I came by to see how the wine glasses worked out," he said. "Were they what you needed?" Lame. Lord, he sounded lame. But he cared not about how he sounded or if it took her two years to answer his question, as long as he could look at her.

Her smile said that she didn't care what excuse he gave, either. She said, "Come in, sit down, please, Sam, I so want you to."

He stepped into a spotless house with hardwood floors in the den, oriental rugs, and original art on the walls. It was clear, uncluttered. The stereo was playing low. He could smell food cooking in the kitchen. He thought, Hmm, that Bridges guy must have left her well off.

She closed the front door. He was inside. She reached for his arm and led him to the sofa. "Sit, sit," she said.

"Yeeeeeeeeeeeeeeeeeen!" The teakettle in the kitchen screeched a high-pitched noon whistle sound.

He jumped. She grabbed her stomach and laughed. "Oh, my, sorry about that. I was just making myself some tea. Want some?"

"Sure. Yes. Iced, I hope? But I can't stay but a minute."

She took his left hand, winked, and said, "Come on into the kitchen, Sam. Of course the tea will be iced, with sugar. I'm a Southern gal."

They settled in at the kitchen table and began to talk. Just talk. That's all. Just talk. She asked him questions about himself that no one had ever bothered to ask him, not even Renee. Maybe Renee never asked him because she thought she already knew or because she really didn't care. Anymore. He told Gloria about his growing up, being mostly afraid of everything, and always feeling like an outsider. She listened to every word he spoke, sat there with the him that he shared, hanging on his every word.

"I had not realized, Gloria, until just now, how pleasant it could be for someone to actually listen to me. To hear what I am saying."

She touched his arm. "I do hear you," she said, lifting the tea pitcher to refill their glasses. "Sam, I am as comfortable with you as I am stretching out on a pallet in the springtime."

He reached over and picked up her hand. She was older than him in years. He saw that on her hands. She did not care. He did not care. Their souls were the same age.

It would have been better if he'd grabbed her and unzipped her shorts and licked her from the top of her head to the bottom of her feet—eaten every square inch of pear preserves. Then he could have felt guilty and maybe left her and gone home an adulterer to Renee, startled

Renee with his indiscretion, begged for her forgiveness, tried to find a way to find Renee and him again.

But, no, they talked. And talked. Satisfying talk. Being understood talk. Several hours later, the sun set itself into the middle of the western sky, spreading orange and pink through Gloria's kitchen window. Startled, he said, "I've overstayed. I came to check on the wine glasses and I've told you my life's story."

She smiled. "I'm so glad you came, Sam. If buying wine glasses from The Shoppe will get me a visit from such a charming man, I will buy a dozen every week and put on the tea kettle and be ready every Saturday when you come by to check on them. I haven't enjoyed an afternoon like this in I can't remember when. You are so easy to talk with."

He stood to leave. "You were good medicine for me today, Gloria. I could get addicted to it."

"Me, too," she said.

He walked out of Gloria's front gate, his mind and body more alive than in years. He turned and told her, "Gloria, you are a wonderful woman."

She just smiled that smile. He smiled back.

Saturday afternoons became their talk time together. Strong vines began growing around them and sending down deep roots.

*****

One Saturday morning in July, Renee confronted him. "Samone, seems like a man could save some weekend time for his family. Any way that you can finish at The Shoppe by four so that we can go see a movie? Ashley'll keep Janie for us."

"Wish I could," he lied. "I'll be late coming in this afternoon. Go on with some of your girlfriends."

She looked up at him with question marks in her eyes, the only way she ever looked at him anymore, when she ever did look at him. He knew that she didn't need him to see a movie. And she knew that it was Saturday. He hugged Renee and walked out the front door, feeling her back there puzzling over him, unable to figure him out. She was loving him as much as she knew how; she just didn't know how to love him any better. But he needed more than she was loving him.

13.

EVOLUTION

Silver dipped the Q-tip into the peroxide and pressed it against the backs of his concrete-scratched hands over and over, the way that he had lifted her up, over and over, again and again, for his pleasure. His hands burned, but he didn't notice: he was ecstatic.

"She's real," he said aloud. "She's real. She's come off the page!"

This was the last thing he'd ever expected, so he sat on the commode doctoring himself, remembering her: that hair, the way his fingers felt in its tangle. "My God, she is alive!" But he was depleted. And antsy. This forced a complete change in his strategy. He did not like changing anything established with forethought. Just thinking about doing so taxed him.

He put the cap on the peroxide just so and replaced it on the shelf in its rightful place: he liked a place for everything and everything in its place. He sat down in his easy chair to think this through, logically. But how the blood from her lips tasted pierced his thinking. He licked his lips, jerking then in his recollection of how she smelled like lemons.

"That's the thing about magazines," he said to the four walls. "They all smell the same." The remembering unexpectedly aroused him, though he had never in his life been so spent. He followed his instincts like a toddler; he went to his bed and lifted the magazine. The woman on page twenty-eight looked different now. "Renee's hair is brighter, blonder. I think it's longer, too," he said aloud to the neat stacks of books surrounding his bed. One book was slightly askew. He remedied that immediately and then returned his attention to the magazine. Eventually, however, it became apparent to Silver that Renee had messed up his relationship with the blonde on page twenty-eight. Things just weren't going the same way they always did. So he became angry, and in the very face of his neatness obsession he threw the magazine off into the corner. It splayed out as it landed, bending some of the pages, bunching the magazine up, which upset him, but he held it in and left the magazine over in the corner.

He stretched out but could not sleep, so he reached for a magazine he'd not looked at recently and found a brunette. There was no zing. He bemoaned that and twisted and turned, but after a time, he dozed off. The dream came. It was fuzzy that night, hazy; it had changed. A woman appeared with flowing locks. She was Renee, not the girl from page twenty-eight. She was running. He was chasing her. She was alive with what was ahead. She turned, but this time she turned clockwise. In fact, as she turned, he, in his dream, looked down at his watch and the hands moved forward. They made a loud clicking noise as they moved. A page of the calendar flipped over. Renee beckoned him, flapping her skirt up and down, tempting him with what was naked underneath, which he then knew was what had been under what he folded neatly, very neatly, and placed inside the glove compartment. This time, Renee didn't have a gun and he didn't get to grovel. He wanted to grovel, but she wouldn't let him. She took up all the time. Why wasn't she cooperating with his fantasy? He reached for her at the edge of the cliff, which had turned now into concrete, with a top made of vines into which a thousand eyes looked, watching her in his hands, slipping off without a face, but smiling anyway, slithering into the sea, leaving him impotent and unsatisfied.

He awoke, sweating and angry. The back of his hands hurt. He tried to find the right magazine. Nothing worked. "She will not get away with this," he said.

He dashed into the bathroom, stared into the mirror, and aimed his fist into it, crushing the mirror and scraping open, again, the scratches on his right hand. He walked back to the bedroom, dripping his blood onto the floor, paying it no mind. He picked up the magazine with the girl on page twenty-eight and unbent its pages, but he couldn't flatten them all out, which he did not like at all.

"This magazine is no good to me now!" he raged, ripping out page twenty-eight, smearing his blood on the face of the girl with whom he had enjoyed so many evenings. He wrote near her now-hidden face, "Renee."

He collapsed on the floor and cried like a baby. After a time, he scrambled around in the medicine cabinet, found some bandages, and wrapped his hand. He scrubbed the floor clean and dressed in fresh clothes before he drove to the nearest hardware store to buy a new mirror for his medicine cabinet. He spent the entire night installing it.

14.

TEST QUESTIONS

I had scabs on my neck that I had to camouflage. After everything I'd tried, the blue and wine plaid scarf would do it best, I thought. In addition, its colors would tie my blue shirtwaist and wine jacket together. It was the only jacket I had to wear. The tiny pearl earrings that Samone gave me the day we married looked simple enough and would soften my hairdo: I planned to put my hair up in a bun.

I admitted that I looked ready for an office instead of a kitchen. But I still had mixed emotions. In fact, when I dropped off Janie I told Mother, "I'm dreading this."

She quickly turned from me—that was just her way—and took Janie's hand. "Don't be silly. Everybody works. You'll do fine. Get up and get going." She never once looked me in the eye.

"Okay, I guess so, Mother," I said, twisting my purse strap.

She frowned at me like I was a child who couldn't seem to get it together. If I live to be half a century old and she is still alive, I guess she will still look at me that way. I don't understand it.

"Yes, well, there's no guessing to it," she said. "It is exactly the right thing for you. Time for you to get into the world again." Just like that. Do it. Vintage Mother. You don't argue with a drill sergeant with opinions tighter than a drum skin. Just rubs against 'em and makes noise. I learned that years ago—just stand way back with her and don't get close. Plus, clearly, she and Ashley were in cahoots. I was outnumbered. Always had been.

She turned soft for a moment and spoke it out: "I'll feed Janie lunch. Take your time getting back. Break a leg." She tried to smile over her deep-seated angst. Sometimes she almost broke through.

"Okay," I said. I leaned over and kissed Janie on her cheek. As I walked back to my car listening to her talking with Janie, I thought, Why do I want to succeed at an interview for a job that I don't want?

Mother's words filtered through. "Made you some new clothes for your doll, Janie, come and let me show you."

She never talked to me like that. How did she learn how to do it? Something in me that felt totally alone shouted back to them both: "Thanks, Mother. See you this afternoon, Janie."

Neither acted like they ever heard me. I wondered sometimes if I was on a planet with people or if this was a dream.

*****

I took a deep breath and entered Lawson and Keyes, Attorneys at Law, directly across from the elevator exit on the tenth floor of the Mirror Place Center.

A personable sixtyish woman welcomed me in a high-pitched squeaky voice, "Good morning, how can I help you?" I liked her immediately.

"I'm Renee, Ashley's sister, here to meet her for an eleven-thirty interview," I replied.

"Oh, yes," the lady said, "I'll let her know you're here. She's expecting you. I am so glad you've come. If they don't find somebody for this front desk, I may have to miss being there when my first grandchild arrives. And that would never do. Please, have a seat, make yourself comfortable."

"Thank you," I said, thinking how her tiny head was made up mostly of nose, with pointed ears and dark eyes. How she reminded me of a squirrel. I sat down on a pale blue modern sofa, above which an oil painting of a waterfall hung. Together, the sofa and the painting were a pleasant vignette, the soft blue of the sofa moving up and into the edge of the light blue water, eventually turning aqua, gradually changing upward into a deep navy blue and, finally, a faded blue-gray at the top. An unusual coffee table stretched the length of the entire sofa, its base of enormous tree branches topped with thick beveled glass. Atop it lay a swirl of magazines and a copy of a locally published alternative news-paper. I picked it up and began flipping through. On page fifteen stood a bare-chested man modeling slacks for a high-end men's clothing store. Silver! A girl was standing by him with her hand on his chest. Fear rippled through me, flushing my face. Beads of sweat popped out above my lips. I pulled the issue closer to my eyes, searching unsuccessfully for Silver's last name.

The receptionist saw my alarm and asked, "Are you okay, Mrs. Sims?"

"Yes, thanks," I said. "It is just a bit hot in the room."

"I agree. Sorry about that. I'll ask maintenance to adjust the thermostat," she said.

Ashley walked in. "Hey, Renee, you look great. I like that scarf. I'll have to try one with a shirtwaist. It looks good."

"Thanks, sis," I said, continuing to sit with the newspaper. I reached into my purse for a tissue.

"Come on back," she said. "Mr. Lawson and Ms. Keyes, the managing partners, are just down this hall in the main conference room. You'll enjoy meeting them."

"Okay, let me dry my nerves," I said, dabbing above my lips.

"You are going to be fine," she said as she smiled at me.

I rose, dropped the newspaper on the table, and followed her into a conference room where a man in his midforties and a woman about the same age sat on the far side of a conference table. They stood, smiled, and walked around to the end of the table, offering their hands, him first. He said, "Hello, Mrs. Sims, good to see you again. I'm Paul Lawson; this is my partner, Ms. Keyes. We came over last year, after Samone—"

"Yes, thank you," I said, interrupting him. "I remember." I dropped my head. Sweat trickled down my midriff from up under my arms. Would they be able to see that? I did not want to be here in the glare of fluorescent lights talking about Samone in an interview for a job that was supposed to help me learn how to forget about losing him. I said, "I'm sorry I interrupted you, Mr. Lawson; I'm not usually so rude. I guess I'm nervous."

He just kept smiling at me, still facing me, and stepped back, gracefully, so that Ms. Keyes could reach over and shake my hand. She said, "We think the world of your sister Ashley. It is such a pleasure to meet you." There was a lilt in her, something that made me think of spring. I had not expected such lightness in a job interview. She walked to the far side of the table and looked at Mr. Lawson.

He took the cue and said, "Know this has been a hard time for you. We are glad, though, that you have come in today to look at the receptionist position. Please, let's all sit down."

"Thanks," I said, taking the chair across the table from the two of them. After I did, they sat. Then Ashley, standing behind me and to my left, took a seat on my side of the table. She looked so professional, a file and pen on the table neatly in front of her, not at all like my sister who left a trail of clothes through her room and dishes stacked in the sink for days when Mother and Daddy weren't there. She smiled another reassuring smile at me. I smiled back. It loosened me up some.

Mr. Lawson looked toward Ashley, acknowledged her with a nod, and said, "I told Ashley last week that we really need some help on the front desk. Our receptionist is moving out of state to be with her daughter who is having her first grandchild." He sat, then, in silence, waiting for me.

"Yes, she told me," I said. "My Janie is the first grandchild on both sides. They are very special."

"They certainly are," Mr. Lawson agreed. "I believe that Ms. Keyes can tell you about grandchildren."

She smiled and said, "There aren't enough good things that can be said about grandchildren. I'll take an oath to that."

We laughed. The air in the room lightened up even more. Mr. Lawson moved directly into the matter: "Well, I appreciate Ashley having you come in. It is very important to have someone at the front desk who can give a client a good first impression."

"I can understand that, Mr. Lawson. But to tell you the truth, I don't have that much work experience outside the home." I realized I had just broken the second rule of job interviews, having already broken the first earlier: don't interrupt the interviewer.

He continued as if I had said exactly the right thing. "Are you interested in getting into the workforce, Mrs. Sims?"

"Well, yes, I think so," I said. I didn't want to get into anything, really, except bed, by myself, and stay there the rest of my life, but I smiled and feigned interest.

"Good. Do you mind taking a few tests this afternoon that we use for the position?"

"Sure, certainly, yes, I'd be glad to," I said, as upbeat as I could possibly be, wondering as I spoke what in the world he was talking about.

"Great," he said, looking me directly in the eyes. "Do you have any questions?"

"Well, Janie will be in kindergarten, and they leave school at three, so I'm not sure about the hours," I said.

It didn't deter Mr. Lawson. "Yes. Ashley and I talked about that. We have a clerk who can handle the front desk after three. Any other questions?"

I said, "No, no, I really can't think of anything to ask."

He smiled, not a condescending bone in his body, stood, came around the table again, and reached out his hand to me for another handshake. "Well, we have to run," he said, seeming to take me into his confidence. "Billable hours, you know."

I responded to the handshake, feeling somewhat surprised at how quickly this had gone. I thought interviews were long and drawn out and places where a person had to tell things about themselves and what they knew.

"Thank you, Mr. Lawson," I said. "And Ms. Keyes." I looked at them both as best I knew how. I liked them.

Mr. Lawson turned as he was leaving the room and said, "Ashley will take care of everything. She's been the administrator here from the outset. We couldn't do without her. It was very nice to meet you." He smiled wide.

Ms. Keyes stood and blinked at me like she was on my side. She, too, came around the table, reached out for another handshake, and said, "Know you will ace the tests. Look forward to working with you." They left the room.

"Tests, you didn't tell me I was going to be taking tests," I said to Ashley.

She laughed out loud. "Sis, if you can't pass the tests I'm going to give you, we've got bigger problems than this job."

I completed some paperwork for Ashley and said to the receptionist as I walked back into the reception area, "I wish you luck with your move."

She grinned wide, relief showing. "Thanks, Mrs. Sims. You, too."

The phone rang, and she turned to answer it. I grabbed the newspaper with Silver's picture inside and tucked it into my handbag to hide him from Ashley and anybody else who might come into the room. It dawned on me when I did it that, except for Samone's life, this was the first thing that I had ever stolen in mine.

15.

MEMORIES AND MOMMAS

Five a.m. I was awake, hovering in the darkness. Worrying. It was my first day on the new job that I didn't want. I questioned why any legitimate business would want me working for them. What if I couldn't do the work and I messed up and Ashley got in trouble? I was not a modern working woman. I was a failed wife and a semifunctioning mother who had spread her legs for a stranger who folded her panties and put them in the car's glove compartment.

But I realized that at the office, Samone's clothes wouldn't still be hanging in a closet—I hadn't been able to bring myself to clear his closet out. When I opened the closet door and went in there, it still smelled like him, which I had not wanted to lose, not just yet. I kept wondering if there was something he needed me to do, so he would turn me loose, but I didn't know what it was. Plus, if he told me what it was, I couldn't trust him. Any man who would do what he did to Janie and me was not trustworthy. It came to me that I had been locked in a world with closets around every corner with no escape, my eyes not able to see far enough.

So, I played tricks on myself: I pretended nothing in the closet ever happened. It did, though. Some days I hated him for everything. Some days I ached for him. Some days I wanted to slap him. Some days I wished I could hold him like I wouldn't let him hold me. And I didn't have the energy to face any of it, much less worry about what to wear to a job. I wanted to stay in a ball curled up in a corner of the world. Alone. But I couldn't. Janie was there. She needed a momma.

Mommas are people who don't know how to be who they are, who try to help their children be who they are supposed to be. Mommas wear smiles and wag fingers at our kids, pretending we know what we are talking about and telling them to listen to us, and all the while we are lost. We try to keep them safe, knowing full well that it is not safe to be or love or live. We don't know anything and we can't learn. Damn liars, all of us.

I ran the shower at six-thirty and an hour later walked out into the garage dressed in a black skirt, a white blouse, and black pumps with my hair rolled up into a bun, again. The neck was healed. I did not have to wear a scarf. I walked Janie to the car holding her hand. She'd said over her cereal, "I gotta wear my Sunday shoes, Momma. That is 'portant." I didn't have the heart to tell her that she couldn't wear her black patent leather shoes with a strap all day during her first day at kindergarten, because I knew her feet would be hurting by midmorning, so I let her wear them and tucked her sneakers into a bag with a note explaining everything to her teacher.

The day at the office went easily. Ashley spoon-fed me what I needed to know. Everybody smiled at me and acted like I was supposed to be there.

Janie liked kindergarten. She talked nonstop on the ride home, and when we walked into the kitchen that afternoon she tugged on my skirt and looked up at me, blinking, "Momma, I wuv you. Come play dolls with me and I will tell you 'bout the school."

"I will, sweetheart. Yes, I will. Go change out of your school clothes. I'll be there, in a minute." As the words came out, I realized I had just done to Janie what I did to Samone that night I was baking the chocolate cake and he said, with a twinkle in his eye, "Renee, it's ten o'clock. Let's go to bed."

But to him I had countered, razor sharp, "Ashley's asked me to bring this chocolate cake for our Florida trip tomorrow, Samone. I've gotta bake the cake."

His face dropped.

"Don't pout," I said, putting him off. "You'll get a slice of it when I finish, chocolate cake with chocolate icing."

He looked at me with tired old eyes and said, "Okay." He turned and walked out of the kitchen and said in afterthought, "Wake me when you come to bed, Renee."

Half listening to him, I stirred the batter and said, "I will." I didn't even do him the courtesy of looking at him. When I crawled in under the covers, he was snoring. I was tired. I fell asleep.

The next morning the three of us sat at the table together in our kitchen and ate our breakfast.

Janie crawled up on his lap. "How much do you wuv me, Daddy?" Janie asked Samone.

He squeezed her, stretched his arms as wide as they would stretch, and said, "Wider than the world, sweetheart, wider than the world."

He brought his arms back in to rest on Janie. She giggled and pushed his arms out again and said, "Say it one more time, Daddy."

He laughed and stretched his arms again and said, "Wider than the world, sweetheart, wider than the world."

She hugged him, jumped down, scooted off.

Samone pushed his chair back and motioned for me to sit on his lap. I did.

"Pretty playful, aren't you, mister, for a Monday morning," I teased.

"You didn't wake me last night," he said sweetly, like a man who'd never been denied anything he'd ever wanted from me.

"You were snoring; couldn't do it," I said, feeling ashamed.

He lifted my chin and looked at me as if what he was about to say was an important instruction of some kind, for a rite of passage. "Enjoy your trip, Renee, you and Janie. Be safe. See you in a week. Regardless of anything, Renee, I love you, I truly do."

I never told him I loved him. I never even answered him back. Why didn't I answer him? Something? Anything? Even "Okay." Just "Okay."

Janie called me. I pulled loose from Samone like we had the rest of our lives to talk about loving each other. I slipped down off his lap and walked toward Janie. He followed me to hug me. I didn't let him. I reached for Janie. Over my shoulder I said, "See you in a week." She scooted off, again.

"Yes," he said, and then he put his hands on my shoulders and turned me toward him. I warmed and looked at him and smiled.

He smiled at me with a seriousness I'd never seen on his face before. He said, "When you get back in a week, Renee, we have to talk."

"Okay. About what?" I asked.

He didn't say anything. He took the answer with him to the front door. But then he turned and walked a few steps back toward me, his mouth open to say something. We were maybe three feet apart. He spread his arms wide for me, like he'd done for Janie at the breakfast table, to hug me. I didn't step into his arms. I looked at them and his mouth about to speak and, in the face of every invitation of his to meet him and hear him, I yelled down the hall to Janie something about making sure she didn't leave her flip flops, which she'd need for the beach.

She squealed and said, "Oh, boy, beach! Where are they, Momma?"

I raised my eyebrows at Samone and shrugged my shoulders, saying with my body language, Oh my goodness, what next?

He looked at me and closed his eyes hard. He shook his head. His arms were still open. I threw him a kiss and waved and said, "Let me go find her flip flops." I left his arms open without me in them. I never heard what we needed to talk about.

That's how I see him now in dreams, when he comes, and he does, sometimes, with his arms open, waiting on me to hug him, his mouth trying to tell me something important. I cannot stand it.

16.

81110 Connie Street

Saturday afternoons, Gloria was always ready when Sam arrived, her eyes sparkling when she opened the door. He'd go home the other six days wanting Renee to want him and wanting to want her and not dream about pear preserves, while he lay alongside Renee's body, tiny, skinny, with Renee off in some place he didn't understand while she was right there beside him, oblivious to his thrashing around tangled up in an invisible net that wouldn't let him breathe.

He couldn't sleep on the seesaw. His blood pressure went sky high. The doctor put him on medication and said, "You are young to get high blood pressure, Sam. Working too hard?"

Sam smiled at him and said, "Yes, probably, Doc," thinking, as he looked at the doctor, about Gloria's voice, how it sounded when they sat on her deck and she'd turn and say, "Sam, let me get us some more tea." Or, "Sam, do you mind checking the birdbath? It's got a leak and the sparrows don't visit anymore." Or, "Sam, I really like talking with you," after they'd sat in an easy quiet for a time.

Months passed. The web grew tighter. Their hands touched, occasionally; their eyes, always.

*****

Renee and Ashley and Janie went to the beach for a week, but Samone refused to go. "I can't, Renee; I've got inventory to work. That sale coming up. I have to work."

All of it was true, but he lied. It was as much as done in the lie, amidst which Renee looked at him and said, "Samone, I know I've been hard to get along with lately. I want to try."

Samone's heart was not in her last ditch effort. He didn't care if she tried or wanted to try or not. He didn't want to go anywhere with Renee, not to Florida, not to the kitchen. A person's heart has limits, and after a heart has been smashed to smithereens the pieces get lost and some of them can never be found again.

Renee called as soon as they arrived at the beach and said, "Samone, we are here. What you doing?"

"I'm working inventory, Renee. Have a good time. Take care of Janie. Don't let her get out in deep water."

"Wish you had come with us, Samone. The water is beautiful." The whine in her voice was like that of a kid who wanted her way, not a person speaking to be who she was for him, but a person attempting to keep him in the box she'd believed he was in all the time, an item tucked away to access when it was convenient for her and her happiness.

But he was no longer an item in Renee's box, so he spoke like he might speak to a vendor about an order: "I bet it is beautiful, Renee. You all have a good time."

His voice was hard. Hearing his voice being hard hurt him. She had heard the hardness. "You okay, Samone?" she asked. Her voice dropped with his name, a drop that was an "I've had about as much of you as I can take."

Maybe this was the first time she'd heard him in a very long time.

"I'm fine. Just tired. Just lots to do here," Samone said. He wanted to scream, but he didn't know what to scream. Renee was hearing him, Boobs Samone, the person she found back there on that school bus, and there he was not caring and smelling pear preserves and losing her and them with a calmness that frightened him. But if he had known what was going to happen, would he have stopped, attempted to back life up, and turn down a different street to seek them? No, he would not have stopped. He would have revved it up faster.

17.

A Handful of Yellow Mums

Everything was coming together at the same time. The excitement was agonizing. He couldn't think straight anymore, but the crazy thing was he believed that for the first time in a long time his heart was doing the thinking.

Sam was not a touchy-feely guy. He didn't understand it. But he'd trudged that rutted road, mile after mile after mile, empty, his feet shackled, blinders on, trying to move forward, going nowhere with Renee. He loved her, but she'd closed her arms and wouldn't let him out of the rut. She couldn't hear him begging her. She couldn't hear him.

One day, he looked up in Mac's Coffee Shop and there was sunshine, gentle, kind, a lushness that he didn't even know was possible. The ruts looked different in that sunshine.

On the phone, Gloria's voice had that sunshine in it: "Sam, I have a great big ole blanket to take with us on the picnic. Picnickers have to have a place to stretch out and take a nap after eating homemade deviled eggs." She giggled. He felt sixteen. His skills were rusty. He knew that.

He said back, "Love me some deviled eggs, dear lady. And for sure the nap, before and or after the deviled eggs."

She laughed and told him about the menu. He held his breath to be able to hear every syllable she spoke through the magic of the telephone. Before Gloria, had he been walking around dead? Just thinking he was living? Had she birthed him? The world was upside down.

"We're on, then?" she asked. "Our place at Florence Lake at ten, tomorrow?"

Oh my God, her voice even smelled like pear preserves. Isn't there something holy about pears? Sam wondered. Hadn't he read somewhere that pears were sacred? He needed to look into that.

"A team of wild horses couldn't keep me away, Gloria," he said, his heart racing so fast when he spoke that he felt like it would come out of his chest.

She laughed again, this time a satisfied laugh with relief in it. He sighed.

"See you tomorrow," she said, sunshine all over her words.

"I will be there. Tomorrow. I can't wait!" He hung up the receiver and set his coffee cup on the counter, thinking what a fine woman she was and how he felt a glow inside himself when he talked with her. A cloud drifted into that glow: he had to face Renee and tell her the truth about Gloria; he should have already told her. He'd always told Renee the truth, until this. Sam rinsed the cup and set it in the sink. The phone rang. It was Renee.

"Janie and I are headed home, Samone," she said. "Be there late afternoon tomorrow. How are things?"

There was a new lilt in her voice that puzzled him.

"Great, Renee," he lied. "'Bout what time do you think you'll get in?" Waiting for Renee's answer, he looked at his watch, calculating how much time he and Gloria would have on the blanket before they would need to fold it and put it in her trunk.

"Oh, it'll be late, maybe dark. We are stopping at Ashley's favorite place in Mobile for lunch and taking Janie to a doll exhibit there," Renee rambled on.

He listened with Gloria right up close to him. A person might judge him, Gloria being there in his heart during his conversation with Renee, but, honestly, if he were completely truthful, Gloria had been there ever since she first arrived.

Something different happened, though, during Renee's call: Renee's voice sounding round reminded him of the roundness of Gloria's breasts, which he had not touched with his hands, only his eyes, so he listened to Renee, anticipating his first taste of pear preserves.

The unfaithful thoughts about Gloria while he talked with Renee were not deliberate. His feeling for Renee was gone.

He said, "Drive safely, Renee. Don't hurry. I have a lot to do tomorrow."

Renee said, "Okay, we'll take our time. Here, Janie wants to tell you something."

Janie was hyperexcited, wanting to tell him their whole week in a few sentences: "So much water here, Daddy, and it jumps up on my legs and things tickle my toes in the sand. Coming home and bringing you some stuff we bought in a store. Oops, Mama says don't tell you that." She giggled and mumbled something to Renee and then directed her words back at him again and said, "Wuv you!"

"I love you, Janie. Have fun." He wanted to hug her. His eyes watered. Renee came back on the line. He said, "Be safe, Renee." His words came out as flat as something he might have said to a person he'd just chatted with in an airport who stood to go to his plane. Renee dropped the tone of her voice like she knew he wasn't there. Which was, in a way, a compliment to her that she had actually paid enough attention to begin to notice his absence.

That night he slept with cantankerous questions, restless babies, never still. He woke, emotionally battered and bruised. First thing, he stepped out onto the back deck and picked a small handful of yellow mums that he tied together with a slender white ribbon to make Gloria a bouquet. It was not nearly enough, but it was all he had. He carried the bouquet to the car, placed it on the car seat, and backed out of the driveway, not seeing Mrs. Mabel Morris a few feet away, puttering in her flowerbed. But her wave caught his eye. He felt guilty. His face turned red. He waved back. She yelled, her voice muted outside the car, her mouth moving and her eyebrows going up and down. He stopped and rolled down the car window.

She smiled and shouted, "Samone, you look particularly spiffy this morning. Heard from Renee?"

"Well, thank you, ma'am," he replied. "You look nice, yourself. Yes, Renee called yesterday. She and Janie will be home tonight." Renee's name sounded hollow out against the fullness of the morning.

Mrs. Mabel folded her hands on her round tummy and smiled a sweet rumpled garden goddess smile. She said, "Have a great day, Samone. Know you'll be glad to get 'em home." What a beautiful bouquet of mums, she thought. I need to grow more mums, particularly on the east side of the back yard.

"You, too, Mrs. Mabel. You bet!" he said, waving back at her, thinking how absolutely irresponsible he had been to have walked out into the open, across their front yard, carrying a handful of yellow mums for another woman.

He could barely breathe. In his dreams of late, when he was suffocating, Gloria would come to him and he would place his face between her breasts and, when he did, precious air would flow into him and he would breathe. He needed to breathe. He pointed the car toward Florence Lake.

18.

RED MUD ON HIS BOOTS

I needed the Florida trip and the vastness of the Gulf of Mexico. Ashley cared for Janie, often, so I could spend time alone on the beach, where the rhythm of the waves relentlessly pounding the shore mirrored for me my own pounding of Samone with my anger at life's ups and downs.

"I have been thoughtless for a very long time," I told one of the beach birds that helped me eat my sandwich. And I wept.

A week later the three of us arrived home about dusk, tanned and rested. I needed to see Samone, to have the talk he wanted to have, to listen to him. I really had not listened much to him at all since his daddy died. As we began unpacking the car, Janie tugged on the bottom of my shorts and said, "Momma, wet me go home with Aunt Asht, okay?"

She and Ashley had become big buds during the week.

I handed Janie her beach ball to take inside. She set it on the grass and ran over to Ashley, tugged at her shorts, and asked, "Can I, Aunt Asht, can I?"

"Janie, it's not nice to invite yourself to someone's house," I said, laughing. "Here, let's get our things out of the car and inside."

She totally ignored my instructions, tugged at me again, and said, "Not invitin', Momma. Aunt Asht told me on the beach 'mi casa su casa'; you know what that means?"

"And Janie is exactly right, sis," Ashley said, laughing. "Grab your doll, Janie; Mother will want to see you and hear about the shark you saw. I'll bring her back after a while, Renee."

They drove away, Janie waving. I began unrolling the water hose to set the sprinkler out. The grass was brown; Samone had obviously not watered it since we left. I heard the phone ringing, dropped the hose, and ran inside, expecting to hear his voice on the other end. I'd missed him. And the more I'd pondered us and how I'd let him down for so long, the further away he'd felt to me, like we were more separate than usual, wider apart.

I lifted the phone to my ear. "Hello!" I said, listening for his voice.

But a formal voice that I did not recognize said, "May I speak with Mrs. Sims?"

"This is she," I said, thinking that I didn't want to deal with anybody right now, not a salesperson or anybody other than Samone. I wanted to tell him that I loved him.

"Mrs. Renee Sims?" the voiced probed.

"Yes," I said, annoyed that someone was busying up the telephone line. Samone might be trying to call right this minute.

The man hesitated and the silence was loud. I felt heaviness in it. Right at that moment, in that silence, I knew something wasn't right. After what seemed an eternity, he continued, "Mrs. Sims, I have some bad news for you. I think you should meet us at the hospital."

"What news? Why do I need to meet you at the hospital?" I hung on the voice, its words.

"Are you married to Samone Sims?"

"Yes, yes, that's right. What's wrong?"

"He has been shot."

"Shot! What are you talking about?" I dropped the phone.

I ran. Out the front door. Screaming. I did not know what else to do, but as my foot hit the top step off the porch, I knew that I could not outrun this.

Mrs. Mabel Morris was in her front flower bed next door. I fell in front of her.

"Dear, what in the world is the matter? What is wrong, Renee?"

"Thank God you are here, Mrs. Mabel," I said as I grabbed for her.

She dropped her clippers and squatted in front of me, my hands on her arms, and asked, "Renee, what is going on? Are you all right?"

"Samone has been shot," I said. "They just called me. He's in the hospital. I've got to get to him."

"Oh my God! Yes, you have to get to him. We've got to get you to the hospital. I'll drive my car," she said, steady, in control. "Wait here.

I will get my car keys. How did he get shot, Renee? Does he keep guns at The Shoppe?"

I did not answer her. I did not know. I needed to see him. I needed to tell him so much.

Mrs. Mabel drove as meticulously as she gardens, stopping this side of every yellow light. "Run it, Mrs. Mabel," I said at one intersection.

She didn't, and she didn't say a word back to me. When we arrived at the hospital, she pulled in under the ER canopy behind an ambulance parked at the curb. Two stout men were carrying a stretcher from it with a man on it wearing Samone's boots. Yes, those were his boots.

I jumped out of the car and ran to him, but the hospital personnel all around him pushed me back, "I'm sorry, ma'am," one of them said, "we have to get him inside."

"I'm his wife," I said. "I am with him." That did not help. They ignored me. They wheeled him through the double doors and left me standing there.

But you would have thought they already knew we were coming: a woman that looked official walked over to Mrs. Mabel and me and said, "Come this way, Mrs. Sims." She didn't smile or try to talk with us. She opened the door to a tiny holding room, a cubbyhole of a pale green-walled space with two mismatched straight back chairs on either side of a small, naked table pushed up against the wall. A cheap picture of an eighteenth-century family hauling their belongings across the prairie hung lopsided and off center above the table.

"Please, Mrs. Sims, wait here, if you will. Somebody will be with you in a moment," the woman said, firm, direct, distant, like she didn't want to get us on her hands. You would have thought we were here to buy a driver's license or pay for a speeding ticket.

I didn't want a chair. I didn't want to sit down. I paced. Eventually, I said to Mrs. Mabel, "I can't stand it any longer."

Mrs. Mabel said, "Stay here, Renee. It's best."

I whispered angrily at her—not wanting anyone to hear me and stop me, "How dare they close me off in a room away from my husband!"

She let me leave. I crept down the corridor toward the murmur of voices in the treatment rooms along either side. I was lucky. I found Samone. Well, I knew it was him. It had to be. He had on his hiking boots. And they were so muddy. Red muddy. Thick red muddy. He was on a table inside one of the treatment rooms, only a few steps down the corridor from the cubbyhole where they had stashed us. The door was slightly ajar, so I just stood out there, very quiet, not making noise, because I had to see and I did not want to be shooed away.

When I peered through the opening in the doorway, I saw the doctor working on Samone, trying to get him to breathe. He wouldn't. At the far end of Samone's bed, I could see his head—or where it should have been—but it had no face, just red bloody flesh dripping out onto his shoulders. I could make out his left ear. One time I kissed that ear, when we were scuffling together on the sofa right after we got married, before we lost each other.

I smothered my mouth with my hands and got down on my knees in the middle of the corridor. Hiding.

My mind was playing tricks. I was certain of that. How else could I be looking at my husband with no head—except for an ear—and be getting bent out of shape about there being mud on his boots when it hadn't rained in weeks? The ground was as dry as dust. And the mud was packed on his boots. I just couldn't understand that. But it was just me, not wanting to look at where his head was supposed to be. I guess the boots were safer.

The doctor spoke to his assistant as clear as anything, saying, "This damage was close range, all right. Look at the powder burns. Damn, he blew his brains out."

It didn't seem like I could be hearing all of that with my own ears. It didn't make any sense. Surely I was in a dark well looking up, seeing and hearing that doctor off somewhere talking about somebody else, not Samone, not like he was an index card with markings the doctor was checking off. I had to be dreaming. Yes, I was dreaming. I would wake up and then this would stop. I would see Samone.

"What happened, do you think?" the nurse asked, turning toward the doctor as she spoke.

The doctor said—mind you, he had no idea I was standing off over here outside the door listening—"The authorities said this man killed himself. A forty-five. It came out the back. Absolutely no evidence of anything else except suicide. Gun lying right there. The coroner, of course, will have the final say so. He'll be here in a few minutes."

"My God," the nurse said, "why would a man this young kill himself? I just don't understand it."

The doctor covered Samone's head with the sheet and removed his plastic gloves. Easy as that.

The nurse, too, just went right on living, clearing the stainless steel side table, tossing bloody gauze into a big trash can. She dropped a wad of it on the floor and bent over to pick it up. But she was messy and left a smear of Samone's blood on the floor.

I crumpled over, the doctor's voice drifting off into the distance, sounding like a gong, "Never know why people do what they do. A man's got to have a passel of troubles to take his own life. Yes, a passel of troubles . . . a passel of troubles . . . a passel of troubles . . ."

I came to with a tall man wearing green standing over me. He moved me back to the cubbyhole. After some time—time didn't matter anymore; it never would—a nurse, wrinkled and tired, skin brown from cigarettes, and a large mole on her right cheek, came in to me carrying a tray with a syringe lying on it, stark, alone. I told that nurse that I didn't want any shots. I needed to be alert. That seemed sensible to me, since I'd been kidnapped and was being held in a haunted house with costumed goblins talking about Samone killing himself and forcing me into a sliver of a room with a lopsided old picture. Those hospital people couldn't have really been there with me. They just thought that they were.

Then I was very clear in what I said. If the nurse had listened, she'd have heard it. I said, "I want my husband." But she wouldn't listen to me no matter what I said. Mrs. Mabel nodded at her and the syringe. I saw it, every bit of it; they were conspiring. In a minute, my mouth got dry and I couldn't talk plain and I needed to ask questions and talk to my husband. Never go to a hospital to find life.

Out of the maze, it hit me. Janie. Oh, my God, Janie. "How do I get to her?" I asked Mrs. Mabel.

She held my arm, walking me toward one of the chairs, and asked, "Get to whom, Renee?"

I tried my best to explain, but it was useless. This whole thing was useless.

The nurse stepped in between Mrs. Mabel and me and took my arm. She said to me, "Sit here for a few minutes, Mrs. Sims, before you leave, why don't you. It's going to be all right."

It was all I could do not to slap her. What in the Goddamn hell did she know?

"My baby," I said. "I have to get to my baby."

And then the rest of the day became a race in slow motion. Now, of course, it is just a heavy fog. Like it was talking with Janie. But everything sped up too fast for me to keep up when I talked with her. I still see it. Pristine. Clear. I didn't lie. I just didn't tell her the truth. I said, "Your daddy has gone away on a trip for a time. He didn't have a chance to tell us good-bye." I was thinking, though: He fucking planned to kill himself and did it and didn't bother to tell me.

But he did try to tell me good-bye. He did. I didn't let him. Maybe that killed him. Maybe my walking away from his arms and not letting him hug me and not letting him speak what was in him forced him to pull the trigger.

19.

COUNTERCLOCKWISE

About a year separated my losing Samone and my losing Grandmother Tracy. In fact, Grandmother Tracy died exactly two weeks after the gazebo, on a rain-weary day at the tail end of a week of summer downpours.

We had her funeral in the church she had attended for decades, a tiny used-to-be-white, one-aisle holy place, about a quarter full of mourners, tucked back up in a sheltering grove of pine trees, complete with a leaning steeple and wood floors with cracks wide enough for lizards to slide in and out. Steam oozed up into the church out of the moss-covered churchyard and glued the pages of the hymnals together. Even at eleven a.m., the mist in the air would have been perfect for filming a murder mystery.

To get in the church to say our good-byes, we had to fight off swooping bluebirds that chirped like they were auditioning for the choir. One of the ushers who stood sentry at the front door in a shiny light blue suit with too short pants waved his scrubbed dirt-ingrained hands to try to help protect us from the birds. He said, "Y'all be careful now. Must have 'em a nest a eggs somers nearby."

As the choir of some half dozen people in white choir robes sang Grandmother Tracy's two favorite songs, Beulah Land and I'll Fly Away, a couple of the birds plopped down outside on the weather beaten windowsill within arm's reach of me, seemingly mesmerized by the music, jerking their heads around to keep a look out so as not to get caught.

Rev. Jones, the Missionary Baptist minister, only infrequently inserted Grandmother Tracy's name into his sermon and, in fact, mispronounced it, saying "Cavalier" as if it were spelled "Cabalier." Despite that, he could have won a most-fervent preaching contest. He raised his voice high and dipped his arms low, wiping the sweat off his brow with a handkerchief. He greatly overachieved at using the occasion of Grandmother Tracy's funeral to try to "save" us all. If Grandmother Tracy had been alive, it is my guess that she would have told him after the funeral that he'd overdone it by a long shot. But she was dead. Everybody was dying. I was overwhelmed.

Mother was sad. She forgot to take with her the philosophy that strong people don't let things get to them. I never did like that saying, anyway.

As we left the church, Mr. Lawson came over to us and said, "I'm so sorry for your loss. I know you will miss her. Please don't try to come back into the office for a few days, Ashley and Renee." We thanked him and walked together to the grave site to watch them bury her.

It is a pitiful sound, the creak of the casket dropping into the open hole and the thump of the clod of dirt on its top. A pure pitiful sound.

One afternoon, a few days after Grandmother Tracy's funeral, I began making an early supper, pasta with red sauce, one of Janie's favorites. The phone rang. I kept stirring the pasta with my right hand and reached for the phone with my left.

"Hello," I said.

"Renee?" the voice on the other end said.

"Yes . . ."

I waited. No sound. Must be a prank caller. I frowned and reached to lay the phone in the cradle.

He spoke, "Renee, this is Silver."

"Silver?" My gut tightened in fear. I listened hard.

"You've already forgotten me?" he asked, annoyed.

"I have not forgotten you, Silver," I said.

He burst into song, the one that was playing on my car radio that day I had driven us down the interstate toward the unexpected horror of the gazebo. The same words. He was singing them, again. The same inflection. I didn't want to hear the song. I didn't want to hear his voice. I shut out the lyrics. I held the phone out away from my ear. I closed my eyes. Nausea welled up in me.

Janie walked in, dragging her big girl doll. "Who's that, Momma? Daddy?"

"Hold on a minute, will ya?" I said into the receiver.

"Yeah, I will," he replied. He began whistling on the other end, an I-guess-I-will-have-to-wait kind of whistling.

"No, sweetheart, it's not your daddy, it's a friend," I said, laying the receiver on the counter and sitting down in a kitchen chair to be closer to Janie's face.

She looked puzzled, hugged her big girl doll tightly, and said, "I wuv Daddy wider than the world, Momma, wider than the world."

She waddled out of the kitchen telling her big girl doll, "That's what I'll tell him when he gets back from there."

I picked up the phone, thinking I'd tell this crazy man a polite good-bye, but I didn't have it in me to even deal with him. I set the receiver in the cradle.

I smelled burnt pasta. We ate sandwiches for supper.

*****

Janie had been in her bed for about an hour when the doorbell rang. I looked at my watch. Nine-thirty p.m. Who in the world would be coming here at this hour?

I went to the door. There stood Silver wearing a tee shirt and jeans. That lock of red hair was drooping down over his left eye. He looked bedraggled, not anything like the together man with the red fuzz on his arms whom I had met in the intensive care unit's waiting room.

"Hey, Silver," I said, startled that he was standing on my front porch at this hour. "What are you doing here?"

"Hi. Can I come in?" Silver asked, pushing back the red lock of hair.

I did not open the door.

"It's late. How did you find me?"

"I followed the roses," he said proudly.

"What?"

"Didn't you get them?" He shifted on his feet and, nervous like, pushed higher the already rolled up short sleeves of his tee.

"Yes, they were beautiful. I wish I could invite you in, but I just put Janie to bed. I'm right behind her. I have a new job, have to be at work early tomorrow." I tried to smile.

"It's a long time 'til morning, Renee," he said, a begging in his voice. Then, without saying another word, he pushed in the screen door, which I thought was latched. He walked inside. I stood there, speechless. He swaggered in and around the living room and kitchen, scrutinizing everything like he was there for an open house.

I tiptoed down the hall and checked on Janie. She was sound asleep. Gently, I closed her door, came back to the living room, shut the living room door into the hall, and locked it.

Silver had his back to me as I came into the living room. He twisted toward me in a burst of anger and said, "You hung up on me!"

"I didn't," I replied, trying to ease him away from that.

He raised his voice and said, "You didn't? What do you mean 'you didn't'?"

I put my finger across my lips and said, "Shh, you'll wake my daughter, Janie. I hung up, Silver, not on you, but because Janie walked in and heard me on the phone and thought you were her daddy."

"Her daddy? Is he here? I thought you said you weren't married," he argued, flinging back that lock of red hair, over and over. I could have sworn the red fuzz on his arms bristled.

"No, I'm widowed," I replied, as calmly as I could, "but Janie doesn't know that her daddy is dead."

"Doesn't know that he's dead? What do you mean? Are you hiding that from her? Why?" He shot the questions, pop, pop, pop!

Flabbergasted, I stood there, not saying anything for a time, not sure what to say. Who was this man?

"Well, say something, damn it," he said, like he owned some kind of right to my words.

I became angry, so I shot it out, plain and simple: "He killed himself, Silver. It was my fault. I couldn't tell her."

Silver turned pale. A sinister grin of satisfaction spread across his face, like he'd been hit with some unexpected good news. He sat down on the sofa, flipping that hair back again from over his eye. He shook his head in disbelief and said, sarcastically, "So, your daughter thinks her daddy is alive out there somewhere."

"She thinks that he might come back. Yeah, I guess so," I said, realizing how it sounded.

"He may be dead, Renee, but he's not really gone. Is he?"

I stood still and listened to his question. I couldn't hear it.

"Why did he kill himself?"

I didn't want to answer that question. I didn't want him to ask the question. I began to cry. Finally, I said, "I don't know."

He spat back, "You don't know, but you say it's your fault. What kind of woman are you?"

I sat down on the sofa. Silver just sat there staring at me. I think if I live to be a hundred, I'll never forget that empty hole inside me at that moment. I dropped my head. He reached over and began trying to wrest my hair from the clip holding it.

"Please, please don't do that, Silver," I said, "I am tired."

He flew into a crazed madman rage. "Tired. What are you tired from? Who'd you fuck today?"

"What?" I could not believe he'd said that to me.

"Stand up and take off your clothes, Renee," he said, like he was ordering his eggs over easy.

"Silver, you have got to be kidding. It is time for you to go." I stood up and walked toward the door.

He kept sitting.

"Maybe we'd better call it an evening, Silver," I said.

He didn't budge. He said, "No maybe to it, Renee. I'm not leaving here tonight until I get what I came for."

"What?" I asked. "Get what you came for? It's bedtime, Silver. Janie is just down the hall. You have to leave."

He stepped in front of me and reached for my hair. As he pulled the big clip that held it up off my neck, he pushed us toward the sofa. My hair dropped. He ran his fingers through my hair and said, "You've made your bed, Renee; now lie in it counterclockwise."

"Counterclockwise?" I asked, befuddled. "What do you mean?"

"I will show you," he said, "and if you don't do what I tell you, Janie will know a lot more than that her daddy is dead."

He began moving in on top of me, without my consent, but I didn't say anything. I let it happen and pretended to be somewhere else. It seemed the only way. Funny what irrational things a person thinks about when they are in fear. I was fixated on probably not smelling clean because I had not washed up after I had burned the pasta and done the dishes.

He began unzipping my shorts and unbuttoning my shirt. I just let him, praying that Janie would not stir. I thought, He's right, Renee, you asked for this.

"Your underwear, too," he said, and he waited on me to remove them.

I took them off and handed them to him. He folded them neatly and laid them on the arm of the sofa. He pulled us up and into the center of the room, me naked, exposed, shaking, he still in his clothes. He began turning me around and around by my shoulders.

"Slowly, very slowly," he said, "keep turning like that, Renee, slowly, very slowly."

Then he took his hands away, knowing I was in his grip. I moved like a wind-up doll, too fast to suit him, I guess, because he kept telling me to slow down. I felt a taste in him that was outside of us, arousing him, directing us, a faceless technician. I didn't care. I didn't give a happy hallelujah. What in the name of God did it matter who directed what? I had stood in that very room on that very square foot of hardwood floor and I did not let my husband hug me. The world came to an end there.

I could turn and twirl from then until kingdom come and back, naked as a jaybird, on that spot, where in one place the wood wanted to buck up and down, and I could take Silver however he came. It had about as much effect on those loving open arms I turned my back on as time had had on my heart to heal me.

Twirl! Twirl! Twirl.

But he wanted me to barely move. I didn't care what he wanted, so I followed his directions. My hair swished on my shoulders and brushed across my nipples.

"Toss it back and forth, Renee," he insisted.

He thought he was there with me, but Renee was very far away.

At some point, Silver stepped into my nakedness. I became angry. Trapped, I did not want him against me. I pushed him. To my surprise, it caught him off guard and he fell on my floor. I could not believe it: he lay there with himself, begging me to turn and smile at him over my shoulder. At first, I was unwilling to play his game. Then, I succumbed. It did not matter. He seemed very pleased. As soon as he finished, I grabbed my clothes and covered myself. He slipped out the door. I stood there. A thing.

He turned when he stepped out onto the porch and said, "Don't you ever hang up on me again. Ever. Do you hear me? I don't like it."

I didn't respond. I latched the door.

*****

All the showers in the world could not have cleaned me, but I took two.

If there had ever been fresh air and sunshine and breezes and the sound of birds chirping, they were gone. It was dark there.

I will just not look, I told myself. Maybe I can stay sane that way. I will never speak a word of Silver to anyone. I cannot. How would anyone ever understand?

*****

The next day I called the hardware store. "Mr. Calo, this is Renee Sims up the street."

"Hey, Renee, what can I do for you today?" I could hear the cash register drawer opening and closing in the background and another salesman talking to a customer.

"Do you carry reinforced storm doors, Mr. Calo?"

"Sure do. What do you need?"

"I need one for the front and one for the back," I said, without asking a price.

One of his carpenters came that day and installed them. I kept them locked.

Silver didn't call or show up again. Time passed. I began to gain some emotional energy.

PART TWO

ANOTHER WORLD

20.

REDMAN

Josh Bridges could spit good and put a hit on you, easy. The corners of his mouth were always brown from suckling Redman, which he kept in the foil-lined pouch in his right back pants pocket, across from his heart, his wallet, in the left.

He'd mumble like a phonograph record playing on a too slow speed, pinch up a chew of Redman, tuck it into his cheek, and smile the contentment of a baby at its mother's breast.

After getting his chew, he'd roll the top of the pouch back down, crease it slick, and ram it, haphazardly, into his right back pants pocket, so that every right back pocket on every pair of his pants had stretched, over time, into a thin, limp, impotent bulge.

*****

Josh Bridges and Gloria were married, so far as the folks in Gargagun knew, but it was a set up from the get go, all business, separate bedrooms, no sexual relations, fronts for whatever the Raleigh Mafia needed fronted.

If every man in the entire universe had been lined up from which Gloria could pick and none of them suited her, Gloria would have done without a man forever before she would have entered a genuine relationship with Bridges. However, she was the light of his eye.

"I love that woman. No question about it," he'd say.

And it was true. He was, without any question, as deeply in love with her as a man with no heart and the impulse control of a four-year-old could be in love with anybody.

Gloria realized from the outset that living with him was the worst assignment she could have ever received. But she was strong and patient, with the ability to remain calm right past the juice in the corners of his mouth and his temper when she was not "payin' him enough mind."

In addition, Bridges drank a little whiskey every day, preferably Jack Daniels, to, as he called it, "stay in balance." For without a little alcohol in him, he was, as he admitted, "wilder 'n a loon."

And he binged. Often. When the insatiable craving to guzzle grabbed hold of him, he'd drink, wreak havoc, and then pass out to stink up a piece of God's earth somewhere for a few days until his own stench brought him to, at which time he'd scrounge around and beg his way into a breakfast beer, aiming, again, to "stay in balance," swearing through his crocodile tears never to ever put himself through it again.

He suffered from a short memory.

And, regardless of any of his promises to anybody, the setting of the sun always signaled for him serious drinking time. His declining eyesight was, in a way, a friend, for it blurred the sun's location in the western sky so that it looked lower and lower earlier and earlier every day, which beckoned him, of course, to spit out the Redman and twist the cap off the Jack earlier and earlier in the afternoon. "Ahhhhhhhh, sweet," he'd say and step again into the gateway to euphoria.

On occasion, however, even in the throes of euphoria, he bungled it. Like one night when he was making a business deal over at a man's house and something crawled down his pants leg. Startled and antagonized, he staggered up out of his chair, swirling and pulling on his leg, a cursing hound chasing his tail.

"What's the matter, Josh?" the man asked.

Bridges didn't answer. He was engrossed in circling himself, searching for his attacker.

The man's wife ran to the kitchen for a can of wasp repellant and rushed back into the room to witness a soft gray creature drop out of Bridges' pants leg onto the top of his left boot. It sat there, didn't move. Bridges poked it with his index finger, jerking his finger away to avoid being bitten, all the while saying, "What za hell?" as everybody stared and the woman with the wasp repellant moved in close enough to spray his attacker, if it became necessary.

Bridges ripped the creature off his boot and flung it up into the air. Everybody dodged and covered their heads. The man's wife screamed. It landed on the back of a chair and unfolded itself, slowly, into a pair of dirty jockey shorts.

Nobody laughed. It was quieter in that room than before God created the universe.

Bridges grasped the stupidity of what had just happened, even in his whiskey-induced euphoria. So, like the drunk who comes home at two a.m. and jumps his wife for not having his breakfast cooked, Bridges jumped the man in whose house he stood, accused him of planting dirty jockey shorts in his pants. Everybody at the meeting drifted out of the room silently, like worshippers departing a Good Friday service.

Despite Bridges' accusations, the man offered to drive him home. Bridges replied, "I gin drive this som of bitch anywhere I pleeze," pointing to the jockey shorts.

The man and his wife stood at the picture window in the living room, shaking their heads in disbelief as he stumbled across the yard, got his pants leg caught in the pickup door, fell, lost his keys on the ground, finally found them, cranked the pickup, and crept out of the driveway.

"Messed-upist man I ever saw," the man said to his wife. "Ain't doing no business lessen we can talk to Gloria."

*****

The string of these incidents came to a head the night he was in the kitchen by himself, drunk, trying to halve a lemon—he liked to suck lemons—when, out of the blue, in his whiskey-wet mind, Gloria was on him about his Redman. He could have been recollecting some old remark she might have made, like "Josh, Good Lord, please wipe that stuff off your mouth," which he would have likely interpreted to mean that she was coming between him and his chew. Or maybe he just needed her to give him attention.

Or maybe the sudden middle of March's unseasonable summer-ness somehow coaxed him to believe what wasn't true, for it had also provoked azaleas to bloom and sap to start rising and farmers to start thinking about things twisting in the bud.

I don't know.

Whatever it was, his warped mind, infected with rage and the stench of cheap whiskey, directed him to go outside and push Gloria off the metal lawn chair where she was sitting in the peaceful darkness, breathing in the strong scent of sweet olive, listening to the early evening critters, and fantasizing about getting out of Gargagun for good. He pinned her arms back and straddled her, waving his Redman pouch in front of her face.

"The hell you say, woman, you ain't running my life bout no Redman . . . nothing else from nothing . . . better keep yore mouth shut . . . bitch . . . know what's good . . ."

His attack caught her off guard. Redman and Josh Bridges hadn't actually even been in her thinking. Oh, she'd seen his pickup parked over on the side of the drive, off sideways in the grass like he'd already downed a good bit of his bottle. And she'd heard him rambling around in the kitchen, but she wasn't paying him any attention.

He damned her to hell. Said, "Ain't nobody ever accused me of niceties, Gloria. You knew that fore you got here." He balled up his fist. She did not flinch. Flinching was not much in Gloria. Of course, he knew that. But whiskey sometimes gets a man confused. He sat back on her long silk legs like she was a quarter horse he'd proudly mounted and slapped her hard across the left side of her face. Immediately, it swelled.

She slapped him back.

He slapped the other side of her face to even it up.

With the calmness of a Buddhist priest meditating in a garden, she lifted her immaculately manicured left hand and evened up his face quite nicely, and within the width of a breath, she closed her right hand into a beautiful fist and punched his crotch. Pain rollicked through him. He toppled like a bowling pin.

Gloria stood up.

He began crawling around on all fours, discombobulated, crying like only a drunk can cry, sputtering incoherently, "Damn women got no respect for a man, nuthin' in 'em understand importunt . . . get yore ass over here . . . nothin' Redman about it . . ."

Like lots of chronic drunks, he had a way of knowing when he had to change his approach to a situation. So, he got up and staggered to the back entrance to the house. It took him three attempts to open the screen door, and not before he ripped the spring out of the eyehook that held it to the jamb.

The next morning, Gloria called Seth Maddox, who'd been the Raleigh Mafia's boss since his daddy had died.

That afternoon Maddox summoned Bridges; he took the reassignment badly and begged, "Seth, let Gloria go with me. She ain't no good here by herself."

Seth Maddox didn't give a rat's ass about Josh Bridges. He shook his almost bald head, fringes of red combed slick behind his ears, looked out of compassionless eyes, and asked, "Bridges, you done gone and got yourself messed up with this woman?"

"Naw, Seth," Josh answered. "No way. You know I wouldn't do that. It's just that I do better, get better results, when she's involved. It's the pair of us has put Gargagun on the map as the hot spot." Bridges pulled at his ear.

"If Gargagun is a hot spot, we all gonna freeze smack to death, Bridges."

A sheet of fear slapped Bridges' back. He wished he had him some Redman. And some Jack.

"She's gotta stay in Gargagun," Maddox said. "She's been working with me, Bridges, since we were kids. She can read my mind. I can read hers. I can get more information from her quicker than I can get from anybody. I need her . . . in Gargagun. I need her. Do you get it, Bridges?"

A cold sweat broke out on Josh Bridges' face. "I get it," Bridges said. He really needed to pee.

"Well, and get this, too, Bridges," Maddox said. "If you ever again lay a hand on her, make peace with your maker. Do you understand?"

"Hell, yeah, Seth. You know I wouldn't touch a hair on that pretty woman's head." Bridges leaked onto his khakis and the stain widened down toward the knee.

"Get outta here and don't go back over to that house or anywhere near Gloria, ever. One of my men will help get you settled up toward Jaylo 'fore sunup."

Seth Maddox did that. Gave a man enough rope that if he killed you, it was, in his mind, the last thing left for him to do.

*****

Gloria moved into a small new cottage in a quiet neighborhood in Gargagun. One of Seth's lawyers filed the unnecessary papers for divorce in the Chancery Clerk's Office. The Petition for Divorce carried a date of a marriage that had never occurred and Gloria's real signature. Bridges did not contest it. The Divorce Decree was signed the first term of court after Bridges was duly served with process and the time under the statute had run.

21.

Night Moves

One night, some months after the Bridges' divorce was final and a couple of weeks before Samone pointed the car toward Florence Lake, Josh Bridges crept his old gray pickup down a narrow gravel road outside Gargagun. He turned into the driveway of an almost hidden farmhouse back up on a knoll. Pulled up near the carport. Parked. Laid his right arm across the truck horn. Honked it, steady and long. He rolled down the driver's window and stuck his head out, spat, and yelled, "Anybody home?" Spat again. Several barking hound dogs circled the truck, raring up on the front fender.

Inside the farmhouse, a redhead pulled aside a dingy flowered curtain and peeped out the window. "Shit! That bastard'll wanna sit out there in that truck and talk in this heat," he mumbled under his breath. He jerked on the swollen wooden door leading into the carport to open it. He yelled, "Hey, Josh, give me a minute. Gonna get me a Coca-Cola on some ice. Hot out here tonight. Want one?"

"Naw, don't drink them things; take your time; get whatever you need; we got us some strong talking to do," Bridges said. He slapped his arm. "Damn that mosquito!" It fell onto the truck seat. He didn't bother to brush it off.

"Okay, man, be right out," the redhead said, flipping back a stray lock of red hair from over his left eye.

Bridges opened the driver's door, put his left foot on the ground, and spat again. He stepped back into the truck, leaned across, and rolled down the passenger window. "Need a breeze through here in the worse way." Air fluttered across him. "Damn, that feels good," Bridges said.

All of the beauty of a hoot owl screeching mellow over the symphony of the cicadas was wasted on him. He never noticed it.

He reached into his shirt pocket and pulled out a photograph that the man had taken of Gloria and some big, good-looking hunk in hiking boots, the two of them sitting on a blanket under a tree. The man that snapped it for him had said, "No sir, they weren't touching, Mr. Bridges, just sitting there sorta google-eyed like teenagers. Not doing anything wrong."

Bridges focused the flashlight beam on the photograph, shook his head at Gloria's likeness, and said with the sadness of the hoot owl, "It's that smile on your face, Gloria. Gonna get that son of a bitch killed."

The breeze picked up.

Silently, Silver approached the truck under an almost full moon, its rays flirting with that little breeze that Josh Bridges had lured inside the pickup.

Bridges shivered to look up from Gloria's face and, unexpectedly, see Silver standing there, having made not a sound. Bridges remembered that he'd heard that Silver's mama had been part Cherokee and her husband a mean-ass raven-haired man that beat her most Saturday nights. How one day the raven-haired man just up and disappeared. Unexplained. Didn't anybody look for him or want him found. Sure not Silver's mama.

Silver twisted the door handle, still without making a sound, and slid inside the cab.

"Hey, Bridges, what's happening man? Got a fist of that chew for a fellow?" Silver used Bridges' vernacular, getting on his good side, though Silver'd been told the man really didn't have a good side.

Bridges handed Silver the pouch. Silver reached in, drew out a wad with his thumb and index finger, leaned his head back, shoved the wad deep up into his left jaw, sighed, returned the pouch, and waited.

"Ain't much better'n that first taste of baccy, is it?" Bridges bragged, scrunching up his nose, grinning. Maybe it was the only good feeling he'd ever fully understood, baccy in his mouth. Maybe that's why something encouraged Bridges to just abide Silver's sitting there with the Redman before he lit into the reason for his visit.

There they sat, two men inside the cab, wide awake, not moving a peg. Guess the hounds caught the tenor of it. The biggest and laziest of the three, sleeping off in the yard, roused and sniffed and began howling. Low. Lean. Long. Lonely.

Eventually, Bridges broke the spell and grunted, "Silver, got me a need for a bit of help. It ain't gonna be no regular help. Gonna put you in Seth's line of fire."

Silver laughed. "Hell, Bridges, I ain't skeered of Seth or his line of fire if what's in it for me is worth the shit. What you got?"

"What's funny, Silver?" Josh asked. To him, weren't a damn thing funny about Seth or his line of fire. A shiver ran down him as he remembered the last time he'd talked with Seth. He shifted around on the stickiness of the sweated-on front seat.

Silver pushed the dangling red curl back up over his eye again. "Nothing, Josh. What's on your mind?"

Bridges handed Silver the photograph. "That pretty thing of mine has done gone and moved into town, been there no time afore she got herself mixed up with a fellow runs a place called The Shoppe."

Silver viewed the couple. "Even without this moon's glow, Josh, anybody can see these two are into each other." Silver spat out the passenger window. "One of 'em or both of 'em, Bridges?"

Bridges did not immediately respond. Silver sat there waiting for Bridges' answer, like he was waiting to pick up his order at a fast food window.

"It oughta be both. Hell, I know it oughta be both, but I can't do it. I love her too much. Plus, Seth'd kill me. He's liable to kill you, anyway, if he finds out, and you know he's got folks every which way knowing everything. But I've got plenty of folding green."

"Yeah, I know, Josh. Name your price, man, and quit beatin' round the bush. I ain't got all night. I gotta git me some sleep." Silver laughed again.

Bridges laughed with him this time and said, fast: "Fifty thousand. Twenty now. Balance when obit runs."

Silver flipped the red curl back up off his face, reached for the door handle, and said, "You must think I got not a lick of sense. I wouldn't step off into this mess for less than twice that much. But, I would screw the woman!"

Bridges cranked the truck. "She ain't for you nor nobody to screw. That's the problem. A hundred thousand. That's all I got!"

Silver grinned in the moonlight and replied, "Half on the front end and balance when done."

"Okay. Deal. I'll be back tomorrow night 'bout the same time with the down payment," Bridges said.

Silver got out of the pickup, showed up around at Bridge's window, and spat again. He reached into his mouth, found the wad, and threw it off into the grass.

The hound that had been howling gazed at the wad, ambled over, sniffed it, and turned around, with disgust in his haunches. He returned to the flattened place in the grass, still warm with his scent, curled up on it, and closed his eyes.

Silver said, "Just honk that damn horn when you drive up, Josh. Make it in hundreds."

Bridges said, "Will do. See you tomorrow." He crept the pickup back out onto the gravel road to begin the hundred-mile trip back to Jaylo, the right broken taillight on the truck winking back at Silver.

Silver swished Coca-Cola around in his mouth to rinse out the Red Man, spat a hunk of dirty looking stuff on the ground, and drank down the rest of the cola. He peed on the ground in the dark, sighed, zipped his pants, and walked back inside. "Where have I seen that man on that blanket?" he asked himself as he crawled on top of the sheets under the ceiling fan. It hit him—that day, several weeks earlier, when he'd been taking a short cut through Gloria's neighborhood, he'd seen a man walking from her house to a van with some kind of fancy lettering on it. That was the same man in the photograph. He'd paid him no attention. Assumed he was a deliveryman. Gloria liked pretty things and she liked for people to deliver them to her.

"Bridges is sure as all get out gonna stick his tail in a crack with Seth, fooling with anything to do with Gloria," Silver spoke his thoughts. "Oh, well, I don't ask questions," he reminded himself. "I just hit." Realizing where he'd seen the man, though, took it off his mind, so, in less time than it took for him to turn over on his right side and tuck the end of his pillow under to better suit his neck, he began snoring.

22.

MOONLIGHT IN THE BOONIES

A couple of hours after Silver fell asleep, his open-mouthed snoring shook him awake. He sat on the edge of the bed, naked, to get his bearings. His mouth was dry. He splashed water on his face and over his hair from the thin stream in the bathroom sink, cupped his hands and slurped, gargled, and spat. He pulled on denim shorts, poured a double whiskey, and sauntered barefoot out onto the unpainted wooden front porch, easing shut the screen door. Ole Bartow approached, panting, wagging his tail.

"Damn, I hate being stuck out in the boonies with nothing but my whiskey and you dogs, Bart, but I guess I'm here feeding you hounds for a roof a while longer, at least until the Bridges job goes down and I've got rent money for something decent." Silver sat back in the rickety old rocking chair, downed the double, propped his glass on the chair's slant arm, and thought some. "Keep my seat for me, Bart, while I refill this glass to help me think my way on through how to pull off this Bridges thing." The dog looked at the rocker, declined the invitation, turned, and ambled off down the front steps, plodding across the grass back to his warm spot.

In a few moments, Silver returned to the rocker, his glass full to overflowing. He dripped good whiskey on himself and the floor. Lucy Lou, another hound, obese and lazier than Bart ever thought about being, slouched her way up onto the porch and began licking the whiskey off Silver's feet. She raised her face occasionally to breathe her rank breath on him. He stroked her floppy neck skin, thinking about being overdrawn at the bank. He drank the last of the whiskey in the glass. Loosened inside, now, enough to sleep again, he opened the front door to return to bed.

But strong headlights topped the hill, coming in toward him from the same direction into which Bridges' taillight had blinked only hours earlier. "Hell, I hope that is not that son of a bitch changing his mind on me." He pulled the wooden door shut and locked it. The headlights swung up into the driveway.

Silver tucked the forty-five into the front of his pants and stepped out the side entrance in time to watch Seth Maddox slam the door on a late model Ford and walk into the carport.

"Well, I'll be damned!" Silver whispered and stepped out directly in front of him.

"How long you been there?" Seth asked, unstartled.

"About all my life," Silver said.

Seth chuckled. He stepped over into the moonlight, a rumpled, older-looking version of the bare-chested Silver. He leaned in to better see Silver's face, grasped Silver's shoulders, and linked 'em together, the rough and tumble moonlight-caught degenerates. Arguably, they favored those robust Biblical characters stretched naked across old cathedral canvases, trying to connect with God and each other and angels.

But, of course, Silver and Seth were not Biblical characters and they were not naked and their getting an angel assignment seemed pretty far-fetched, though the covered-up conniving members of the underbelly of Gargagun, standing on a tiny carport on a knoll at the end of a gravel road needed an angel in the worse way. Yet the strong discernable aura of something strangely sacred in and about the scene could not be denied: Seth's hands atop Silver's shoulders, then removed; Silver still; Seth clearing his throat like he had something in it.

Silver broke the silence: "Pop, what brings you out here at two in the morning?"

"Well, you know it ain't for no picnic. You got any of that Jack in the house?"

"Hell yeah, come on in. The day I don't have Jack in the house is the day I'll have to rob a bank." They both laughed.

Lucy Lou wandered into the carport, yawned, and wagged her tail at Seth, sniffing him, friendly. "Now that's a real watch dog," Seth said. "She'll catch the crook and love him to death." They laughed again. Lucy

Lou kept sniffing Seth's feet. He raised his voice and said to her, "Git back, now, hound dog. I got business to talk over here with my boy." Lucy Lou cowered. Wobbled off. Usually, everybody cowered around Seth, everybody except Silver.

When Silver switched on the kitchen overhead light, two roach bugs scampered off in opposite directions. One slid in under the lower cabinets. "Nasty things," Seth said.

"Can't get rid of 'em under these oak trees," Silver said. He set a squatty little glass on the pine table and reached for the Jack above the sink. He tipped the lip of the bottle into Seth's glass. "How much?"

"Aw, 'bout to there'll do," Seth pointed halfway up the glass. Silver topped it off with tap water.

"Pop, it's for sure good to see you. How's the whiskey taste? Did I put too much water in it?"

"It's perfect, son, only way it'll get better is for me to drink more of it." Seth wrapped his wide fingers around his drink and waited for Silver to find another glass, pour himself a drink, and sit down at the table.

"Pop, you sure are looking good."

"Silver, don't shit a shitter. I'm warmed-over looking and you know it."

"Naw, now, don't make me pull rank on you, Pop. Nothing warmed over about you, but you've sure got something on your mind. Shows all over you. I could tell it before you stepped into the carport tonight."

Seth sat there thinking his way through his words and shook his head at Silver's offer of a cigarette. "Not tonight. I'm trying to quit those things."

Silver lit his and blew smoke back up over his shoulder away from the table. He set the pack on the table by the Jack.

Then, as if he'd finally found the way to say it, Seth spoke: "Josh Bridges has done up and gone crazy over Gloria and attacked her drunk. I've sent him off to Jaylo permanent. He don't like it. He's crazy as five hundred hells. Gonna have to take him out of the picture. Can I count on my own flesh and blood to handle that for me, Silver?"

"Hell yeah. I could a done it tonight if I'd known. He was here a few hours ago hiring me for a similar job on a fellow he swears is making it with Gloria pretty regular."

"Name Samone." Seth stated it rather than asking.

"Yeah. That's him."

Seth scratched his chin, set the glass down, and ran his index finger around it, thinking. "What's he gonna pay you, Silver?" Seth asked.

"A hundred grand. Half when he comes back tomorrow and the other half when it's done."

Silver tapped a new cigarette on the table and stuck it in the corner of his mouth. Seth picked up the Bic and leaned in to light it inside Silver's cupped hands, guarding the tiny flicker from the night breeze coming in the window. Silver pushed his chair back and waited to hear what Seth would say.

"Okay. Take the half tomorrow," Seth said. "Do his job, which is gonna have to be done eventually anyway. Let me think on when and how we oughta finish Josh."

Silver smiled.

As his daddy's car pulled out onto the gravel road, Silver stripped out of his shorts and lay down naked with the magazine with the girl with the blonde hair on page twenty-eight and the woman on the front wearing leather. Afterwards, he stretched out on the sheets and said to the four walls, "Gonna have enough money to leave this chicken coop and get back into the world. Don't have to drive over there and convince Pop to let me make the money, and, best of all, the world won't have to put up with Bridges much longer."

As he drifted off to sleep, his momma came to mind, looking like she did when he was a first grader, the back of her hair flowing long and loose as she left the house that last evening. She'd turned back and smiled at him, showing such beautiful teeth. He would always remember her hair and those white teeth and her weightless laugh, which convinced him that, as she stepped out that door that evening, she was readying to fly off into the sky.

A funeral happened. Folks along the road where they lived came, as did a stranger whom Silver had never seen before. The stranger had red hair. And he cried. Out loud.

Human Services placed Silver in an orphanage. He was lost there, in a bad way. He was away from his momma and wanted to go over to the cemetery and find her. But he was also lost inside the orphanage, in a good way. He was away from her husband, the man with the raven hair whose eyes would suddenly flash without warning and who would back Silver into a corner, touching him with monsters, which he continued to do in Silver's dreams, even after the raven-haired man up and disappeared that day, years before Silver's mama died.

Silver didn't know a thing about praying; nobody ever taught him how; he wouldn't have believed in it if they had, because no God would ever make a boy like him and set him down to live with a raven-haired man. So Silver talked to an imaginary friend and said to him every night before he went to sleep, as regular as brushing his teeth, which he had to do in the orphanage, although he did not like that part of it at all, "Please hold on to the raven-haired man, wherever he is, and please don't turn him loose, or he'll come back and get me."

One day, when Silver was about ten, that man with red hair who had stood out by his momma's grave and cried out loud drove up at the orphanage with a file of papers in his hands. He spent hours in the office with the man who ran the place. Afterwards, he came out on the playground and told Silver, "Son, I'm Seth Maddox. I'm taking you home with me."

A bunch of people were there when Mr. Maddox drove 'em up hours later into Maddox's yard, his car loaded up with Silver's little suitcase and a pile of other stuff they'd bought him on the way in. Maddox told 'em all, "Want you to meet Silver, a close relative of mine who'll be living with me from now on."

Mr. Maddox treated him real good. Mainly just left him alone and didn't bother him. Still and all, it took Silver some time to get used to being treated good by anybody on a regular basis. Silver never knew, though, who Seth really was until after his twelfth birthday celebration. All the people who worked for Seth came and brought their families. Some of their kids helped Silver blow out the candles on a big chocolate birthday cake. After everybody had long departed and just the two of 'em—Seth and Silver—were sitting there in the yard, Seth said, "Silver, my birthday present to you is not just the party tonight. I want to finally tell you the truth."

"What truth, Mr. Maddox?"

"Son, we are flesh and blood."

Silver didn't quite understand it, so he asked him, "How can that be, Mr. Maddox? I never even saw you till a few years ago."

"I loved yore mama, Silver," Seth said and burst out crying.

"What you crying for, Mr. Maddox?" Silver asked. "That's good news. I ain't never had nobody before."

Seth got up and blew his nose.

It was never a subject between them after that, unless it slipped out on its own, without words, like it had in the moonlight floating across the carport, and they saw it in each other's faces. But the nightmares about the raven-haired man continued, regardless of where Silver lived or how old he got, 'cause everything about that whole thing messed Silver up pretty bad from then on out.

23.

COMING TOGETHER

Sam maneuvered his pickup alongside Gloria's car tracks on the muddy dirt road to the old barn at the north end of the lake. It was their place, in a way—they had rendezvoused there a few times for talks.

Always secluded and pleasant, that day the place seemed hauntingly empty. Private. A peaceful easiness settled in over Sam, knowing that he would soon see Gloria and be alone with her. At the last turn, there she stood, tall in a denim skirt and a button-up shirt like the one she'd worn that first day she came into The Shoppe, the top button unbuttoned.

Behind her was a mishmash of stout-legged crepe myrtles and buxom nandina, over and around which ran golden tipped honeysuckle and blackberry vines, bundling up on a falling-down fence to create a tall hedgerow that secluded the open space outside the old barn.

She smiled and waved.

He rolled down the window, stuck his head out, and said, "Morning, Gloria, you look so beautiful."

She blushed. "Hey, Sam! So good to see you!" she shouted, running toward him even before he had parked behind the hedgerow and stepped out into the aroma of pear preserves.

There she was. He looked into her eyes and handed her the bouquet. She took it and fondled the blooms. "Thank you, Sam. What a thoughtful thing for you to do."

They came together on her blanket in the seclusion of the old barn, but wide open to the universe that had brought them there. Afterwards, they dozed off, whispering to each other things they had wanted to say for so long. But they never consumed the sandwiches or the deviled eggs from the picnic basket. Footsteps came before they could.

Gloria woke him by saying, "Sam, I hear footsteps, someone walking toward the barn! Can you hear that?"

"Yes, don't say anything. Keep your body under mine. Stay against me. You'll be okay," he said. He pulled her in close. Covered her with his body. They were safe.

The steps drew closer. Louder. Heavier. Resolute. Did the person want to be heard? Yes, the intruder must have seen their vehicles and was being politely noisy so whoever was inside would have prior notice that someone was approaching.

Sam turned to see who was entering the barn, so he could ask them to please step back long enough to let them dress. He gazed into the face of a redheaded man pointing a forty-five at them. Although the man couldn't have possibly seen Gloria the way Sam was covering her, he said to Sam, "Get away from that woman."

Gloria screamed.

The man flipped back red curls from over his eye with his left hand and motioned with the forty-five toward the clearing outside the barn. "Move over there, mister, now."

Sam sat up, in front of Gloria, continuing to keep himself between her and the intruder. She was shivering.

Still believing the man was making a mistake, Sam asked, "Who are you? Let's talk. Put your gun aside, please, let us get dressed. We have a picnic lunch with us. You can join us. We'd like that."

"Don't do this, Silver. Don't do this," Gloria pled with the redhead before he could answer Sam.

Amazed, Sam asked her, "Do you know this man?"

"Yes, he will kill us, Sam, unless we do what he says."

They rose together. Stood naked in the barn holding hands. She continued begging the redhead and swinging their clasped hands up and back, emphasizing with the swinging her pleading. "Please don't do this, Silver. Please. I beg you, in the name of everything in our lives. It's not his fault. I love him."

The man with the forty-five just wouldn't hear her. He pointed the gun, then, directly at her and said to Sam, "I'll kill her first if you don't do as I say. If you love the woman, leave her and go outside."

Sam understood, then, that the redheaded man had not just accidentally wandered in on them. Naked, Sam moved into the clearing, holding his arms out and up toward Silver. "Mister, I don't know who you are, but let's talk. If Gloria knows you, you and I ought to be able to work this out. Please, for God's sake, don't hurt that woman. This is all my doing."

Out of a great emptiness, Silver looked into Sam's eyes, moving only to flip back that loose lock of hair.

Gloria ran toward Sam and clung to his legs. "Go back, Gloria. Go back. Go back. Dear God, go back," he said. She would not obey.

Silver stepped toward them in the clearing and addressed Gloria calmly, perfunctorily, as if he were requesting the front page of the newspaper after she finished reading it. "Gloria, please move over there so blood won't get on you."

Silver had picked up Sam's clothes; he threw them toward him and said, like he was his prison warden, "Put you some clothes on. It'll look better for you that way. I got nothing against you."

Gloria dropped her hold on Sam's legs. She knelt in front of him, trembling, as he dressed.

Sam looked at her and saw in her eyes what was in his. At that very moment, he knew beyond any shadow of any doubt whatsoever that Gloria loved him. It was the most exquisitely beautiful thing he had ever seen, a pure alive steadfastness that did not blink in the turmoil.

Janie stepped in. She called his name and smiled. Sam reached for her with his own smile and she caught it and held it in her arms like a treasure, then threw the treasure back to him: "I wuv you this big, Daddy!"

Renee came out of nowhere into the aisle of the school bus and stood there strong in front of him. He felt a rush of love out of her. She smiled like she used to, winked, and called him a rascal. She laid Clem in his hands, along with Janie's smile, and said, "Here, you take these, Samone. They are yours."

Clem looked over at Gloria and spoke words Sam did not understand. Gloria smiled. Renee asked Sam if he had another frog in his pocket, and Charlie patted Renee on the back and said, "Sam, everything is going to be all right."

Gloria said, "Indeed."

Was his life running across before his eyes? He had heard that happened. He did not know, but it soothed him to see it. And, it all fit together and brought to him the surest sense that they had all been together in this from the very beginning, just moving into the spaces already outlined for them, as Silver stepped in and touched the forty-five to Sam's temple.

The gun felt as cold as Silver's vacant eyes looked, but Sam was, unexpectedly, not afraid. He did not feel alone.

Silver was good at what he did. The shot pierced the skull precisely where he had intended. He did, however, have to turn the body over, to get Sam's boots on him and lace them up. He wiped the mud off his hands onto his pants legs. "Damn hell hole of mud out here," he said to himself, completely ignoring Gloria. But she never noticed what he was saying. She was crumpled up in a ball, writhing around naked on the open ground, sobbing.

She couldn't have heard anybody say anything, not even the noise of the approaching truck, until it rattled to a stop on the other side of the hedgerow and the truck door slammed loud enough to startle her. She ran into the barn, grabbed her clothes and the bouquet, and wobbled back outside the barn, disoriented, crouching behind shrubs near the entrance, shaking uncontrollably.

The vehicle didn't faze Silver. He had known it would come. For his watch said twelve noon. Loud squishes accompanied whoever was walking from the truck toward them. Silver pushed the pistol under the front of his pants and waited.

Josh Bridges thrashed his way through the honeysuckle and stepped into the clearing, a piece of the honeysuckle vine hanging off his hat. He looked like a comedian on Hee Haw when Silver saw him, but Silver did not laugh.

"Did ya do it?" Bridges asked, wrestling with the little piece of honeysuckle, trying to remove it.

"Oh, hell yeah! Job done. There. Look it over."

Josh threw the piece of vine to the ground and grinned. Walked over to the body. Spat when he saw it. Stood there looking at the mass of flesh where a head was meant to be. "Damn, Silver, you popped him, man!"

Silver laughed. "Yeah, I guess I did. Got the rest of the money?"

Bridges didn't even bother to inspect the rest of Sam's body. He turned back and walked toward Silver. "Uh huh, dang, you did it, now.

Silver, I didn't know a face'd splatter like that," Josh said. A tiny queasiness surprised him.

Silver closed the sale: "Like we decided, weren't no need of you having to wait on no obit. When the deed was done, you needed to be able to see it for yourself. Does it suit you?"

"Oh, you better believe it. Suits me fine, Silver. That son of a bitch is shot. Shore is a mess, ain't it?" Josh reached into his dirty plaid coat and pulled out packages of one hundred dollar bills, neatly wrapped. He handed them to Silver. "Here's the rest of the deal. Take your time. Count 'er out."

Silver did a quick look-see and said, "It's all here, Josh. Sure good to do business with you." Silver put the money in a pouch he'd strapped across his chest under his shirt. He lifted his head and said to Bridges, like it was an afterthought, "Hey, Josh, you got a minute? I've got something real interesting you might want to see up there in the barn. I've been thinking it's exactly what we need."

Now feeling on top of the world, Josh spat his baccy again. His queasiness was gone. "Hell, yeah," he said. "I got all day, now. Got the work behind us."

As he approached the barn, Josh spied Gloria for the first time, huddled up, naked, trying to cover herself with her wadded-up clothes, holding something yellow. She was trembling and weeping. She stumbled out into the clearing toward Silver, away from Bridges.

Bridges sniggered at her and yelled, "Guess you won't be getting no more of that, Miss Gloria, now will you?"

Silver motioned for Josh to go on in ahead of him. Said, "Let me check on her, Josh. She's a mess. I'll be on in behind you."

"Aw, she'll be all right. She's seen more'n that a fore," Josh replied and began walking toward the barn. He turned and yelled at her again, "Ain't that right, now, Miss Gloria?" A slight breeze pushed at his hat and he reached for it, to set it straight. The bullet came in under his right ear. He really didn't feel a thing.

Silver wiped off the forty-five. Two cartridges had now been spent. He walked back over to Sam's body and, using a handkerchief, worked the gun into the dead man's hands, printed it, and flipped it off just a bit right of the body. Silver had done his research and calculations long before. He zipped Bridges' body up in a bag full of dry ice after he removed the man's plaid coat and stuffed it in the duffle he had brought in afoot at dawn from the farmhouse, located just a short piece as the crow flies up a narrow logging road.

"Whew, I don't know why the world ever put up with you this long, Josh Bridges," Silver said, touching the packet under his shirt to double-check that it was still there, pondering making it to the cooler down in Cairo with Bridges' body before five o'clock.

His hardest task of the day was getting Gloria dressed and into her car. "You gotta drive this thing, Gloria, and follow me on out now."

She was in a daze and didn't say a word.

"I hate to do it to you, old girl, but it's the only way this'll work. He cranked Bridges' truck, as messy inside as Bridges ever thought about being, and pulled out, noticing the vehicle tracks in the little pretend roadway were mostly mush. Plus, a summer thunderstorm had begun. "It'll drop some rain and help do away with even these tracks," Silver said to himself.

Yeah, there came Gloria, driving her car right behind him. He grinned and congratulated himself, thinking back on how he had put things together to pull this off. "That tap on your phone, Gloria, was worth a million. I only made a hundred grand out of it. Gonna have to raise my prices." Silver said out loud, laughing at the incongruity of having made the money he'd just made, out in the boonies, on a hit for a man who'd taken a hit himself.

"Damn, it has been a good day," he said.

He looked into the rearview mirror again. Yeah, there she was, still back there behind him, driving that car.

PART THREE

The Unraveling

24.

BLACKBERRIES AND BODIES

A little over a year after Silver drove Bridges' body out, some kids picking blackberries stepped on his foot under the hedgerow near the old barn at Florence Lake.

Shortly, after the Sheriff's Office had identified and removed the body, a game warden checking fishing licenses approached a man named Cal Hough sitting in a truck full of fishing gear near the hedgerow.

The game warden told a reporter later that day, "To tell you the truth, there was almost no arrest. The man's fishing license was up to snuff. I was about to wave him off when I saw that plaid coat down in the front floorboard. I knew the coat and the man that always wore it, Josh Bridges. And I'd just heard the broadcast over my radio unit about Bridges' body having been found a few hours before under that hedgerow."

The reporter from the capital city's biggest newspaper did a double take. He didn't even know the name of his own next-door neighbor. "Sir, how could you possibly know the owner of the coat? Lots of coats in the world, aren't there?"

"Absolutely. But, see, everybody around here knew Josh Bridges, an ornery sort of fellow I had a run in with a few years back over a license. He was wearing that coat that day, and I had seen him wear that ugly plaid thing around town no telling how many times. It really wasn't a coat; it was a thick cotton shirt. Never kept it clean as long as I saw him wear it, or himself, either. But he wore that coat, hot or cold."

"So, what did you do when you realized Cal Hough had Josh Bridges' coat in his pickup?" the reporter asked.

"I suppose the correct answer would be that I asked myself what Mr. Hough was doing sitting out at Florence Lake with the coat of a dead man in his truck parked no more than fifty yards from where Bridges' body had been found. And then, of course, I asked Mr. Hough about the coat. He blew a fuse. Acted like he did not know anything about the coat even being in his truck. He said, 'I ain't had no coat, seen no coat 'til you pointed it out just now; I ain't put no coat in the floorboard of my truck; and I don't want the coat. Who'd you say it belongs to, anyway?' He acted clueless."

"Did you believe him?" the reporter asked.

"Sir, I didn't know exactly what to believe."

The reporter asked, "Well, did he ever explain why he was parked where he was in the first place?"

"Yes, he pushed his fishing license in on my chest and said, 'I come over here to meet a fellar and fish, parked my truck, sat on the bank, didn't have no luck with any of it, and I come back to my truck to eat them ham sandwiches my wife sent up here with me.'"

"So you called the sheriff?" the reporter asked.

"Yes, exactly. It was Sheriff Bill's judgment to arrest Mr. Hough."

"Has anybody found out who this Hough fellow actually is?"

"The sheriff indicated that he appeared to be a drifter sort who had only worked a short while for a refrigeration plant in Cairo, down toward the coast."

"Is that right? A refrigeration plant?" the reporter asked, his wheels turning.

"Yeah, the sheriff said Mr. Hough was a common laborer, though the plant owner was well off. That anybody with any beef cattle in that area, and there is a lot of cattle down there, took him, the owner, for a godsend because of his walk-in coolers. Said there have been cattle trucks lined up, sometimes, all the way back to the highway, just trying to get in."

"So the only thing you knew connecting Hough to Bridges' murder was his being where Bridges' body was found at Florence Lake with the dead man's coat in the floorboard of his pickup truck?" the reporter asked.

"Right. I don't know anything about the sheriff's investigation to this point, nor if there is any link between Bridges' body and the one they found out near there a year ago. A suicide, I think they said the other body was. But, they'll know soon. The big guys out of the capital are in on the investigation."

The reporter jumped on that and probed for information about the "other body," but the game warden couldn't recollect much about the earlier suicide. He said, "I'll be glad to find out what I can and get back with you on it."

The reporter thanked him, but said, "I've got a deadline to make. I'll check back with you if I need anything further. Appreciate your help."

"No problem. Anytime."

25.

THE POTATO CHIP BAG

As the reporter traveled back to the capital city to get the story out and the game warden began inquiring about the suicide at Florence Lake that occurred the previous year to satisfy his own curiosity, Charlie sat down with a cup of coffee to process the news he'd just seen on television.

"Sometimes I'd rather not know stuff," he said aloud. "Just leave it where it is, even if that is thinking your very best friend in the whole world killed himself a year ago within twenty-four hours of his calling, saying, 'Charlie I need you to meet me out back of Mac's.'"

When Charlie drove up, Sam had been standing by his car, stiff, like he was a knight in one of those metal suits. Charlie almost didn't recognize him.

The first words out of Sam's mouth were, "Charlie, go get that fender fixed. A rusty, floppy fender does not fit your image. And while you are at it, get it washed, too."

The fender did rattle a little: Charlie had hit a bridge abutment a while back.

"Sweet Jesus, Sam, when did you become my papa?"

"Charlie, I ain't nobody's papa but Janie's, but I am damn sure your brother, been so ever since that Indian ceremony on your back steps. I need your help," Sam said, awash in seriousness.

"Sure, what kind of help do you need? What's going on?" Charlie would have done anything for Sam.

Sam just stood there. Silent.

Charlie put his hand on Sam's shoulder and prodded him by saying, "Sam, you've brought me out away from my work and lectured me on my not caring for my car and told me what to do and you want my help and you just keep standing there, looking like there is some life or death matter you can't talk about and need to. Just ask me, Sam! What kind of help do you need? Anything. Just ask me."

Sam stared out of the eyes of a man Charlie had never met. He said with a straight face, "Charlie, do you think I still have any Boobs Samone in me?"

"Good Gawd, Sam, have you brought me down here to ask me that? You been drinking?"

"Naw, Charlie, I ain't been drinking, but I am about to find out if the boys on the bus were right about me. That's what I need to talk to you about." Despite his seriousness and his sudden irrationality, Sam looked young. Clear-faced. Blissful.

"Have you been smoking weed, Sam?"

Sam laughed, pushed back from Charlie's hand, and shook his head, an uncompromising stranger.

"Okay, Sam," Charlie said, "let's get in the car and sit down and talk. What is going on?"

Sam just stood there. He wouldn't move. Finally, he spoke: "Charlie, you remember that day that woman came into Mac's and you said she was mixed up with the Raleigh Mafia and, as we left, I asked you if you smelled pear preserves?"

"Uh huh," Charlie said, thinking Sam must be under too much pressure.

Suddenly, a strong burst of a breeze that felt like it could have lifted both of them up whizzed an empty potato chip bag in front of them so close that they could feel it. Charlie raised his arm to dodge it. Sam laughed. It broke the tension. For a split second, they were kids again.

Sam said, "Charlie, you know that I was always the misfit growing up, the nerd, the guy that didn't have it for much of anything."

"You were smart, Sam, and today you are a successful businessman. What's going on?"

Sam dropped his head. He spoke slowly, not looking now at Charlie, "I think I'm in another lifetime, man."

"What? What are you talking about, Sam? What do you mean 'another lifetime'?"

"This woman that smells like pear preserves has lit something in me. I'm alive inside for the first time in a long time. Alive. I can't explain it to you, Charlie, why I wasn't alive before or why I am alive now, but—"

Charlie interrupted him: "Alive, damn Sam, you've always been alive. What in God's green earth are you talking about? Tell me what is going on."

The potato chip bag blew back across in front of them, landed in a scraggly bush, and got trapped there in the rough breeze, holding on for dear life.

Like Sam seemed to be. He leaned over on the hood of his car and kept his head down, his face hidden, though trying to speak out in the open. Finally, Sam said, "What's going on, Charlie, is that if I don't get to taste those pear preserves, I'm gonna wither up and blow away, empty, like that potato chip bag that almost hit you."

Charlie began sweating.

"And Renee won't even notice I'm gone. She hasn't noticed me for a very long time. She's cut me off."

Charlie didn't know what to say. So he said, "Man, let's sit down in the car and talk. You need to talk."

But Sam wouldn't budge.

Charlie continued, "I had no idea, man. I'm sorry as all get out, Sam. You are my brother. You always have been. There is nothing you can do that I can't handle. Whatever it is, it won't affect our friendship, but I sure as hell hate to see you do something you can't take back, something that might end things for you and Renee."

Sam was a million miles away.

Charlie tried again. "Sam, this is a small town. It ain't no Manhattan here. Whatever happens, everybody's gonna know it." Charlie shuffled his feet around and kicked the gravel in the parking lot. "Renee loves you, Sam, and you've loved her from that day on the school bus when you dropped Clem into her book bag. She's never gonna quit loving you, Sam. But you might lose her. You don't want to lose Renee, do you? Or worse yet, find out that you, yourself, don't want her anymore."

A soberness spread across Sam's face. Charlie couldn't believe he'd just said that to Sam. For a time, the two of them stood there as lost and trapped as the potato chip bag.

Sam said, "Charlie, you've just said a bunch of stuff I've known but couldn't say. I'm in a mell of a hess. Been here a long time, it seems, almost ever since we saw her that day in the coffee shop."

"It might go away, you know, if you give it enough time." The words rattled worse than the fender on Charlie's car.

Sam wasn't finished with what he wanted to say. "Thank you, Charlie. You've always seen about me. Don't want this to sound wrong, but I sure love ya, man." He reached for the door latch on his car and got inside, started it, and rolled the window down. He pulled the gearshift into low. He turned back and said, "Charlie, I need you to promise me something."

"Sure man, whatever, just ask me."

"If anything ever happens, please see about Renee and Janie. They'll need you."

Charlie went weak.

"Aw, man, quit that kind of talk. That's crazy now, but you know, bro, ain't nothing would ever keep me from caring for your family except you doing it, which you are gonna be doing, with or without that Gloria woman." Charlie's hands got all clammy. His chest hurt.

Sam smiled at him like a parent smiles at a kid who has asked him for the moon and he knows he can't give it to him. "Thanks, friend," he said. He drove off.

As Charlie walked back to his sedan past the bush, he picked up the empty potato chip bag and took it with him. He drove home and sat there thinking. He didn't have a good feeling about anything at all.

The next evening, Ashley called Charlie and told him that Sam had killed himself. Charlie hung up the phone and screamed at Sam, on the other side, "I bet that damn woman wouldn't let you lay with her, Sam, and you couldn't bear it and you killed yourself. Damn her and the coffee shop she walked into."

When Sam would come to Charlie now, in his dreams, it would wake him up and he couldn't sleep, trying to figure it out, replaying it, what he could have said or done differently.

Charlie quit going down to Mac's on Wednesdays; he just couldn't bring himself to do it. Once he saw Gloria coming down the street toward him; he turned and walked in the opposite direction, stepped inside a store until she passed. He couldn't look at her.

The week after they buried Sam, he had 'em put a shiny new fender on his cream-colored Chevy sedan and had the car custom washed, all as his memorial to Sam.

Now, a year later, after seeing the day's TV news about a dead body being found and an investigation being opened on Sam's death from last year, Charlie went out and just stood there looking at that fender and got as mad at everything that had happened, whatever it had been, as he did last year when Ashley had called to tell him Sam had committed suicide.

And a new fear struck Charlie. He realized that he had a monkey on his own back if Sam had not committed suicide. For if Sam didn't shoot himself and Charlie didn't tell somebody what he knew about Sam and Gloria, he might be helping Sam's killer go free, but Renee's knowing the truth that Sam had told him about Gloria would tear her apart.

He was in a "mell of a hess."

26.

REVELATIONS OF OLD

As Charlie struggled with the news that Sam might have been murdered, Renee admitted to Ashley, "Sis, I needed this job. I never would have guessed I did or that it would help me. But when I help a nervous or worried client and make them more comfortable, I forget to be anxious."

Ashley smiled. "Thanks, Renee, for telling me that. We're glad you're here; you are doing good work. We need you."

As she turned to go to her office, Mr. Broom, a long-time client, entered the waiting area, reached out his perfectly manicured hands, took Ashley's fingers, and delivered a hand kiss with the gentility of a French aristocrat. They chatted. She excused herself.

"How is Mrs. Renee today?" he asked, performing the same gentleman's ritual with her.

"I'm well, Mr. Broom. Thank you. Can I get you something?"

"No, thank you, Renee, I'm fine. Guess you saw the noon newscast." His face sparkled like that of a child who'd discovered a wonderful secret and was bursting to tell it.

"No, I didn't. Anything special?" she asked, remembering he was an accomplished gossip. And it seemed, she realized, that she was positioned to be the recipient of his latest.

"It's breaking news. Hot off the presses."

"Really? What is it?" Renee asked politely, knowing that Mr. Broom was famous for his enormous imagination, which was rivaled only by his bank account, but he was, on occasion, prone to plump up the gossip he shared to the detriment of its reliability.

He beamed. "They found a man, a pretty mean one from what I can gather, dead at Florence Lake. He'd been murdered."

"Murdered, my goodness," Renee said. "That's just a few miles from my house. How terrible, Mr. Broom."

"Certainly was, Mrs. Renee. Some children picking blackberries found him. It frightened the children so, that when they ran home and told their mothers, they forgot exactly where they'd stepped on him, which made it difficult for the sheriff to locate him. His shoes were covered in red mud, packed on."

"Red mud on his shoes?" Renee rose and walked around to the front of the receptionist's counter to get in closer to Mr. Broom, to hear him better. Her hands began sweating and beads of sweat popped out on her upper lip.

"Yes, indeed, the only place anybody could get that kind of mud on his shoes around here would be Florence Lake," he said, finally sitting down in one of the waiting room chairs.

"Oh, really, Mr. Broom. Is that so?" Renee asked, watching his face.

"Yes, some kind of seismic activity centuries ago left over a hundred acres of land around Florence Lake redder than a rooster's comb."

"I surely didn't know that," she said, seeing Samone lying on that hospital stretcher with that red mud on his boots.

"I saw a documentary a year or so ago about a natural spring under that lake that seeps water into it all the time. Keeps it wet and muddy, red muddy. Strangest thing."

"The man was murdered?" Renee asked, to bring him back to the subject.

"Yes, Mrs. Renee. The news indicated the deceased had been shot in the head."

She thought, Samone shot himself in the head and had red mud on his boots.

Mr. Broom shifted in his chair and continued talking. "They didn't say it on TV, but a man whose uncle knows a person at the sheriff's office said he overheard that just because it looked like a new murder, it might not be. That they are testing the body to determine if it was, instead, an old murder, whatever that means."

"An old murder! I've never heard of such a thing, Mr. Broom, have you?" Using the words "old murder" unsettled her. She didn't know why. She began to tremble.

"No, I certainly have not, Mrs. Renee, and hearing such a phrase brings on a curiosity in me." Mr. Broom leaned forward, dropped his voice almost to a whisper, and said, "They've arrested a man for the murder, you know. Swift action."

"No, what you are telling me, Mr. Broom, is the first I've heard. Who did they arrest?"

"Well, I do not remember the name of the man they arrested. He was not from this area. I am getting information that it might have been a drug killing."

"A drug killing?" Fright moved through Renee.

"Yes, but there is an even more interesting rumor."

"Oh, really? There's more?" she asked.

"Indeed. The man they apprehended insisted that he was innocent, said he hadn't killed anybody, but that he knew who did. I saw him speak those very words directly into the TV cameras."

Renee relaxed. Defendants said that kind of thing all the time. But she smiled at Mr. Broom like she understood. He was a nice man.

Mr. Broom fastidiously surveyed the area to ensure no one else was in the room. He rose from his chair, stepped in close to Renee, and lowered his voice. "I received the most critical part of this news only moments ago from one of the street people we feed regularly at church. He was sitting out on the sidewalk as I came in."

"Well I declare, Mr. Broom," she said, thinking Mr. Broom was now hitting the bottom of the barrel, to be gathering his gossip from street people. She smiled at him and returned to her seat.

"The street man, who comes in the church kitchen all the time, used to be a merchant of some kind, very successful, but he fell on hard times. It can happen, you know, to any of us. Anyway, he said not to speak it to a soul, and I know you certainly would not, but the word going on the street is that they found another man dead out there a little over a year ago."

Renee gulped. She sat down. Before she could speak, Mr. Broom continued, "I'm sorry to say that I do not know who the other dead man was: I was in the hospital for a necessary surgery about that time; I was not getting news regularly. So, having just gotten this information, I haven't had a chance to check it out, but the critical piece of it is that the other man was supposed to have committed suicide. However, now they're expecting that he might have been murdered, also, and are considering the possibility that the same person who killed this fellow they found out there today may have also killed the man last year."

The blood drained from Renee's face. Her heart raced. She said, "Mr. Broom, about a year ago? Murdered?" She stood up, again.

"Yes, that is precisely what the street person told me, Mrs. Renee. It has been my experience that these street people get news before anybody else. Have their ears to the ground, so to speak."

Mr. Lawson buzzed Renee's desk, requesting that she send Mr. Broom back. She did and then she dashed to the bathroom, hugged the commode, and lost her lunch. After she cleaned up, she told Ashley.

Ashley's professional persona imploded and she said, "My God, Renee, do you think Samone might have been murdered? This is unbelievable."

"I don't know."

Ashley regained her composure. "Paul and Leisa have friends in the District Attorney's Office. Let's not believe anything any different from what the authorities told us until we can find out more. Sit tight. It may take awhile," she said.

27.

DUMB AS A FOX

As Mr. Broom departed Lawson and Keyes, Mabel Morris flipped on the television in the kitchen and seated herself on a red stool to debone a chicken and watch her daily *Columbo* program. The detective questioned a suspect on the balcony as the aroma of onions and garlic and celery and rosemary drifted up out of the chicken broth. "It just doesn't get any better than this," she said, "cooking and watching *Columbo*."

An announcer, young enough in Mabel's eighty-five-year-old eyes to need a chaperone to even be out on the street alone, replaced Columbo on the screen. Tie askew, he began speaking, robot like, "We have an update on earlier news reports regarding the body of Josh Bridges which was found today at Florence Lake."

Mabel washed her hands and turned all of her attention to the television screen just in time to hear, "Samone Sims' body was found approximately a year ago near the spot where Josh Bridges' body was found today. The cause of Sims' death was previously determined to have been suicide. Sources reveal, however, that both men were shot in the head at close range with a forty-five caliber weapon. A forty-five revolver and two spent cartridges were found last year near Sims' body and the revolver bore Sims' fingerprints. Authorities have called in a team of forensic experts from the state capital to investigate both deaths in order to determine where and when Bridges' death actually occurred, the actual cause of Sims' death, as well as connections, if any, which may have existed between the two men and their deaths."

Mabel dropped her dishcloth. Recollections stampeded in over her: that last day of Samone's life, Renee out of town, his looking so spiffy, carrying that tiny bouquet of yellow mums. Whose mums were they?

The rook club rumors, disregarded previously, were pertinent now: a few months before Samone's death, one of the busybodies with whom she played rook had said, "Gloria Bridges may have divorced, but she must be well off; she sure seems to be buying out The Shoppe! The owner is doing a lot of Saturday deliveries."

The other busybody had laughed, brushed back her stringy hair from her always devoid of makeup forehead—which Mabel deemed sufficient evidence of one's being unkempt—and said, "Well, my hubby said that Shoppe owner might just as well get a standing room reservation for Friday nights over there 'cause he gets there so early every Saturday morning."

The third woman at the table had scowled. "Ladies, ladies, behave. It is not nice or Christian to envy someone who has things."

"I had ignored them," Mabel said aloud to the blank TV screen, disgusted with the plaster-faced newsman and Samone and herself. She flipped off the television and poured herself some more sweet tea and put lots of lemon in it. "I knew he made deliveries and I just believed the busybodies didn't like Gloria Bridges, but I'll declare. I've been blind, deaf, and stupid."

Being blind, deaf, and stupid did not fit Mabel's self-perception.

She took her glass of iced tea to the enormous kitchen window, clear of any covering, and looked out over the yellow mum bed she'd created as a tribute to Samone. It grinned up at her. Mocked her. "You're sad. Admit it," she said. "Getting this news after a year has torn a scab off. Lord, what it must be doing to Renee!" Tears welled up. She wiped her face and nose with a paper towel and began itemizing aloud to the four walls around her what she knew to attempt to control what was happening. Making lists gave Mabel a sense of control.

"Number one: the rook club gossips gossip, but they aren't liars. Number two: Gloria was a free woman, could see anybody she wanted to see in her home, Samone or anybody, delivering anything. That's not their business or mine. Number three: I sure don't blame her for divorcing that mean Bridges man; don't know why she or anybody else would have ever married him in the first place. He didn't even smell good when I passed him on the street. Number four: I just can't picture Samone having an affair. He loved Renee and Janie. But I saw him myself that last day. And nobody could look any happier than Samone looked that last day, dressed all fine, carrying a bouquet of mums in the morning. Happy people don't just up and kill themselves. That does not happen. Number five: I never did believe he killed himself; yes, he and Renee had spats before he died, but people don't kill themselves over a spat or two. If they did, everybody'd be dead. Number six: I don't care how many spent cartridges were found around Samone's body or who else was found murdered anywhere, Samone Sims wouldn't harm a flea. And, he didn't."

Mabel grabbed a chunk of the chicken meat. It tasted better than she had expected. She set the separate containers of chicken and broth in the fridge. "I'll make the potpie later," she said, continuing to ramble on with herself, the only sounding board for a woman who lived alone. "Later, that's it, later!" she said. "If Bridges was killed before today and one of the two bullets from the forty-five they found by Samone's body, a year ago, killed Bridges, why did Bridges' body not turn into dust by now? Why was it not found when Samone's was found? Where has it been all this time? How did it only get found today? If Samone killed Bridges and then killed himself, how could he have hidden the body without help, and, if he had help, why would the help not have stopped him from killing himself?"

She grabbed her gardening gloves and dashed to the Samone mum bed to weed and deadhead and work the pieces of the puzzle around in her mind. "Columbo, I need you here to help me on this," she said, standing in the lushness of fluffy yellow all around her feet.

So, later that day, after another television report about the arrest of some man at Florence Lake for Bridges' murder, Mabel quickened to the only possible connection between Bridges and Samone: Gloria. And pondered it as she assembled the chicken potpie.

Afterwards, she called Lawson and Keyes, Attorneys at Law, and spoke with Renee. "I just heard the awful news about a body being discovered out at Florence Lake and someone being arrested. Are you okay?"

The phone sounded dead for a time. Eventually, Renee replied, "Yes, Mrs. Mabel. I'm okay, but I'm a wreck. Thank you for calling; thank you for everything. Today has taken me back to that day that you drove me to the hospital." Renee began to cry.

Mrs. Mabel shifted nervously in her Queen Anne chair, upholstered in an intricately patterned tapestry, sipped on her day's third glass of sweet iced tea, and said right out, "Renee, I've had you on my mind. I sure would like for you and Janie to come to supper. It would do me good to be with you two tonight."

"Thank you, Mrs. Mabel. Oh my goodness, yes. You know that day at the hospital, I heard it with my own ears, that he killed himself. I've lived with that now, over a year, blaming myself. What if somebody killed him, Mrs. Mabel, what does that mean?"

Without any hesitation, and with a great degree of resolve, Mabel said, "Well, Renee, this is all very confusing. We shall face the confusion, as friends, together."

"Thank you, Mrs. Mabel. I'm turned upside down right now, can't think, don't know what to think. Thank you for asking us to supper. I don't know what I'd do without you."

No sooner had Mabel Morris hung up the phone than her front doorbell rang and there stood a man, whom she described to Renee later that evening as "Sergeant Rodger White, too blasted skinny and some kind of arrogant to go with it."

The skinny man's sidekick was George Carlson, short and pimpled faced, an intern investigator from the District Attorney's Office, so wet behind the ears, in Mabel's eyes, that a whole box of Kleenex wouldn't dry him.

She, of course, invited them in for some sweet iced tea.

They accepted her invitation, grinning knowingly at each other, mistakenly relying on Sergeant White's previsit assessment of Mrs. Mabel, which was based solely on seeing her name and age on a list of neighbors: "Little ole lady, next door neighbor of a victim, good place to start an investigation and get the lay of the land without her even knowing it, George."

"Yes, sir," George replied, though he wasn't sure exactly what "the lay of the land" was or how a person got it, but he'd only taken Criminal Justice I, so he reasoned, without saying anything more, that he'd likely get the definition of that in Criminal Justice II.

Mabel listened intently to the two men. On the trip to the kitchen to assemble a plate of cookies to go with their iced tea, she concluded that Sergeant White was dragging the lake for a body. She had no intention whatsoever of being the lake, and George had not yet found the lake and wouldn't know the body if he stepped on it.

The two men eased into their seats in Mrs. Mabel's immaculate, well-appointed living room, sipping the iced tea and crunching the cookies. It was an unexpected lagniappe.

But not so were any investigative discoveries from Mrs. Mabel. For she kept the investigators sufficiently off balance with, "Oh I do so love feeding handsome gentlemen. I wish I'd known you were coming, I'd have baked a German chocolate cake for us."

It was very difficult to object to such talk from a sweet little ole lady. George realized right away that she reminded him of his great-grandmother. Sergeant White's inflated ego lured him to the edge of his chair to deliver a soulful Barney Fife impersonation. "Now, Mrs. Morris, do you have any knowledge of the Raleigh Mafia?" Admittedly, he was not standing and raring back and tucking his thumbs in his belt, like Barney, but the glass of sweet tea in one hand and the cookie in the other made that almost impossible.

In any event, he deemed his remarkable communication skills about to deliver their bounty when Mabel batted her eyelashes, rolled up the edge of her apron with deceptively frail looking hands, and replied, "Sergeant, unless that is a new rose they've come out with, no, sir, I don't believe I do. What exactly is the Raleigh Mafia, Sergeant? Please do explain it to me."

Sergeant White's head swelled a bit more at her request for information from him, and he Barneyed, again, which rather amused both George and Mabel: they accidentally caught each other's eyes, and, quickly, in defense of themselves and each other, dropped their glances and refocused on Sergeant White.

George coughed.

Sergeant White said, "Well, Mrs. Morris, it is not a new rose they've come out with. It is a group of thugs who thug their way around Gargagun and Jaylo and traffic in drugs and prostitutes and everything else you wouldn't want to have around this pretty house."

The phone rang, interrupting Sergeant White's arm spread. Mabel stood and walked across in front of him to answer it. He frowned. "Hope you can make it quick, Mrs. Morris, we've got some more important questions for you."

"Oh, yes, indeed, Sergeant. Please excuse me, gentlemen, but I simply must take this; I am expecting a call from a relative." It was a lie.

Of course, Mabel Morris never lied. She considered such a remark an honest attempt to assist unexpected circumstances in helping her control a situation that required control. Of every talent she possessed—and there were many—maintaining control was her greatest.

She picked up the receiver and said, "Hello."

"Hello, Mrs. Mabel, this is Renee. I hate to bother you and I sure hate to invite someone to eat with us tonight, but I think it would be the thing to do if you don't mind."

"Sure, Renee, absolutely. Do I know them?"

"Charlie, Mrs. Morris, Samone's best friend. Do you remember Charlie?"

"Of course I do, one of the finest people, great artist," she said. "I follow his cartoons." She shielded the receiver and whispered back over her shoulder to the perplexed investigators, "I'll be right with you. Please have another cookie." She moved her left hand from the receiver to point toward the cookie plate, now half empty.

Sergeant White nodded and wiggled in the chintz chair, visibly deliberating the cookie offer. He set his tea on the cut-glass coaster on the side table and picked up a cookie, bit into it, and smiled at its deliciousness before he caught himself and then said, silently, with his eyes, "Yes, Mrs. Morris, we have a lot of things to do today. For God's sake, hurry up!"

Mabel saw the nod, the smile, and the eye language; she appreciated the smile, acknowledged the nod, and ignored the eye language, continuing her conversation with Renee to assure that she felt comfortable that Charlie was welcome.

"See you all three at six; quit your worrying now," she said and hung up the phone. It appeared, to her pleasure, that the phone interruption, combined with Sergeant White's successful cookie deliberations and his two empty glasses of the best sweet tea in all of Gargagun, had sufficiently deflated the investigative energies to near zero when she reentered the living room.

"Sergeant White, that was Renee Sims, such a lovely woman, certainly upset over today's news. She's coming to eat some chicken potpie with me tonight. Oh, such fine neighbors. None of us will ever get over losing Samone. Simply dreadful. For goodness sake, Sergeant White, you and George be careful out there now with that group you told me about, that . . . I can't remember what you called them . . ."

"The Raleigh Mafia," he replied.

"Oh, yes, yes. Sounds simply dreadful. I can't imagine such." She clinked more ice into their glasses, dropped in a sprig of mint, informed them about the importance of the correct amount of sun for herbs, why her daylilies thrived on a shaded bank despite their name, and quite a few other important things. She did not reveal any information about Samone, Renee and Samone's arguments, how spiffy Samone was that last morning, yellow mums, or the rook club rumors, rationalizing she had no idea of their importance until they asked her a question about it.

The two men departed much better informed about how to throw a dinner party, select a church in Gargagun with the best choir, and/or deal with the unsettling nature of fluctuating interest rates.

Mabel Morris closed the front door behind them. "Whew, they wore me out!" she said.

Sergeant White brushed cookie crumbs off the front of his suit coat and straightened his tie, thinking how a good nap would help give him a second wind for the rest of the afternoon's investigations. "Well, now, sometimes, George, you just gotta scratch folks off your list that don't have any information, like her, a confused—but, don't get me wrong, very endearing—lil ole lady. Have to admit she makes a dang good cookie. Only reason we'd ever need to talk to her again is to try some of her German chocolate cake." Sergeant White laughed.

George didn't catch the joke.

Mabel cracked the dining room blinds and watched the men depart. She made the crust for the chicken potpie and muddled through the afternoon, worried.

*****

Renee called Charlie and invited him to supper. A relief fell over him that she'd called. He would have the chance to see for himself how she was handling the news. And get to see Janie. He'd been checking in with Renee regularly by phone and he'd seen her out and about with Janie. Once he'd even joined them at a restaurant for a meal.

"Yes, Renee, we need to talk, for sure; so much has happened today. Have you heard anything new in the last hour or so?" he asked.

"Nothing other than the newscast. I just don't understand why anybody would kill Samone, Charlie." She began to cry.

"Oh, Renee; I'm so sorry. It's sure getting to me, too." He could hear her wiping her face and sniffling. "Will you be okay until tonight?"

"I guess. This news today, Charlie, it just turns the world upside down."

*****

Charlie stepped into the steaming shower that evening. "I really don't know how to handle this, Sam," he said, aloud. It seemed to him that Sam heard him. Later, he parked his washed and waxed sedan in Renee's driveway. Renee met him at the door, hugged his neck, and said, "Thank you, Charlie, for coming tonight. This news today has me pretty confused. It will be good to have a meal with you."

Charlie picked up Janie, gave her a squeeze, and said, "Janie, tell your mama it's time to go eat. Nothing happening we can't handle."

Janie giggled. "Nuthin' we can't handle," she said.

28.

CONDOLENCES

Silver drove past as Mrs. Mabel served the chicken potpie. He drove around the block and parked along a side street that gave him a clear view of Renee's house, dark inside that night, the front porch light on, a Chevy sedan parked in her driveway. He swept his high-powered binoculars across the lawn and adjacent houses. There. He saw her. There. In a neighbor's dining room picture window, soft, behind the sheer curtains, sitting across from some man, strong looking, passing her a dish of food. She took the dish of food and gazed up at him, smiling. Their mouths moved. The man nodded at her, smiled.

"Look at that smiling, Goddamn it," Silver said.

The man reached out and patted her hand. Renee and the man kept looking at each other.

"I don't like it one bit, some man smiling at you like that, Renee, patting on you, Goddamn it, Renee, touching you, and you smiling back at him like that," Silver said to her from behind the binoculars. "I killed off your husband, who was fucking behind your back. You oughta be grateful to me, but no, you ungrateful bitch, I catch you with another man."

A warped mind is warped.

It kept speaking out loud, "I should come in there right now and get it cleared up in front of everybody, Renee, that you had better get it through your thick skull that you can't be doing this."

He spun the binocular dial to get a closer view of her, how her hair fell on her shoulders. She turned to look at an older woman and then back at a little girl.

151

Silver didn't care about them. He cared about how her hair swished. Which sidetracked him. Derailed his interrupting the supper to make his announcement. So he seethed. Started his car. Let it idle. Sat in it on the flat pavement outside looking up into the window at her and became aroused, because her long blonde hair kept swishing over her breasts. His passion subsided. He returned the binoculars to the case. He pulled the gearshift into low. He drove directly to Gloria's house with Seth's words, from a year ago after Florence Lake, ringing in his ears.

"She's gone slap dab crazy. Can't nobody talk to her. She won't say a word. Can't get her eyes focused. Just stares off into space. She's not gonna say anything, 'cause, first, she just ain't—I've known her long enough to know that. Second, she's like a dead woman, can't say much without getting lost saying it."

So Seth had insisted to Silver before he drove to Cairo with Bridges' body that he leave Gloria at the headquarters and that she remain there until she could get it together.

One afternoon shortly after the murders, while they were all three sitting in the headquarters, Gloria suddenly slapped Silver. Slapped him again. Spat on him. Said, "Your mother should have killed you in her womb. You aren't Seth's son. You are from the seed of the devil."

Without changing the look on his face, Seth said, "Gloria, don't you know that kind of talk won't do?"

She turned to Seth, looked directly into his face, and said, "Seth, don't you know Silver's killing the man I loved won't do?" She screamed and stumbled toward the bedroom door, drunk with sorrow. She turned toward them in the doorway and said, "You owed me more than this. I'll never forget it. Never."

Not a sound came out of her bedroom for days. The seasons changed before Seth finally drove her home and had his guys take her some groceries.

"Something tells me I need to re-remind you, Gloria, now, even after all this time, to keep your mouth shut," Silver mumbled.

*****

In the kitchen before supper, out of the hearing of Charlie and Janie, who were in the living room playing checkers, Renee unloaded her feelings with Mrs. Mabel. During supper, all three of the adults guided the conversation away from any "Samone talk."

Charlie said, "The chicken pot pie is delicious. A favorite of mine."

"Thank you, Charlie. You'll never know how glad I am that you came with Renee and Janie to supper." Mrs. Mabel passed him the bowl for seconds. "Well, Charlie, I do hope that it won't be your last time at my table." He's as charming as he is savvy, she thought. And, despite her protests, which bordered on flirtation, Mrs. Mabel found herself one step behind Charlie after supper, as he cleared the table, which endeared him to her even further.

Mabel and Charlie returned with a tray piled high with dishes of vanilla ice cream and toppings; Janie jumped up and down, grabbed a dish, and asked, "Mr. Charlie, can I have chocolate syrup?"

He winked at Mrs. Mabel and said, "I think Janie is on to something, Mrs. Mabel, don't you? We do have chocolate, don't we?"

"Oh, yes, indeed, chocolate or strawberry or caramel or all three. Take your pick," she said. It was fun being in cahoots with this delightful young man.

Janie went with chocolate.

Renee smiled, relaxed fully for the first time all day, sipped her sweet tea, and thought how Samone would be happy if he could see Janie now, with the chocolate smeared across her face and hands, swiping at the chocolate with her clean left hand.

Charlie handed her a paper napkin. "Nuthin' we can't handle, is there Janie?" he said. She grinned and nodded, her mouth too full to respond.

Mabel sighed. Her eyes felt wet. "This might be the nicest dinner party I've ever thrown," she said.

"Uh huh," Janie muttered. Everybody laughed.

Oh my goodness, how good it feels to laugh, Renee thought.

Charlie thought how he'd never really noticed how beautiful Renee was until that night.

At Mrs. Mabel's insistence, Janie spent the night with her. "You grown folks could use some time to talk," she said. "Much has happened today."

Charlie and Renee walked back to Renee's house across the monkey grass clumped on the landline between the houses. He steadied her on his arm. "Do we just walk through this or is there a pathway, Renee?"

"There's a pathway, Charlie. It's wide enough for the both of us."

He caught her eye. "I like that, Renee, 'wide enough for the both of us.'"

They sat on Renee's front porch in the cool of the night replaying the recent news about the dead body and how it might be linked with Samone's death. "There's really nothing we can do right now but wait, is there, Charlie?"

"Right, Renee, we will wait together. I'm with you through this. Thanks so much for inviting me over tonight. I needed to be with you and Janie," Charlie said, thinking how he felt strong when he was with Renee and how that night he'd understood for the very first time why Sam had put Clem in her book bag.

"I can never thank you enough for tonight, Charlie. It meant so much being with you after today's news, but I need to confess something to you." She got very quiet. Charlie waited. "I'm ashamed I haven't been able to bring myself to tell Janie her daddy is dead. I've led her to believe he's just gone away and is coming back. My folks think I've gone bonkers."

He lifted her chin. "You have not gone bonkers, Renee. You've done the best you could with the hand you were dealt. We all have. Cut yourself some slack. The right time will come for telling Janie. And, when it does, I'll help you." He was thinking how he had things he, too, needed to confess to her, things Sam had told him that would hurt her too badly if he told her right then.

Her heart fluttered, unexpectedly, when Charlie spoke. "Wanna come on inside for a bit, Charlie?" she asked.

"Nothing would please me more, Renee. Thanks for the invitation, but I have a big day tomorrow. And right now, talking won't help us solve this confusion. We need to know the real truth about how Sam died. Also, at some point, I need to come over and talk with you about some things that are on my mind. But not tonight." He winked. Kissed her on the top of her head. "I'll talk with you soon, Renee. Call me if you need me for anything at any hour."

"I will, Charlie. Night. Sleep tight."

Talking with him had lifted weight off Renee's shoulders. "I've been carrying it all alone, until tonight," she said, aloud. She felt lighter. When she heard Charlie's sedan door slam, she turned and floated inside, pulling the door in behind her. Charlie helped her feel safe. It was a good feeling. In her floating and feeling so safe, she forgot to be afraid, so she didn't lock the new storm door. She flipped the lock on the handle of the inside door, out of habit, and slipped the burglar chain across in place.

*****

As Renee showered, Silver pulled into his own driveway, went inside his apartment, stripped for bed, and found the magazine. It did not go well. Exasperated, he walked through the apartment to the kitchen and found the whiskey bottle. He sat naked on the plastic dinette chair, which stuck to his rump. He unscrewed the top of the bottle and drank from it. "Ahh!" He burped and began gulping the cheap whiskey, pushing its warmth down inside, into the emptiness.

*****

After she showered, Renee picked up the day's mail and her cup of tea and settled into what used to be Samone's easy chair, about which Janie had said that morning, "It smells like Daddy."

That night, smelling Samone hadn't upset her so much. She felt still inside. The lopsidedness of her guilt for Samone's suicide had somehow been sawed off now, possibly taking her out of his death's equation. She was strangely relieved that he might have actually been murdered. "I don't know. Relief, Renee, that Samone may have been murdered? What kind of woman feels relief that her husband was murdered?" she argued aloud with herself.

Ashamed, she shifted in the chair, upsetting the stack of mail. A red envelope fell out onto the floor. What was that scent? Pear preserves? She picked up the envelope. It was addressed, in great big rickety black letters, to "Mrs. Renee Sims" at her correct address. She took a sip of tea and set her teacup on the side table. She held the envelope out to see it better. "That scent is coming from that envelope," she said. She sniffed it. "How strange!" She opened it. A safe-deposit box key attached to a signature card fell out into her lap. A pink notecard was inside the red envelope, on which was written in cursive, in that same rickety black ink, a perfectly symmetrical note. It read: "Renee, I knew your husband through The Shoppe. My condolences to you for your loss. We should talk. But if I don't reach you by Labor Day, it is very important that you contact Carl Rather, Caleon Bank, sign the signature card, and return it to him for access to Box #506, with this key. Gloria Bridges"

Renee turned the notecard over and over. She examined the envelope. It had no postmark. It had to have been dropped directly into her mailbox that very day. "How bizarre! Condolences today from the woman who used to be married to that man whose body they found today." She tried to settle back into Samone's scent, but the scent of the pear preserves mixing in with it somehow upset her. Also, her tea was cold. "I think I've had all the news I can handle today. I'm going to bed. I'll worry about this tomorrow."

29.

HOME COOKING

Sheriff Bill slammed shut the cell door on Cal Hough, who was throwing a tantrum, yelling, "No, I ain't calling nobody. I ain't got nobody to call and I ain't got no money. I want a lawyer!"

It was true: he had no bank account; the few coins in his pocket and the three one dollar bills in a plastic wallet were all the money he had.

"Okay, Mr. Hough, I'll tell the judge your situation about needing a lawyer," the sheriff said. "Just let me know, though, if you change your mind about making a phone call." Sheriff Bill walked back out front and assigned an around-the-clock guard for the cell block to protect Hough. His arrest had made the national news.

The sheriff told his clerk, "Strange situation. The coroner's first words upon seeing the Josh Bridges corpse were, 'This body has likely been frozen.' And there this fella Cal Hough, who works for a Cairo refrigeration plant, sat in his pickup at Florence Lake carrying the dead man's coat in his pickup which was parked where the corpse was found and where the body of the man that they had thought committed suicide last year was found. But Hough has refused to make a phone call out to anybody, not even down to the refrigeration plant."

In his cell, Hough hunched over on the metal cot with its urine-splotched mattress. He frowned, dropped both his hands in disgust, and cradled his head in them. Antsy, he rose to pace and stubbed his toe on the left front leg of the cot that jutted out at an angle.

"Dang nab it!" Hough said. He sat down again, took off his shoe and his white sock, and began rubbing his toe. It was swollen and bleeding. Hough didn't know that the previous inhabitant of his cell, who had weighed twice his 150 pounds and had mental problems, had hallucinated and ripped the cot's left front leg off to attack the sink, which collapsed the cot and crumbled the sink's front, leaving it a jagged instrument looking for a prisoner's jewels. Nor did he know that county maintenance had ignored the sink and was unable to reattach the cot's leg—it was pretty well bunged up—so they substituted a leg from a broken down cot in the warehouse, but since it didn't exactly match the stub leg, they wired the misfits together, resulting in the cot's replacement leg's awkward misalignment and a cot that rocked.

That first night, Hough's restless leg sent the cot on a creaking binge. He got up and walked most of that first night to try to stop his shaking legs and ease his frazzled nerves. Bit his fingernails. Spat 'em out on the floor.

*****

The next afternoon, around one p.m., sunlight filtered in through ancient dusty ceiling-high windows and lingered like a loyal puppy dog over counsel behind the rail in the county courtroom. In that mellowness, Circuit Court Judge Carlo Bailey responded to Cal Hough's request for a public defender, appointing Phillip Cavenaugh Jones, a mild-mannered trusted local, as Hough's lawyer.

"Thank you, Judge," Jones said.

"No, thank you, Mr. Jones, for serving this fine state." After Jones conferred with his client, Judge Bailey read Hough the charges against him and asked for his plea.

Cal Hough said, "I'm not guilty."

Judge Bailey said: "Under the circumstances, defendant will be held without bond. Flight risk."

Jones watched the color drain from Hough's face.

"Mr. Jones, I wish to hell I'd never come up here. Give everything I got. But he ain't even settin' me no dollar figure for getting out. Oughta be some amount set for me. Where am I gonna fly to?"

"We'll talk about it back at the jail," Jones said and walked with his client and his deputy escort to the jailhouse.

Inside the cell, Hough sat down on the rickety cot and began wringing his hands. "What the hell we gonna do to get me outta here, lawyer? I ain't done nothing. Thought they'd a figured that out for sure this morning."

"We'll request the court reconsider bond, Mr. Hough." Hough's restless legs kicked in. He held them down and began chattering, "It's a coat, a dirty coat got 'em holding me here, a dirty coat."

Jones listened. He was good at listening.

"I didn't see narry a coat down there in that there floorboard with all them empty beer cans, newspapers and such, Mr. Jones, when I reached over to get them fishing lures from the glove compartment. Hell, somebody planted that thing on me while I was a fishin'," Hough begged at Jones.

Jones listened.

"Who dun it had to've brought that lug wrench and setter right back in on the coat, 'cause I sure as Jesus didn't put narry a coat in there nor nowhere and I sure didn't trouble to drag a lug wrench around and put it under it. I ain't got no education. Left fifth grade, but I'd know a heap sight better'n to sit out there where a man's body's done been found, if I'd killed him, a carryin' his coat up in my front floorboard. I ain't stupid."

Jones kept listening.

"Hell, I've been stupid 'bout this whole thing in a lot of ways I'm beginnin' to figure out, but I'm not no 'shoot myself in the foot' stupid. I am mad, madder'n a pile of snakes, 'cause I've been framed."

Jones said, "Mr. Hough, these are pretty serious charges against you. Two murder charges: one on this Bridges and, now, Samone Sims, back a year ago."

Hough stopped talking. Lots of thinking started running across his face. Fast. It got as quiet as snowflakes falling.

Jones looked directly into his client's face and said, voice lowered, "Mr. Hough, did you ever hear of this fellow they found dead out there, Josh Bridges?"

"Not no, but hell no!"

"What about Samone Sims, the man they found out there about a year ago? What was your relationship to him, Mr. Hough?"

"Relationship? Hell, I can't even pronounce his name. Wouldn't know him from Adam's house cat. Goddamn it. I'm in a nightmare!" Hough dropped his head in his hands. Eventually, he looked up, a lost hopelessness in his being. He said, "Mr. Jones, I swear on a stack of Bibles a thousand high, I didn't know nobody'd been killed. Not this week, last week, fifty-two weeks ago, or anytime in between. I'm innocent."

"I'll file an appeal on the bond," Jones said.

Hough snapped at Jones like he was his enemy, "When you reckon that peal'll be heard, lawyer?"

"Well, I'll get the appeal filed immediately; the state will object. It might take awhile."

"Goddamn with awhiles, lawyer! Goddamn with awhiles!"

"I'm gonna do the best I can do to help you, Mr. Hough. Whatever else you believe or don't believe, you can believe that." Jones rapped on the wall to get the deputy. He turned and said to Hough, "I believe you, Mr. Hough. But there's something not fitting in. Think if you will on what you might want to tell me that will help me help you."

A palpable fear gripped Hough. "Mr. Jones, you ever hear about being between the devil and the deep blue sea?"

"Sure have, Mr. Hough. What do you mean?"

"Let me just say it like this: these murder charges is the deep blue sea."

"Okay. Think on how you can help me understand that better. I'll be back tomorrow."

30.

THIRD TIME IS THE CHARM

It began after midnight. I stumbled from the bed, half asleep, to answer the doorbell. There he stood, staring in on me through the narrow width of space that the burglar chain exposed. His wild eyes seemed to be sprouting out of the moon behind him. Protected by the thickness of the door and the clarity of my mind, I looked directly at Silver and ignored him. I had no intention whatsoever of his coming inside my home. I knew him, now; I could see into him. He was crazy, mean crazy. He flipped up that red twig of hair over his face. I looked at it and did not watch it.

As I stood fenced off from him, it hit me that maybe God had sent him to test me further, knowing that I had failed the test twice. But I would not fail it a third time. No. At that moment, Silver was, for me, the least important person in the whole world, standing in a sliver of light along the door facing, so I lied, for convenience, to be able to go back to bed.

"You woke me, Silver. It's awful late. What time is it?"

He stuck his nose into the gap between the door and the door facing and grinned. "You're sure right about that, Renee. It's awful late. But plenty early," he cackled.

A shiver of repulsion ran down my back. I said, "It's good to see you, but I'm not up to company tonight, Silver. I got some sad news today. I'm exhausted. I've got to get some rest. I'm afraid we'll have to get together another time." The part about getting together another time was, of course, a lie.

"Rest?" He laughed the laugh of a spook in a Halloween house. "You think I'm getting any rest, you over here entertaining men?"

I pulled my bathrobe tighter around me. Had he seen Charlie there earlier in the evening? "Silver, it is not your concern whom I entertain. You must leave," I said as I reached to close the door.

An energy flared in his face and without any forewarning he raised his arms, crossed them, and used them, along with his feet, as weapons, to rip the burglar chain out of the facing. The burglar chain dangled. I'll always remember the way it dangled.

Once inside, he turned and slammed the door shut behind him. He locked it at the knob. I turned to run. He grabbed me. "Not my concern? I must leave? Who d'ya think you are, Renee?" He whirled in on top of me and slapped me with both his hands, back and forth, back and forth.

I tried to cover my face with my arms. He dropped me. Jerked back. Pulled a gun.

"God, Silver, what are you doing?" I looked up into his face. He was off somewhere far away; I was the parking meter, its time ticking with the metal of his weapon twisting, bruising slots into my temple. Reckless.

Monster sounds erupted from him. He gritted his teeth. He reeled in over me, spreading on my skin his unbathed smell alive with cheap whiskey and mixed with that same sweetness of pear preserves I'd smelled on the envelope.

I saw it, then, the red envelope with the pink notecard inside. When I had stood to go to bed earlier, it had fallen out of my lap onto the braided trim on the chair cover and the envelope was, as Silver pressed the gun into me, pressing into the brown on the chair. With the gun to my head, I had a crazy thought: the red envelope matches the braid on Samone's chair. And, right in the middle of being held at gunpoint, I became irrationally worried that the envelope might fall to the floor and upset Silver even more.

But, as abruptly as he'd pulled the gun, he pocketed it and grabbed me with both his hands and pressed me up against the back wall of the living room. So much was happening so fast. I opened my mouth to try to speak. He balled up his fist and punched me in the jaw. I heard him hitting the bone. It sounded so much louder than I would have ever expected. I crumpled. He pulled the gun from inside his pocket, again.

My mouth wouldn't move. Was it just not moving because I was so afraid? Or was it not moving because he'd smashed my face? Finally, I found words, dry words: "Silver? What do you want?"

He staggered in on me, mumbling, drunk, reaching for my throat with his left hand, the gun in his right, "What's between your legs, you whore."

"Leave. Leave me alone, for God's sake, Silver, leave me alone. Please. Silver, go. You have no business here. Go!"

He grinned and tried to focus his eyes on me, but he couldn't. "Business. You don't know the first thing about business."

I tried to reason with him.

He slapped me over and over with the gun. Held it to my temple and pretended to pull the trigger. "Pow! Pow!" He laughed.

I begged him for my life. Finally, I gave up begging. I understood that he was going to kill me. So, I balled up in a fetal position in the middle of the living room floor, grateful that Janie was not there. It worried me, though, that someone might tell her how I died. I did not want that. I wanted her to know the good in me. I concentrated on that and forgot Silver for a time, although he circled me like he was sizing up a crippled animal he'd happened upon. Then, without any forewarning, he grabbed me, a plastic bag of garbage that needed to go to the curb. He dragged me to the corner of the room, dropped me, and kicked me as far into the corner as he could, seemingly preoccupied with my body fitting into the corner.

I know it makes no sense what I am about to tell you, but it seemed like the right thing for him to do, to get me out of the middle of the living room floor, where he had held me hostage before. I did not want him to have the pleasure of repeating that evening, after I'd told him not to come inside.

My face and eyes were swelling; it was a strain to get my eyes open enough to be able to see him. He was a blur, a wild blur moving around me, taunting me with the tip of the gun. I racked my brain to try to understand what I'd done to him to turn him into this monster. "What have I done to you, Silver, to cause this?" I spoke in my mind, but the words would not come out. I closed my eyes and prayed, silently.

He held the gun up in the air, in victory, and said, "I've got you now, you bitch, I've got you." He kicked me, over and over, trying to push me further up into the corner. I dodged like that starved stray puppy, the one who first met him and enticed him by dropping the Cosmopolitan between us.

Why, dear God, did I do that? I'd give everything in the world, except Janie, not to have done that. It was my soul speaking. Silently.

He circled me, dancing around, waving the gun, pointing it at me, cocking it . . . uncocking it . . . laughing . . . cocking it . . . uncocking it . . . laughing. Without provocation, he pocketed the gun and screeched a straight back chair across the hardwood floor, setting it beside me, its right front leg touching my head. He sat down in the chair and began to sob like a disappointed baby. He pulled out the gun again and pointed it in my direction, but it wobbled around, loose. "You've messed it all up."

"My God, dear God, Silver, what have I messed up?" I wanted to see him answer me. See the look on his face. If I could see the look there, maybe I could understand. But I could not. My eyes were swollen almost shut.

He did not reply. A silence engulfed us. It was a great relief.

Suddenly, he jerked toward me, moving his body around, swishing his stench over me. It seemed he had his ear to me, against my neck, listening with total concentration to hear what was not being said. He rose. I could hear the gun flopping down toward me. He crouched over me again and placed the barrel of the gun in the middle of my forehead, his left hand pushing my head toward the left.

He said, "She turned counter; counter, you bitch."

"What? What do you mean?" I begged. "Tell me, Silver, what you mean?"

"It's too late, you know it's too late. Ever since you, Renee, she won't work with me anymore. I've got the gun now and she turns the opposite way. Hell, you know exactly what I mean. Don't pretend with me, you bitch!"

I sat up. I know now it was a courageous thing to do—to sit up—and probably what set him off to finish. But it seemed like the most important thing in the whole world, to sit up and face him and hear him and correct whatever it was that I had done so he'd leave. So I sat up, believing I could make this whole thing go away. I just sat up.

And he didn't do anything.

After a time, he spilled words over me, talking in a language foreign to me about running and dying and falling. "You understand me, you bitch. Don't act like you don't."

It came to me, as he rambled, what I'd seen earlier before he battered my eyes, the old dried blood that ran the length of the right side of his blue shirt. That was not my blood. I could smell it now; it stank heavy, sweet, old. Smelling it on the stench of his body jerked a glob of the partially digested chicken potpie up into my throat. I tried to swallow it, but it wouldn't go back down. It pushed into my mouth, stubborn, and I held it as long as I could, because I knew it would not sit well with this man if I left right now with his having just been there on that chair weeping. But I had no choice. I ran for the commode in the bathroom right off the living room, which I think is what made him so mad. He ran after me. I spewed my stomach contents into the commode. He stood laughing at me. I finished and wiped my mouth, but my head kept hanging into the seat opening. I simply could not lift it.

He fumbled with the lever and flushed the commode, splashing the contents up into my face. I spat over and over and over to get the slips of food off my lips. But I couldn't, which threw me into a new fit of vomiting. As I writhed, he rammed my face inside the commode seat and sat on me. I heard the robe and gown rip. I don't remember feeling them or hearing them fall off.

The strangest thing of all: Samone's face came to me right in that moment. Oh, he was not angry with me, not for my withholding myself from him in the past or my allowing this monster in my life. Samone said to me, clearly, without words, "Hold on, Renee. Don't give in. Hold on. Remember the school bus. Remember the school bus."

I held the commode seat for all my life. And I saw Samone's face back then when I handed him that frog and how he smiled at me from ear to ear and said in that smile, "I think you are the most wonderful person God ever created."

I don't know why Samone and I were together there in that bathroom on that bus with a monster on top of me, but the central air-conditioning vent began to blow air up into my face—Silver had jerked my head out of the commode and my face was just above the floor being comforted by a rag from my torn gown, flipping and flopping against my right arm.

It and Samone's face and his wordless words, there in the bathroom and on the bus, were to me like the crumpled old photo of a loved one a soldier keeps tucked inside his helmet to fondle in a foxhole to assure himself that something other than what is happening has happened before and will happen again, if the soldier can only hold on long enough.

And so I held on.

He ripped my back with his dirty fingernails. I smelled the flesh rip. I did not want him in my flesh. I did not care how it smelled. I did not want him in my flesh. I begged him. "Stop," I said. "Stop, Silver, stop!"

He didn't listen. He didn't have his mind or his body on listening. And then, when his body wouldn't work the way he wanted it to work, he kept his right foot holding me down beside the toilet and he began rummaging through the medicine cabinet. He found several things that he used to rip me in other places. I sorta went away from there, I guess, because I don't remember everything as clearly as I want to.

"I'm trying as hard as I can, Samone, to hold on. Dear God, I'm holding on," I said out loud. I tried to yell it, but it was mostly a whisper, I think.

Of everything about it all, something important happened. A revelation occurred. At first I was maniacally angry. Then I was afraid, begging afraid. But, after a time, I reached a point where I knew I had no power whatsoever over Silver or what he was doing or would do. I had no control. I didn't care anymore. I turned loose. When I reached that point—however idiotic it might sound—it was freeing. I said out loud, "Forgive me, Samone, I am turning loose the commode seat and the having dropped the Cosmopolitan in the floor and having driven my car to the roadside park." I just gave in, like a human, and listened to the gurgling sound of the ripping from afar. Oh, please, please don't misunderstand. I had said, "Stop! Stop!" How many times did I say it? I can't count them. Anyway, he was too big and I was too small and he knew that and he would not stop until he decided to stop.

But the strangest thing I remember, too. How he pushed me against the bathroom wall, where there is now still blood—I know it has to be there, proof—and made me turn my head counterclockwise, over and over and over, as I bled into the floor and into the commode from the bottom of me and I wept and let it happen—no, no, no, not the rape, no—the bleeding. I just bled. What I don't remember is how, when he left, I dragged myself to the phone to lift the receiver. It seemed so heavy.

Charlie answered.

"Come help me, please, I've been raped." I dropped the receiver. Then I dragged myself across the floor to the living room door and I saw the blood was different coming from the different places and I marveled at that as I collapsed.

Oh yes, I remember something else, too. Something I forgot to tell you. Earlier, when I had opened the front door with the burglar latch on, I asked Silver, "Why are you here?"

And he had said, "To pay your husband back for what he did."

As I waited on Charlie, I asked Samone what Silver had meant. I pled with him to tell me what he had done. Samone would not answer me. He kept talking with Charlie. He kept saying, over and over, "Take care of her, Charlie."

I knew he would. I already felt safe knowing Charlie would take care of me. That kept me alive.

But I could not lift my head. It and my thighs and back were wet and stuck to the living room floor. I smelled an odor. Out of the corner of my eyes, I saw the smell: my own blood, puddles of it, spread out, circling me. The wider I opened my eyes to try to see, the more the pain in me awoke and the more perplexed I became. What had happened? A recollection flashed in on me, and then another and another, dominoes falling, atop which landed an unexpected joy. "Oh my God, I am still alive!" Strange, pain and joy, partners. I had never before understood that.

As I lay there, lost, I did not know that a silent miracle was being hatched in my wretchedness, shifting "me" around inside. Maybe I had not been ripe enough for the miracle before. I could hear my own voice echoing, "You should have killed Silver months ago when he used you as a 'thing,' Renee, for his quick fix here in the center of your living room floor, in your own home. But you refused to look, Renee, like you refused to look at your falling-to-pieces marriage. Did you think if you did not look, it would not fall to pieces? No, you did not think at all. You insulted Samone. And yourself. It's too late now to fix it. Samone is dead and you are dying, where you pretended to live, Renee, back behind in the shadows. Blaming Samone. It was not Samone, Renee, who was not loving you; it was you."

I whispered my knowing, "My God, Samone, there was nothing in me to give to you. You couldn't find me because I was not there to find. I'm bleeding to death in this room where I have always been totally loyal to you, Samone, smiling into your face, absent of my self, cheating you. I am so very sorry."

My last thoughts before the darkness closed in, again, were of a strange quilt: nice forearms . . . why . . . no light . . . I am not that much different from Silver . . . a monster . . . on the floor . . . blood sticky . . . so very sleepy . . . I must close my eyes . . . sleep again like in Samone's chair . . . a red envelope . . . red braid . . . Did I call Charlie? . . . How long ago? . . . he will come for me . . . Charlie . . . I am so sleepy . . .

So I closed my eyes and rested.

When I awoke, Charlie was leaning over me following the stretcher to the ambulance, holding my hand.

"Am I alive, Charlie?"

"Yes, oh God in heaven, yes. You are alive, Renee," he kept saying. And, over and over, "I'm here, Renee. You are not alone. I am here." He had such a strong face.

31.

MERTHIOLATE BURNS

Within a week or so after the rape, Seth Maddox parked an old white pickup alongside the curb. A little shirtless, barefooted kid in blue shorts wobbled his tricycle past him along the shady tree-lined sidewalk. Maddox got out of the pickup. Waved at the little kid. The kid grinned back at him and honked a Groucho Marx handlebar horn to try to scare him. Maddox pretended to jump. Laughed. The kid sat back, then, on the tricycle seat, put his hands on his hips, and yelled, "Hey, mister. Look. See me drive without hands."

Maddox watched the little kid aim his tricycle toward a woman standing in the doorway, holding open the screen door of a modest home. She was wearing an apron. The little kid pedaled toward her, no hands, his dirty little fat legs moving fast, his knees almost banging the handlebars. At the steps to the front porch, the tricycle tipped over and the kid fell off, onto his already dirt-smeared knees. He didn't cry. He stood straight like a soldier and glanced over to see if the stranger was still there. He was.

Maddox said, "A little Merthiolate'll fix it."

"Yikes!" the kid squeaked. "That'll burn."

Maddox chuckled.

The woman shut the screen and walked down the steps to help the kid. She blew on his knee, wrapped one arm around him, and patted him on his head.

She nodded at Maddox. "Thanks, mister." She helped the little kid up the steps and held the screen door open for him to come inside. "Come on in, Billy, and wash up, now. Got you a peanut butter and jelly sandwich on white loaf bread, just like you like it." Billy hugged her legs and wiped his runny nose on her apron. The woman closed the screen door behind her.

Maddox could hear the kid telling the woman how he'd "scared that man out there."

He had. Something in the whole situation had smashed in on Maddox, unexpectedly, when he'd seen the kid. Then, when he waved at him, for a split second, there stood Silver, barefooted, in blue shorts, forlorn, outside the orphanage, without a tricycle or parents. "What's wrong with me?" Maddox mumbled to himself.

He began the few blocks' walk over to Gloria's. After a step or two, he experienced an epiphany, which he spoke, unconsciously, "Nobody ever held no screen door open for me to come inside for a peanut butter and jelly sandwich." It felt strange realizing something so little so late in life that seemed so important.

He turned a corner and walked two more blocks past a cur dog barking behind a fence; some more kids, slightly older than the tricycle boy, jumping rope in a grassless tree-shaded yard, each jump over the rope stirring up dust; and a teenage boy up under a jalopy, his bare feet sticking out, a band-aid on his right big toe. A squirrel scampered across the sidewalk in front of Maddox, stopped, stared at him, climbed a tree, and hid out in the open on the tallest branch, observing Maddox at a safe distance.

"Busiest morning and the most attention I've gotten in a long time," Maddox said, shaking his head. He unlatched the gate and walked into Gloria's yard. "Well, she finally listened to me, she did, and fenced the entire place, front and back." He smiled, feeling good about his influence on her. Balancing on the narrow stone path, he walked the ten to twelve feet down the center of the tiny front yard, stepped off into the grass, and circled around the side to the back deck. He climbed the deck steps and knocked on the back door. Removed his hat and cradled it in his left elbow. Pulled out a wadded up handkerchief and wiped his brow. Listened. Not a sound inside.

A clothesline stretched from the back door to the top of the swing arbor out at the end of the deck. A clean dishrag hung over the clothesline. "I buy you the best Sears clothes dryer ever made, get it installed for you, and you still hang your dishrags out to bleach in the sun. Always gonna be a country girl, aren't you, baby, no matter how long you live in Gargagun."

He shifted his hat to his right hand and fanned himself with it. "Darn, it's hot out here. Gloria, come to the door," he lifted his voice. No sound from inside. He set his ear up against the door pane, listening. Maybe she's playing music. She plays music all the time. No music. "Strange kind of quiet in there, Gloria." A green fly buzzed around in the kitchen and worked its way up under the curtain on the back door pane. Flapped on it. "Gloria, you've never allowed flies in your house. Am I at the right house? Hey, Gloria, come to the door!"

Nothing moved inside the house. A tiny breeze flipped across the dishrag. A bad smell hit him. Was it the dishrag? Maddox walked to the end of the house and peered into the garage window. "Yeah, I'm at the right place; that's your car, Gloria."

He returned to the back door and knocked again. "Well, you're here, Gloria, your car is in the garage. Quit pouting and open the damn door," he shouted. There was no movement inside. None. Dead still.

He noticed that the expanse of Bermuda and rye grass carpeting the back yard was high and scraggily. It had not been mowed in weeks. "You oughta let me get somebody to mow this yard for you, Gloria," he begged into the emptiness. "Dagnabit, I've told you, time and again, to let me help you. You don't pay me any attention. And, you're too dang independent for your own good."

He walked out onto the deck to get a better look at the backyard, passing an old worn-out mop hanging on the clothesline, as a stiff breeze flowed in around him from the direction of the house. A stench engulfed him. "Wheweee! You need to throw this damn mop away and get a new one and let me send them boys over here to mow your yard. And damn, girl, you need to quit this poutin'." He returned to the house, opened the screen on the back door, squinted into the door pane, trying to see into the crack between the cotton panels on the back door. Couldn't see a thing. All the lights were off.

Suddenly, he felt hot in his chest, the boss of the Raleigh Mafia; he felt little and disregarded by the woman inside who was ignoring him, refusing to come to the door of the house he'd bought and paid for and furnished and maintained for her, with a car parked in the garage bought with his money, too. "You ain't never let me in, Gloria, not since we was six years old and you up and grabbed my heart." He could just picture her back then, looking him straight in the face, taking nothing off of him, but battling anybody who gave him grief. He could out strategize anybody about anything, manipulate most anybody, scare 'em, get his way, but he didn't have a clue how to get "inside" with this woman.

Or anybody, really. Never learned much about getting close to folks growing up. His mama's favorite word was "don't," and she could slap a blister on a little fellow's leg for getting in her way or on his arm for reaching for a cookie. His daddy told him in grade school. "Son, the business is gonna be yours someday. Keep your feelings to yourself; don't nobody care how you feel. Feelings can't help you get what you need. Shut yore mouth and listen with yore ears; leave them feelings to the sissies."

He knocked on the back door again. Not a whimper or a peep from inside. The Gloria he'd known all those many years would not play games with him. If she were angry, she would come to the door, open it, let him into the kitchen, chew him out, tell him to sit down, and make him some coffee. She would not play hide and seek. He quit being mad. Standing on the deck in the heat, fear poured over him like ice water. He kicked the back door. It didn't budge. From a table on the deck, he grabbed a metal statue of a naked Greek man and smashed in the door pane, reached in, turned the lock, and pushed open the door.

From inside, the foul, rotten mop smell burst out over him, but it was the stench of old dead, not a rotten mop. He grabbed a dishcloth from the kitchen counter and covered his nose. He flipped on a light. This was not Gloria's house where the salt and pepper shakers were lined up, side by side, at the exact same angle. The dining table was tipped over on its side, leaning against the fridge, a dining chair wedged underneath it. An upside-down sugar bowl lay on the floor, its top cracked into tiny pieces, sugar cobwebbing out from the bowl, feeding a line of ants trotting to and fro from the bowl's edge to the baseboard underneath the sink. Straight ahead, he saw it, a ballooned out body lying on her side in the living room, clothes ripped off, dried blood spattered on them. Her cat, Jingo, dead, too, between her legs. He crept toward her hideousness. His hands were shaking. Seth Maddox's hands never shook. He bent down at her head, talking to her in a low voice, as if she were alive, "Gloria, someone has killed you and screwed over us both."

It was always about Seth Maddox.

Then he saw them: a long red hair caught up inside the loop of the yellow scarf used to strangle her, looped still around the neck flesh; and another red hair stretched out worm-like on the floor by her arm.

Maddox covered the broken window with tin foil and pulled the door shut behind him. His daddy's voice came out of nowhere: "When it's already done and you can't undo it, do whatever you gotta do."

On the walk back to the pickup, not one bird sang, nor did any squirrels scamper or any kids skip rope. And the jalopy with the teen under it had vanished. He sat inside the cab of his truck to get his breath, dry-eyed tinder, ready to explode, listening to the echo, "Feelings can't help you get what you need . . . leave them feelings to the sissies."

"Goddamn, Daddy, don't you ever shut up!" Sweat rolled down his face and into his collar. "Gloria. I cannot make it without you," he said into the rearview mirror, not a soul behind him or in front of him. He was alone. "How could you go and leave me like this?" He blew his nose and cranked the truck. He circled the block past Gloria's house once, just to see how it looked. "Nobody'll notice anything until I get back; it looks perfectly normal from the outside . . . Nothing is ever perfectly normal, is it Gloria?"

Within minutes, he pulled into a service station across the interstate where every person with a lawn mower brought gas cans for fill up, so he would be no more conspicuous filling up a gas can here than he would be ordering a burger and fries at Hardee's. He capped the gas can tightly and drove back off across the interstate.

32.

UNSPEAKABLE THINGS

D r. Clayton propped her elbow by Renee's right arm on the hospital tray, taking her into her confidence: "You've been through a lot, Renee; right now it might be difficult to imagine ever being completely well again, but you *will* be."

Renee nodded.

"It won't happen quickly and it'll be hard work, but you won't be alone. I'm here for you anytime, day or night."

Renee was wounded. Inside. And out.

Dr. Clayton lifted her elbow off the tray and set Renee's medical chart on it, scribbling. She looked at Renee with a steady softness and said, "I want to see you in my office next week, Renee. Okay?"

"Yes. Okay," Renee replied, thinking how glad she was that she had a female doctor.

The Demerol in her flashed Silver's face in the room. She blurted out, "If he walked in here, Dr. Clayton, I would jerk my medical chart from you and bash him with it." She began to cry.

Dr. Clayton let her cry. Didn't rush her. She smiled that steady softness again, reached over and lifted Renee's chin, and said, "You wouldn't have to jerk it from me; I would hand you the chart. It's okay to be angry. But you are going to need counseling, Renee; it is not optional." She closed the medical chart and set her prescription pad atop it, scrawled something on it, ripped off the sheet and handed it to her. "Here's the name of a female counselor, Renee, who specializes in helping women who've been through what you've been through."

Renee tried to stand up to take the sheet. She felt faint. She grabbed the bed rail. Ashley came to her side. A nurse's aide whisked a wheelchair over and helped her in it onto an inflatable pillow. She began perspiring from the pain. She nodded to the doctor. "I will. I will see the counselor," she said, but she was skeptical how talking about Silver with anybody could help anything. She wanted his ass and anything to do with it as far away from her as possible. She shivered at the thought of his ever having touched her. It hurt, even to shiver. And she wanted not to hurt. She became nauseous. The nurse's aide handed her a gold half-moon shaped plastic container. She dry heaved into it.

She was almost too weak to sit, but the aide added another pillow to brace her and strapped her in, wiping her face with a cold towel. "You may want to hold this on your face for the ride home," she said.

Renee was wondering how she had ever let such a monster into her life, but she didn't want to think about it. So instead, in a Demerol stupor, she fantasized about killing Silver while dozing as the nurse wheeled her along the shiny corridor to the exit.

Back home, in her own bed, afloat in the Demerol and with Ashley by her side, Renee felt the pain begin to subside, physically and emotionally. She was able to rest.

*****

As Charlie flipped on the turn signal and rolled his sedan into Renee's driveway, an explosion shook the ground.

"What the heck? You going out on me, you new-fendered son of a gun?" Charlie accused the sedan. He jumped out to check its exterior. It was fine, still shiny from the morning's wash and wax job that would have pleased Sam. He raised the hood. "Looks fine under here, too," he said to himself, slamming the hood to stare directly into a giant marshmallow of black smoke on the horizon. Fire sirens a few blocks over screeched toward the smoke.

Mrs. Mabel opened her front door and waved at him and said, "Look, look at that smoke, Charlie. What do you suppose it is?"

"Don't know, Mrs. Mabel, some kind of explosion. Happened just as I drove up. Thought at first it was my car. It looks to be close."

"The boom woke me," she said. "I thought I was having a bad dream." She stepped out onto the porch in her black-checkered housecoat, hair tightly teased, netted, and flat on one side from her afternoon nap. She worked her way onto the path between the yards, approached Charlie, reached up, and gave him a hug. "So glad to see you, Charlie. You coming to check on our Renee?"

He blushed. Though he hardly knew this woman, he felt compelled to hug her back. "Yes. How do you think she's doing since she got home, Mrs. Mabel?"

"To be honest, Charlie, I don't know. She's had so much to deal with so fast. She's still in lots of pain, though Ashley phoned and said the pain meds are helping and Renee's slept most of the day. This has shaken her up. And right on top of the confusing news about how Samone may have actually died."

Charlie let that reality hold center stage for a moment before he spoke. "Yes, such a shock hearing that Sam may have been murdered. So much for her to handle. I'm concerned about her, Mrs. Mabel. It's gonna be tough on her for a long time. Do you, by chance, know the man who did this to her?"

"No, oh heavens no!" Mabel placed her hands on her hips, tilted her head in toward Charlie, and said, "And it's a good thing I don't. I'd add him to my compost heap. What he did to Renee was unspeakable. Simply unspeakable!" Red crept up her neck into her face. She was embarrassed talking about it.

He took her arm and said, "Mrs. Mabel, you've named it. It was unbelievable. We are lucky she is alive." There they both stood by the old sedan, helpless and angry. "Do you think that she is safe here, now?" he asked.

"Yes, I do. The sheriff sends a car by now and then patrolling the area and he has told 'em to call for anything that seems the least bit suspicious. Ashley's here around the clock. She's not letting anyone in that they don't know. And they are keeping the doors and windows locked tight."

"Good, that's good."

"She's holding up under all of this. She's a lot braver than I understood," she said. Trying not to cry, she changed the subject and turned toward the fire. "Look, I believe that smoke will catch those fluffy clouds up there."

He turned, also, to watch the smoke tumbling around in the sky, red flames underneath creating a glow, seemingly fueling the smoke's lapping tongues. He felt inept. He said, "I am so glad that you are next door. And that Ashley is with her. Sam would not have been able to accept any of this happening to her. He adored Renee."

Mrs. Mabel suddenly straightened tall, faced him, and cornered him. "I sure hate to ask you this, Charlie," she said, "but I must. Did you ever think that Samone was being unfaithful to Renee, having an affair with anyone?"

Startled, Charlie asked, "What do you mean, Mrs. Mabel?"

It was a clear stall. He did not reassure her with words like, "No, no, no. Oh, heavens no, Mrs. Mabel. I never had any thoughts of any kind that Sam was ever unfaithful to Renee. Never." She recognized the stall. Her face showed she'd uncovered something.

Charlie felt pinched.

She moved to the front walk and positioned herself between Charlie and Renee's front porch—he'd have to finish the conversation before he went inside. "Charlie, I heard a rumor, back before we lost Samone, that his car had been seen parked regularly on Saturdays in the yard of a woman named Gloria Bridges—well really, I think she took her maiden name back after she divorced that man whose body they found out at Florence Lake, and now she goes by Gloria Jenkins."

Mrs. Mabel's revelation flashed Charlie back to the day before Sam died, out behind Mac's Coffee Shop. Tears welled up in his eyes. He felt pain and relief and gratefulness toward her, like he might feel toward a doctor who'd lanced a boil on his backside, spilling pus out, soiling everything necessary, to initiate healing.

Mrs. Mabel said not another word. She waited.

Charlie did not speak; he was thinking.

Finally, she interrupted his thinking. Jabbed the scalpel in. "Did you ever know of Gloria Jenkins yourself, personally, Charlie?"

He tried to look her in the eyes, but his own eyes just wouldn't do it, so he looked toward her and said with genuine concern and serious-ness, "Mrs. Mabel, I've heard of that woman and may have seen her around town, but I have never personally met her, no." There. He did not lie. He sighed.

She pressed. "Charlie, you are an awfully good friend to our dear Renee and were, of course, to her husband, Sam. Do you think that Renee ever knew about Gloria?"

It seemed surreal to Charlie that Mrs. Mabel had, within a matter of moments, established that it was a given that Sam and Gloria were in a relationship. He wanted to back away from all this talk. He felt guilty: he'd held the information about Sam and Gloria—exactly what he had held, he did not know—for almost a year. There it was, finally, spread out into the daylight, but he did not know what Renee knew. This time he looked Mrs. Mabel in the eye. "Mrs. Mabel, I'm uncomfortable with this talk. I didn't know that woman, Gloria, at all. I don't know exactly what the situation was; I don't know what Renee knew or did not know, but I do not think Renee had a clue."

She dropped her head and shook it. She sighed. She clicked her tongue to the top of her mouth, "Tst, tst," and said, "thank you, Charlie."

He immediately began mental preparations for her next probe, but she turned and moved toward her house, seeming to brush the subject off her hands by saying, "Okay, well, I've got to get back inside. Supper is in the oven. Thanks, again, Charlie. With Renee in the shape she's in, the last thing that she needs is friends telling her unfounded rumors about Samone. That would hurt her."

"Yes, you are right, Mrs. Mabel," Charlie said, with questions in his eyes.

She turned, then, and looked at him. "Charlie, for the time being, why don't I go talk to Sheriff Bill and tell him about the rumors and explain the situation you and I are in. If you have something more that you want to tell him, fine, but if there is any link between the deaths of the two men, having that information could be critical."

Charlie felt relieved. Mrs. Mabel continued, "Renee sure needs you right now."

"Thanks. I appreciate your saying that. She needs us both," he said.

She sighed. "Yes. We all need each other." Then she changed the subject. "Guess I'll have to spend another ten dollars at the beauty shop tomorrow to get the smell of this smoke out of my hair. I wonder what in the world that fire was."

"You smell sweet, Mrs. Mabel, smoke or not," Charlie said.

"Honey, if I were forty years younger, wouldn't a woman anywhere within a hundred mile radius have a chance with you." They both laughed. She walked back to her house.

Charlie thought how Mrs. Mabel was nobody's fool and one of the nicest people he'd ever met in his life and how he wanted to wring Sam's neck for doing whatever it was that he'd done, while at the same time, he missed him so much he couldn't stand it.

He pressed the brass doorbell on Renee's porch. Ashley opened the door and said, "Hi, Charlie. Good to see you. Please, come in. Renee will be so glad to see you."

"Did you hear the explosion a few minutes ago?" he asked, pointing toward the now almost impotent smoke.

"No, we didn't hear anything; we're on the back of the house in Renee's bedroom with the window AC running. I've moved a single bed in there to be with her day and night. I don't want her to be alone, though I think I may eventually drive her crazy. Not today, though. She's slept like a baby. What kind of explosion was it?"

"I don't know, Ashley. It shook my car."

"Hope nobody was hurt. Already enough hurt around here for everybody. Come on back."

As they walked in, Renee was hanging up the telephone, fright on her face that dissolved at the sight of Charlie. She stretched out her arms and said, "I need a hug."

He leaned in and hugged her, pushing her hair back and kissing her forehead, thinking he'd been hugged more in one day than during his entire last year. "You are looking stronger, Renee," he said. "You're getting pink back into your cheeks. How has today gone, getting home, and getting settled in? Lots of pain?"

"Thank you, Charlie. The pain has eased some. The Demerol is a godsend."

"Good." He cleared his throat and settled into the club chair by her bed.

Ashley crawled up on the foot of the bed.

"That was the female officer that helped us the other night calling to tell me that he's still loose," Renee said.

Charlie picked up her hand. "They'll find him, Renee. But I hope that you and Ashley will please keep the doors locked. I'm so glad you are here, Ashley. You girls please don't hesitate to call me. I can be here in a moment's notice."

"I know, Charlie, I can never thank you enough for rescuing me the other night, saving my life. You know, you saved my life."

"Oh, Renee, thank you for calling me. I'm so sorry you've had to go through all of this."

Renee propped herself up on the bed pillows. She continued with the report from the Sheriff's Office: "The officer said that his full name is Silver M. Conway. They've issued an all-points bulletin for him, saying he's armed and dangerous He was living in an apartment about two miles from here, until this week. He vacated it. Cleaned it out."

"Maybe he left the area," Ashley said.

"That would be good, but I want him arrested. I am crazy to have gotten mixed up with him," she said and began to cry. Charlie got up and sat down by her on the bed. He got her a tissue.

"Here, I brought you and Ashley and Janie some candy. Chocolate, caramel, peanuts, cherries, pecans, got all the food groups covered," he said. He handed her the paper sack full of assorted candy bars wrapped in a big red bow.

"Where is Janie?" he asked.

"She's with Mother for a few more weeks. Charlie, please stay with us for supper. We need you to," Renee said. He did not resist. Renee's face relaxed. "Oh good, Charlie. The weight of it all is so much less with you here."

Ashley got up, without their notice, and tiptoed out to the kitchen.

PART FOUR

THE WHEELS OF JUSTICE

33.

Getting out and About

Just before dawn, the day after the explosion, Sheriff Bill Trailor woke and cupped himself around Anna, his sanctuary, intending to listen to her sleep. But the recent crimes invaded his thoughts. He whispered into Anna's ear, "Two men murdered; one of 'em's wife raped; the ex of the other dead man burned in her own house; the accused rapist raised by Seth Maddox. Maddox is all over this."

Anna did not stir.

He patted her on her behind and slipped out into the silence of pre-dawn, made their coffee, and brought her a tray. He set it on her bedside table, touched her slender hand, and smiled. He returned to the kitchen, grabbed his to-go mug, and slipped out through the dark into the white Buick, the top of which sported a too-long antenna that swayed as he drove the back roads among the people he was charged to protect.

In the year and a half he'd been sheriff, he'd viewed many an early-morning thing: women kissing husbands good-bye on front porches or dragging drunk ones in, nagging them; farmers creeping tractors with blinking lights down pavements toward fields; kids waiting in the dark for a six-thirty school bus, wiping runny noses on their sleeves, scuffling, eating a sausage biscuit; dairy cows ambling toward the barn, mooing, udders full. The sheriff waved and smiled as he passed. In no time, he had endeared himself to the people; they began waving and smiling back. Over time, they developed a morning expectation of greeting their very likable new Sheriff Bill.

He turned into a gravel driveway off the paved road that led up to Seth Maddox's center of operations. A passerby might incorrectly have assumed that the sheriff was pulling in to back up and turn around in front of an old abandoned barn building, for no sign of life appeared anywhere around it except some clumps of scrubby grass and a weak grove of pecan trees out back that trailed off anemic toward the west. Though most folks in the county probably knew that Seth Maddox operated his machine shop and farming business in the building, only insiders knew the full truth of the place: the middle of the building held Maddox's living quarters as well as bedrooms that could sleep up to a dozen; across the back, a ten-stall garage housed a moving van, a late model Cadillac, and everything in between.

Sheriff Bill had long suspected that a lot more happened at that location than farming. If so, his predecessor had left it intact, never confronted it. Also, Bill Trailor had known Seth Maddox at a distance for a few years back in grade school. Bill took him, then, as a hard to understand, closed off boy, apt to kick a person when he was down and lie about it, which he once did to Bill. And though Bill couldn't recall the details of what happened, he never forgot Seth's meanness or how it had made him feel.

As he pressed the Buick's brakes and brought it to a stop, he lifted the microphone from its cradle on the dashboard, pressed and held down the button, and said, "Sheriff's a 10-20 at the Seth Maddox place."

The radio dispatcher in the Gargagun Sheriff's Department replied, "That's a 10-4, Sheriff."

"10-4." He stepped out of the Buick with his coffee cup, took a sip, and set it on the top of the car. "Morning is happening," he said to himself, stretching, watching the blue sky of day riding in behind a delicate pink-toned light from the east that flared out in swoops across the sky like a dancer's organza skirt kicked up high, flounced out. The softness of the color reminded him of Anna, in her pajamas, probably right that minute propped up on pillows in their bed drinking her coffee, adding too much heavy cream to it.

He reached in and honked the car horn, and then shouted out toward the seemingly empty old barn, "Seth, I need to talk to you."

A turtledove hunched down in the scrubby grass off under the eave of the building began cooing.

Sheriff Bill walked toward the barn listening for any response from Seth Maddox. There was none. The bird cooed again. Sheriff Bill sipped his coffee. Listened. Eventually, something stirred inside the building.

The front door swung open. Out staggered a disheveled Seth Maddox, buckling his belt and pushing back his uncombed red hair that circled a round, shiny baldness. He had not even zipped his pants.

"Damn, I could get more done with some of that coffee, Bill. Got any extra?"

"No, Seth, but I'd have brought you a cup if I'd known you were sleeping in."

"Bill," Maddox said, searching for his zipper, forcing a smile, his eyes darting around trying to size up the situation, "now you know, a morning nap is good for a man." He finally zipped his pants.

"Farming and sleeping at the same time, are you, Seth?"

The turtledove cooed again. Long. Low. Maddox turned his back on the sheriff, picked up a flat-sided rock, and skimmed it toward the cooing. "Well, not much farming this morning. Stuff broke down. Men off in the holler fixing it. Waiting on 'em to get back."

The sheriff reached for his coffee cup and took another sip.

"What you doing out this way so early this morning, Bill? You needing some machinist work done?"

"No, Seth, I've got a warrant to serve on Silver. For rape."

Maddox's shoulders lowered and then relaxed. He lowered his head and chuckled an arrogant chuckle.

The sheriff took it all in. He could read a man quicker than lightning. "Seems to me, Seth, nothing much funny about rape. Or my gonna arrest a man you raised."

"Rape? Seems to me, Bill, like my Silver could get all he wants without raping anybody," Maddox said. "So I don't guess he did any raping."

"I don't know about that, Seth, this woman's been torn up pretty bad. She's pushing charges. Gonna testify. Plenty of proof. Hair samples. Fingerprints. It's a done deal. Will Silver turn himself in? Or am I gonna have to find him?"

"You know Silver ain't never been too predictable; I spect you'll have to find him," Maddox said and then grinned.

"Just where will I find him, Seth?"

"I've got no idea, Bill. He's always been a vagabond kind. Haven't seen him in a long time." Maddox kicked at the ground.

"Well, if you care about him—and I sure know you do, Seth—you find him and tell him that it'll go a lot easier on him if he shows up. If I have to run him down, and I will—it's just a matter of time—it'll likely be Marchman Prison for the rest of his life. Course, if he turns himself in, I'll ask the prosecutor to work with him on a plea. You know I can't promise anything. That woman is wanting his hide."

Seth Maddox didn't change the look on his face. He ran his hands with dirty black under the fingernails through his uncombed stringy hair around the bald and asked, cocky, despite his fear, or maybe because of it, "Who is the woman, anyway, Bill, that's saying Silver raped her?" He really did not know.

The sheriff tapped his coffee cup with the little finger on his right hand and said, "Well, that's the interesting thing, Seth. She is Samone Sims' widow, Renee."

"The hell you say!" Red anger flashed across Maddox's face. He whirled, stomped back toward the building, stopped, turned again, and said, dropping disgust into his words, "I'll see what I can do. Ain't never been able to do much with that boy. Course, you know that, Bill."

The sheriff opened the door to the Buick and sat down in the driver's seat. He cranked it. He rolled down the window, poured the last few drops of his coffee onto the ground, and looked directly at Maddox. "Gets hotter than the devil's ass this time of year, don't it Seth? Seemed like we were all gonna burn up last night, for sure. It'll eventually get cooler, though." He backed the Buick out onto the paved road and turned toward Gargagun.

As the sheriff meandered down the county road back toward town, thinking about all he'd learned from that short visit, the soft pink of morning crept into Mrs. Mabel's bedroom underneath the long flowered bedroom draperies. She filled the percolator with Maxwell House, plugged it in, and walked to the front door to pick up the paper. She opened it to huge headlines: "Arson Suspected In Gargagun House Fire Death."

"Well, I'll be," she said, sitting down at the kitchen table to read the article. "'Gloria Jenkins lost her life in a fire in her home. Arson is suspected. A team from the Fire Marshall's Office is investigating the . . .' My Lord in heaven! Now, if this doesn't add another pickle to the jar."

She read the article twice to be sure of what she'd read. She dialed the Sheriff's Office to schedule an appointment with Sheriff Bill.

The woman who answered the phone seemed somewhat preoccupied and disinterested. "Mrs. Morris, is this an emergency?" she asked.

"Oh, no, not an emergency, but, I believe, very important."

"Thank you. I will tell the sheriff that you called and that you need to talk with him, and he'll be back with you in a few days. Will that do?"

"Yes, why of course. Thank you," Mabel replied, perplexed. As she cradled the receiver, Sheriff Bill's Buick climbed a tall hill about a mile from Seth Maddox's center of operations. The dispatcher's voice came in through heavy static: "Sheriff . . . got . . . problem . . . that fellow arrested for those murders . . ."

The sheriff pulled over to the side of the road at the top of the hill and stopped. He turned up the volume on the radio. "What kind of problem?"

"He ain't here."

"What da ya mean, 'he ain't here'?"

"That he's gone. Somehow or another he got the leg off his cot, smacked the guard in the head in the middle of the night, and used his keys to escape. We found the guard when we went in to carry breakfast. The ambulance took him to the hospital a few minutes ago. He was talking, but he's for sure concussioned."

"Concussioned?"

"Yeah, you know, his skull was bad banged up."

"Are you telling me that we hired a three hundred pound guard to protect that little fellow Cal Hough and he overpowered the man twice his size and has escaped?"

Amidst radio static, the dispatcher finally came through, weak of signal and heart, "That's a 10-4."

The sheriff pressed the accelerator. "I'll be there ASAP."

"10-4."

*****

As the sheriff received the news of Hough's escape, Seth Maddox went to the bathroom to splash water on his face and replay the sheriff's visit over in his mind. He mumbled into the bathroom mirror, "One time, just one time, I break a rule I've kept all these years to always let somebody else do the heavy work and the very next morning there stands the sheriff at my door testing me with talk of it getting hotter than a devil's ass this time of year. He knew damn well what he was saying." Seth grabbed for a towel and dropped his head. "Plus, he knows Gloria, knows we've always been friends, but he never one time mentioned anything about her house burning. Not the courtesy to tell me. Fishing expedition. Seeing what he could find out was all it was." He dried his face and sat down in one of the rockers. "No. He didn't come out here to find Silver. But, Goddamn it, every which way I turn, I keep running into Silver screwing up. If I had you here right now, son, I'd wring your neck," he said to himself.

Maddox began tying his shoes.

Someone knocked on the back door. Only "intimates" knew there was a back door, and even some of them had a difficult time finding it.

Maddox picked up his revolver and put it in the bib of his overalls. "Who's there?"

A strange voice answered, "Please Mr. Maddox, open up a'fore somebody sees me and I get hauled back over to that there jail."

34.

Oasis

Maddox opened the door. There stood a lost sheep with bleeding hands. "Damn, ain't you the man supposed to be in jail?" Maddox asked.

"Yes sir, I shore am. 'Preciate it mighty much if you'd let me in." Hough's left hand held his right one, torn open along the thumb and index finger, flesh lying back.

"Mister, I can't be hiding no criminal," Maddox said, pulling the revolver on Hough.

"Please Mr. Maddox, don't shoot me. I ain't lookin' at no harmin' nor no hidin', no sir, just want outta this mess," Hough said, stepping back away from the door a couple of feet, like he'd just leave rather than risk more trouble. He dripped blood on the ground. "Mr. Maddox, I sure got no kinda squawk with you, no siree. My boss with a 'frigeration plant down Cairo way—I've wurked now fer him no more 'n two months—he said, 'Cal, take this here side of beef up there to a man at this address,' a farm not fur from here." Hough saw a fresh look on Maddox's face, a recognition of some sort. Maddox pushed the revolver back into his bib. That gave Hough a mighty necessary bit of comfort.

"Yeah," Maddox said, "your boss and I used to hunt together. He's been here on hunting trips. But how did you know who I was or where I was or how to even find the back entrance to this place, Mr. Hough?" He motioned for Hough to come inside.

Hough stepped in the door. Maddox closed it and locked it.

"My boss jest said, stressin' hard, 'While you in Gargagun, any problems of any kind, drive to Seth Maddox's.' He give me how to get here

191

and get to yore back door. Told me to memory it. Said you an important friend of his. I walked all night gittin' here."

Maddox sat down and motioned for Hough to take one of the oak rockers.

Hough cleared his throat and sat down, still holding his right hand in his left. "And, I sure as hell dun got me a problem, Mr. Maddox. I'm innocent. Ain't never caused no harm to narrin. Never have. Done gone and been rested an I'm innocent."

"How'd you get yourself in such a fix?" Maddox asked, but before Hough could answer, Maddox got up, motioned for Hough to stay put, walked over and knocked on a door off the sitting room. "Fellows, I need a little help here getting this man's cut hand cleaned up and bandaged and we could use a little more coffee, ASAP. Ah hell, make us a big breakfast, too," he said.

Hough heard stirring around behind the door. In a few minutes, the aroma of brewing coffee floated into the room.

Maddox sat back down. "I interrupted you. Can't figure how a nice fellow like you could get yourself in such a fix."

Smelling the coffee caused saliva to run around all over the inside of Hough's mouth. When he talked, it sounded slushy. "Like I said, I dropped a side of beef off over yonder at a man where I wuz told to, at a farmhouse on the south side of the Jaylo Road, three miles out from a innersecshun with Townhill Road. My boss drew me a picture. Wuz easy a find—I'm good at findin'; wuz the only house anywheres around."

Someone came in from the kitchen with a coffee pot on a tray and two black mugs and set them down on a table.

Hough wanted some coffee awful bad. "Mind if I have a sup a that there coffee fore I finish, Mr. Maddox?" he asked, like a child.

"Yeah, take anything in yours?" Maddox asked.

"Naw, black as all get out's the way I usually drink 'er, but they ain't been givin' us no coffee at the jail. Water's all we ever got." Hough held his cup in his left hand and slurped his coffee, loudly. He continued his explanation to Maddox. "The fella took the beef were a tall man with red hair, sorta like yoren, but he wuz lots younger'n me or you, not meanin' anything by it, of course."

"What was his name, Mr. Hough?" Maddox asked, waiting very patiently for a response, holding his eyes on Hough.

Hough pointed to his hand and said, "I shore need sumpin' here for this hand, if ya got it, so's I don't leave narry streak on yore floor."

Just as he spoke, a man walked in with bandages and salve and tape.

Hough continued. "I don't know nobody's name, Mr. Maddox, my boss never give me one, said the man'd know the beef wuz coming. And he shore did, no problem a'tall 'til the fella wanted to write out a paper check. My boss had done told me, clear, 'Hough, cash only; don't take no checks from nobody.' So, of course, I held to it."

Maddox shifted in his chair, uneasy. "Don't blame your boss a'tall. What'd you do?"

"Well, the fella with red hair what took the beef solved it. He said he'd go get cash for the paper check."

"And?" Maddox asked.

"He ast me did I fish. I told him I shore did. He said, 'Well, good, I thought so, just from lookin' at ya; I'll get ya a fishing rod. You can take a spin down to Florence Lake just up the way while I go to the bank and get yore cash and come on out and get ya paid.' His stringy red hair kept getting' in hiz face an he laughed and said, 'Hell, we'll go fishing together to celebrate the deal. What you say?'"

Maddox dropped his eyes.

Hough continued, "It sounded good to me. My wife sez I'll die a fishin'. Didn't need no fishin' rod. Keep 'em in the truck all a time. Told the fella that and went on out there, did some fishin', didn't catch nuthin', but the fella never showed. I came on back to my truck to eat a sandwich fore I went to find him, got 'rested over a coat done been planted in my floorboard."

Breakfast came and Maddox began cutting up his eggs over easy. Hough ate fast; he was hungry.

Maddox asked him, "Why in the world didn't you call your boss and get him to get you out of jail, Mr. Hough?"

"Oh, I couldn't. I shore didn't kill nobody and I didn't wanna get him in no trouble down there at work, not my boss, and then, with me missing the cash for the beef and all. I didn't have no kind of job for months 'fore he hired me, and I need a job bad and I ain't worked there all that long, and I figured I'd get out soon as the law knew I weren't no murderer and I'd find the fella an pick up the cash an go on back home, but my lawyer said there'd be no gettin' me out while they got the paperwork handled. Got left down there in that there jail, so I pulled a broke leg off my cot and worked my way out of there."

Maddox's facial expression did not change one bit. He poured himself some more coffee in his mug and refilled Hough's.

Hough said to Maddox, "Mister, I wouldn't murder a wiggle worm. Somebody's done set me up good. Don't know who'd wanna do such, but I sure 'preciate yore helpin' me out, shore do, Mr. Maddox. Just hope my boss'll take this good as you."

"He will. It'll be fine," Maddox said. "Finish your breakfast."

While Hough was in the shower there at the headquarters, dressing for his trip home, Maddox picked up the phone and dialed Silver.

"Hello," Silver said.

"Get your ass over here today, noon, if you want to keep it. And, for God's sake, Silver, don't get caught headed in this direction," Maddox said, and then he dropped the receiver in the cradle.

Hough departed in one of Maddox's cars around midmorning with a driver's license for a Gerald Jones, a couple of thousand dollars, and a map for the back roads to get him out of the area back toward Cairo. But Hough turned north instead. Near Memphis, he gassed up and found a pay phone to call his wife. "Honee, we dun got us a bad sitiation," he said, "a real bad 'un."

Her voice sounded tired and anxious, "What'cha mean, Cal, a sitiation? Been worrieder than anything bout ya. Vorene told me, sed, 'He's jailed up. Bound to be a mistake. They'll let'em out once they seez it.' Course I didn't have no money to get up there and 'fraid to go over the 'frigeration plant and ask for any. Might lose you your job. You ain't hurt nobody, has you, hun?"

Hough looked around from inside the phone booth. No one had followed him. He said, "I'll splain it when ya get here. Pack us some clothes, borrow some money from Vorene, catch yoreself a bus fer Nashville. I'll pick ya up at the station. Wait on me there 'til I 'rive. You and Vorene don't talk to nobody bout nuthin'. Our lives rest on it."

She gasped.

They didn't have much more than what they had on and a few pots and pans. The landlord owned everything else. So, she just carried a paper sack with a few belongings with her in the cab to the bus station. She caught the three o'clock bus to Nashville.

35.

Holding Up

For days after Renee came home from the hospital, all the minutes in all the hours were pain tangled up with memories. She wept a lot. The meds gave her some relief. So did Ashley's help rearranging pillows under her knees and situating her in the new recliner Charlie brought her for the bedroom.

Sleep was her refuge. But even it haunted her, sometimes, with nightmares. One she remembered, vividly. She was in a cold sweat looking down into a hell hole, the scent of Ivory soap mixed with her own vomit that was rising up, but she knew it was a commode, at the bottom of which was an enormous carousel of faces dancing on poles, circling and taunting her, with Silver, smiling and aroused, caressing her hair and neck and using carnival music in the background to seduce her. Suddenly, his face filled with rage and he backed her up against the inside of the commode alongside Samone, who was lying in bed, peacefully snoring, and she knew it was the last night he would be alive, so she struggled to get to him, but she was too late because she was lying beside him, smug-faced, deliberately not waking him, refusing to touch his hand.

*****

After a time, she began to be able to move short distances around the house without hurting by taking tiny steps, first around the bed and back and forth to the bathroom, and then further distances inside the house. There was hope in her movement.

"We are going to have to get you some running shoes, Renee," Charlie said.

"Keep your money in your pocket, Charlie; I won't be running for awhile. I feel all wobbly, like I'm going to fall."

The next day he called: "I've got a present for you, Renee."

"Charlie, you can't keep bringing me presents."

He laughed. "Well, Renee, if an outright gift bothers you, I'll just make you a loan of this one for a few months. Then I'll come take it back, get it off your hands after that, if you don't want to keep it."

"Well, I guess, Charlie," she whined. "I don't even know what it is that you are saying that you will take back."

He did not succumb to her whining. "Oh, I almost forgot, we're throwing you a party tonight to give it to you," he said.

"To give me what?" she grouched.

"Your gift."

"Throwing me a party? Good gracious, Charlie. You know I live in my pajamas." Surely he knows I'm in no shape for a party, she was thinking.

"Okay, the problem is solved. We'll make it a pajama party?" he said, lifting his voice at the end to leave it in her hands. He waited on her response.

"How can I not say yes to you, Charlie? But I'm serious about all the gifts. I will never be able to repay you."

He lowered his voice, an uncharacteristic desperation in it, and said, "Just keep living, Renee, and healing and working with your counselor. That's the repayment I need."

She was ashamed she'd been so grumpy and she felt sorry for herself.

"Tell you what, Renee, lie down and rest. Try to get yourself a good nap this afternoon. We'll party tonight."

He arrived in pajama bottoms and a tee shirt. Mrs. Mabel wore pajamas she'd found in a cedar chest; they smelled like the cedar chest. Ashley wore some of Renee's old pajamas decorated in cartoon characters, with a hole in the collar. Janie wore pink baby doll pajamas.

"Ladies, I need to borrow Janie's services for a short while," Charlie said. "Oh, and a box of tin foil, please, Renee."

"A box of tin foil?" Renee asked.

"Yep!" He acted like that was the most normal thing in the world to request. He hugged her.

Charlie and Janie departed and returned in a few minutes, lugging an enormous box wrapped in newspapers with a lopsided tin foil bow atop. They set the box on the patio. Everyone gathered around it. Janie crawled on top and, at Charlie's signal, flung her arms wide.

"Da-da!" Charlie said, "Open it up, Renee. I can promise you that this gift will never let you down."

Janie helped her rip off the newspaper and open the box, crammed full of crumpled up newspaper sheets. Buried in them was a shiny red walking cane.

Renee was speechless.

"Do you like it?" Charlie asked.

"Wow, Charlie! I never in my life would have thought that I'd be glad to be getting a walking cane, but yes, it's very thoughtful. It's beautiful. Thank you."

"You are welcome, Renee. Janie and I have named your cane."

"Named it?"

"Yes, we have named it Mr. No-Wobbler."

"Show her, Mr. Charlie, show her the 'nitials," Janie interrupted, tugging at Renee's leg, jerking the cane out of her hand, and sticking it up in her face. "See, Mommie, 'nitials. See."

And for sure, there, on the handle, Renee's initials had been engraved; underneath them were Charlie's and Janie's, his in large letters, hers in tiny ones.

Tears welled up in her eyes.

Mrs. Mabel reached for Mr. No-Wobbler. She examined it and then grabbed Charlie's leg with the handle. He jumped. "I want one just like it, Charlie. It's perfect for catching a good-looking man."

Charlie blushed. "I can arrange that, Mrs. Mabel—the cane, not the good-looking man." Everybody laughed.

Ashley oohed and aahed over Mr. No-Wobbler. She caught Renee's eye and said, "I could use this, sis, to tame some folks in the office. Right?"

Renee nodded. She set it on the floor. It was the right height; it felt safe when she leaned on it. "Mr. No-Wobbler fits me, Charlie and Janie. And, as much as I love them, Mrs. Mabel and Ashley will have to get their own canes. Mr. No-Wobbler belongs with me."

Janie beamed. Renee hugged her neck and then Charlie's.

He held onto her. Reluctantly, she pulled back. "Mr. No-Wobbler will make a great prod, Charlie, so you best behave."

He smiled. "Behave is my middle name, Renee." His eyes looked wet. Everybody got all quiet, like they were in church.

Renee broke the silence and said, "Gonna test Mr. No-Wobbler. Walk with it." She grasped the handle and hobbled around.

Ashley cleared her throat and said, "Great idea, Renee. When are we going to eat that homemade chocolate ice cream you made for us, Charlie?"

"Now seems about the perfect time," he said. "Let's get inside out of this heat."

He scooped. Janie served. They all sat around the kitchen table together.

Renee recollected the times with Samone and Janie around that very table and how she had taken Samone for granted. An unexpected sadness stirred inside her. She excused herself and lay down to rest.

Her nerves were, of course, thread thin. In addition to sadness, the panic attacks continued. She worked regularly with the counselor. Even so, trying to spew out her clogged-upness was hard work. Sometimes she could only sit in the room with the counselor, breathing air, unaware of what she really thought or felt, emotionally bland. Empty. Lost. Whatever she did or didn't say or do, the counselor accepted it and didn't push her. Renee finally trusted that she did not have to organize her truths to speak them to the counselor, who could tolerate the naked chaos in her.

But counseling was an exhausting process. Sometimes, after a session, Renee would feel like an old rag that had been scrubbed on a washboard. When she would begin to wonder if continuing counseling was even worth it, her own garbled words would spout out something during a session that would corner her with an unforeseen awareness that, sometimes, she could not even put into words, only know inside herself. It was as if a piece of a puzzle would ride in on an experience or realization or feeling and snap into place. Something in her would shift. A barrier in her would fall. Light would come in. Ashley called them ahas.

Renee told her counselor, "It's strange, but sometimes, far removed from a counseling session, I sometimes experience reinforcement of an aha, during a conversation or while watching a scene in a movie or hearing a song, none of which, alone, would normally have any particular significance for me."

Her counselor said, "Renee, the universe is giving you a pop quiz to make sure you got it."

It was true.

She had a pop quiz one afternoon sitting in a sleeveless tee and shorts in the recliner near the air conditioning vent that helped her begin to understand her vulnerability to Silver that day in the intensive care unit's waiting area. The cold air from the air conditioning vent overwhelmed her. She became unbearably cold and began shivering. Irrationally, she panicked and had that old compulsion to save herself. As she scrambled to pull up the bed coverlet, the sun appeared from behind a cloud, hot through the window. She remembered that it was August and the outside temps were actually ninety degrees. And she remembered that day in the intensive care unit's waiting area and her compulsion to run out of a hospital to save herself from dying. And how Silver had sauntered in and saved her from freezing to death in the summertime.

"Oh my God, how I have missed the mark," she said. "With Silver. With Samone."

36.

DISGUISES

Silver parked an old white van out back of Seth Maddox's headquarters, knocked on the back door, and yelled, "It's me, Pop."

Maddox opened the door on a mustached man with brown hair, in coveralls and work boots. Big-rimmed, tinted glasses covered most of his dirt-smudged face. He had dirt under his fingernails.

"Is that you, Silver?"

"Hell yeah." Silver put his hands behind his head. Strutted. "How you like my new disguise?"

Although he'd always been a master at hiding underneath whatever persona he needed, he'd decided personae alone would no longer suffice. He needed a disguise to remain in and around Gargagun, to make his last hit. Then, maybe he'd go to Mexico or some other exotic place: he finally had the money to get out of this godforsaken redneck scrap of earth.

"I almost didn't recognize you, Silver; what's that thing you are driving?" Seth asked, pointing to a white van with the words "Odd Jobs, Cheap!" painted in red on its sides, and underneath those words, a phone number that did not exist.

"It's my work van. Did that myself. Shoot, I look like any other bricklayer or carpenter or plumber with dirty fingernails and a dirty face. I'm even using bad grammar and picking my nose," he said.

Seth Maddox shook his head. "If it's not one thing with you, Silver, it's another. Get in here and close the door. I've thought of putting a hit out on you, going around raping folks you got no business even talking to. You knew better'n that. Got the law out here looking at us," Seth said.

"Now, Pop, you don't believe everything you hear," Silver replied. "Anyway, I ain't afraid of no law; it can't find its ass with both hands. It's sat around all these years, letting us move free, ain't never done a thing, ain't gonna do a thing now." He laughed.

"This is no laughing matter and don't you ever underestimate that new sheriff, Silver. He's not the old law we had. And he is nobody's fool. Says the evidence is there on the rape. If they catch you, you're done for. Neither he nor that DA down there will cut you an inch of slack. I know 'em both, from way back."

Silver swaggered. "You know good and damn well that nobody's gonna catch me disguised like this. Ain't gonna know me. You didn't even know me. I'm not catchable. Plus, if they did, ain't nobody to do diddly squat to me. That woman that says I raped her wanted me real bad. Plus she's a coward. She wouldn't hold up. She'd run like a scared rabbit."

Maddox shook his head, again. "Goddamn it, Silver, scared rabbits can be mighty dangerous. Like that Hough fellow. Now if that wasn't a howdy do. Did'ya lose your mind? Why in God's name did you not leave that side of beef down there? You didn't say one word to me about planting a crop this time of year. What you doing? Running your own damn show?"

Silver's face reddened. His nose twitched.

Maddox turned and walked toward the living quarters. Slumping, Silver followed him and said, "Hough was the only thing that didn't work perfectly. Yeah, I got the cart before the horse, Pop, I know it now, but I got wind it was time to plant."

Seth went to the coffee pot and poured two cups of coffee; he handed one to Silver. Both men sat down in the rockers and rocked for a time. Neither said anything. The air was too full to talk. And Maddox didn't know what else to say. Silver wasn't listening.

The heavy silence, though, eventually pressed in on Silver. He began rationalizing, trying to persuade Maddox, and said, "Anyway we look at it, the Hough thing turned out for the best. He's escaped. Won't be a trial. It's good. It's all good."

"You've gone slap ass blind, Silver. Besides your early and ill-conceived planting unnecessarily opening up that thing from a year ago, you raped the man's widow, painting an arrow directly toward this family. And, you've managed to turn Max Tribling in Cairo into a mad son of a gun."

"Why is that? I got rid of Hough for him. He was about to fire him, anyway, from what he told me. Sorta figured into the planting time, just to tell you the truth. I figured it a win-win. Course I never said it out-right to Tribling, what all was gonna happen, but he was getting antsy over our account. Wanted it closed out. I tried to take care of everything. Guess I oughta have come and talked to you."

"Goddamn it son, leaving all of that aside, which I can't, 'cause it is a damn sure mess up, you could have paid Hough for the beef and left Hough holding Tribling's due, regardless of any planting of anything, anywhere, leaving this operation clean, but no, you thought you were tricking Hough and would hold onto a measly two grand. Sometimes I wonder how we are blood and kin."

Silver never felt very much, ever, but hearing that prickled the hairs on his back.

"Anyway," Maddox continued, "after he escaped, he came here—Tribling's instruction to him if he had any trouble—and I gave Hough Tribling's money, told him to take it to Tribling, trying to cover your stupidity and keep us clean with the best backup a person could find for all we do. Anyway, Tribling called me and said Hough'd taken off to kingdom come with the money. Slipped away like an eel."

Silver hee-hawed like he'd heard a joke and said, "Well, guess it's good then that I didn't pay Hough out of my folding green. If you paid him, whether Tribling got it or not, let's just agree you paid him out of the Bridges' part, just upped what you paid me." Silver slapped his leg like he was delighted. "Wasn't enough money you coulda paid, anyway, for getting rid of that son of a bitch."

"You have gone almighty mad, Silver," Seth said. He slurped his coffee, set the cup down hard, and stood up. "You're not hearing me. The money is not the issue. Tribling is. He's valuable to us, has been for years. Screwing that up could send us to the slammer for a very long time. The man could write a book about us."

"Aww, Pop, he'll get over it once he gets his money," Silver said. "You want me to take it to him? I'll pay him myself."

"Hell no! I want you here, night and day, and out of sight until I can figure out how we handle this whole thing that's turned into a wild octopus. The sheriff's been out here looking for you, Silver. Things are hot." Maddox began pacing the floor.

Silver had never seen him that upset. "I hear you," Silver said. But he was actually thinking how it was just about as perfect as it could get, under the circumstances. For the short term, until he cleaned the slate, Seth's headquarters was the place the sheriff would not come again. He'd already been there.

Maddox stopped pacing and walked over to Silver. "Son, I know you grew into a way of living here. I take it on me for that. And you are welcome to live here with me from now on, but your going out and making decisions without running them by me has to stop. Your arrogance has to stop. You are going to get us both killed!"

"It's gonna be fine, fine. Quit worrying. There is nothing to tie anything to anything."

Maddox said, "Well, looks to me like Gloria is a pretty big tie now, with the fire and all and her up and dead . . . Somebody killed her and not in a fire . . . You know, Silver, I know about fires—sure do know about fires, how they protect and destroy . . . Miss that woman—was my second skin, a sister. Anybody killing her was a horse of a different color. Was no approval coulda come nor woulda come ever from here."

Silver looked him straight in the eyes, cold, emotionless.

Maddox held his own eyes on Silver. "And somebody killed that woman," Maddox said. "Thing is, you know as well as I do that she wouldn't a said a word to harm me or you."

"Well, she ain't gonna say a word now, for sure," Silver replied and walked out of the room.

Maddox listened to the back door slam and the van crank. It skidded out of the yard and revved up as it hit the pavement. "If his mama were alive," Maddox said to the walls, "this would kill her."

37.

THE NEWS

Things appeared to be slowly returning to normal. Ashley resumed work full time and spent only evenings with us, serving up food that Charlie brought in, regularly, from various restaurants.

Mr. No-Wobbler and I became fast friends. I went nowhere without him. One day after the pajama party, we walked into the living room and stood before the picture window, the curtains wide open on a scene even the old masters couldn't imagine. Grass the color of Grandmother Tracy's just-blanched green beans grounded a clear blue sky. Tree branches laughed and waved at me. I was alive.

The central AC kicked on. A whiff of pear preserves floated across the room, reminding me of the red envelope I'd placed in the little cubbyhole in the desk over by the door, after I returned from the hospital. I picked up the envelope and pulled out the pink notecard. Memories of that night slapped me, Silver's smell, a musty version of the pear preserves scent. And his words to me, "I want to pay your husband back for what he did."

Samone would never have had a friend like Silver. Never. So why was Silver so enraged over Samone? It made no sense. Anyway, I did not want to think about that, not then or there in front of the picture window. So I laid the envelop back into the desk cubbyhole, realizing that it was only two weeks until Labor Day.

I coaxed myself to do what was right, to honor the woman who had sent the note. "It probably won't be anything, Renee, a widow's kind words to another widow, or a thank you note because Samone helped her with something at The Shoppe, but, as a courtesy to you, Gloria— may you RIP—since you lost that Bridges man that you once loved,

I will go to the bank as soon as it opens the day after Labor Day and, at least, accept your gift that is in the box," I said out loud to myself.

I picked the envelope up again and removed the note and unfolded it. The words "If I don't reach you by Labor Day" struck me. Why did she say it that way? We just lived a mile or so apart, from the paper's report of the fire. Reach me? Why didn't she just say, "If I don't see you by Labor Day"? Why did she need a bank box, anyway? Why didn't she just put whatever she needed me to have in this note? The more I tried to figure it out, the less sense it made to me, but, from the note, she seemed like a very nice woman. I'll get the signature card back to the bank, I promised myself silently.

I heard a rap at the door. I jumped. I stepped back, away from the bare window, my heart beating in my throat. I tiptoed to the dining room and pulled back the heavy curtains to view the edge of the front porch, without being seen. There, at my front door, stood Sheriff Bill Trailor and a female deputy—not the one I spoke with the night of the rape, a different woman, older, wrinkles on her face and hands. My whole body sighed with relief. I opened the door. "Hello, Sheriff Bill," I said, "and ma'am. Please, come inside."

The sheriff removed his hat and stepped in. The female deputy followed him.

"Good to see you, Renee," he said. "Hope you are feeling better. Anna wanted me to bring you these brownies for Janie." He handed me a paper bag.

"Thank you so much. I've eaten Anna's cooking; you are a lucky man."

"That I am, Renee," he said.

"I promise I will save Janie at least one."

"You do that now, but if you don't, just let me know; Anna will be delighted to make more brownies."

I laid the bag on the coffee table. "I look frightful," I said, realizing I was in the old short-sleeved flowered housecoat with the edge of the left pocket torn loose, my face pale with no makeup, my hair dry and brittle, overdue for a haircut, coming out in handfuls: the doctor said it was the stress.

"You look fine. We should have called," the sheriff said, "but we wanted to catch you while we were on this side of town."

"Please, please sit down," I said, anxious to hear the good news that I was convinced they were bringing me, that they'd caught him.

They both sat on the sofa, I in an armchair. Unconsciously, I began pulling my hair back away from my face and wiping my eyes. They were wet. I had not realized it.

Sheriff Bill repositioned himself out on the edge of the sofa and began fiddling with his hat, as if in the fiddling he'd find the words he needed to say. Finally, after an eternity, he spoke, obviously delaying what he had to say with an introduction, "Renee, I don't know if you know Deputy James."

"No, I don't. Glad to meet you," I said.

She stood and reached over to shake my hand with a firm handshake. She was straight backed, her face open with light. Everything about her announced strength.

Get on with it, I thought. Tell me Silver is in jail.

She said, apologetically, "Renee, I usually work rapes, but I was off duty the night you came in. I wish I'd been there for you. I am so sorry that you have had to go through this whole ordeal."

"Thank you," I said.

"How are you feeling?" she asked.

"I'm better, much better. Still have a ways to go," I said, "but I'm getting around pretty well—with my red cane." I held it up and told them the story of my getting it and its being named Mr. No-Wobbler.

"I like that name, Renee," the deputy said. "Charlie sounds like a real friend."

"He is," I said, realizing I was sitting there thinking that very thing. "He wants me to start getting out some. Moving back into living. So Ashley is taking me on my first outing soon, a picnic."

"Will do you good, Renee. You girls be careful, though," the sheriff said.

"You mean you aren't here to tell me that you have caught him, Sheriff Bill?"

He sat steady, compassion in his face, like a parent comforting a frightened child. "Renee, nothing would please me more than to tell you that we have arrested him, but I can't. It'll happen, though. I'm sure of it. We have some strong leads. But my every instinct tells me that he has not completely left the area, so I want you to be particularly careful, keep your doors locked, don't take any chances, and call us if you need us."

"Okay," I said, disappointed. I wanted them both to leave, to go right then and find him, to quit sitting there with me delivering me brownies.

But the sheriff made no movement. He sat back into the sofa, settled in, set his hat on his right knee. He dropped his head for a minute. Then he lifted it and sat his hat on the sofa between him and the deputy. "I need to ask you some questions, Renee. I know we asked some the night you came in, but I need, now, to ask you some more things that might help us."

"Okay," I said. I could feel my heart beating. It had now moved up into my temples.

"Renee, how long had you known Silver, when he raped you?" the sheriff asked gently, his question nonthreatening.

"I don't know for sure, Sheriff. I met him at the hospital in the ICU while Grandmother Tracy was there. So, months, a few months."

"I believe you told the deputy that night that you had been intimate with him on other occasions before the rape, Renee. Is that right?"

His words hammered across my breastbone. I gulped. What did that mean? Did it mean what he did wasn't rape?

"Yes, I had, Sheriff Bill. I am ashamed of it, but I had, but like I tried to explain, from the beginning it was strange. Everything about it was strange—"

He interrupted me, as if he didn't want me to go down that path: "I'm not implying anything about the rape, Renee; regardless of how intimate you had ever been with him, if it is as you have told us, he raped you. I just need to know as full of a story as I can, to help us. That's all."

"Okay," I said.

"All right, I'm just feeling my way along here, trying to gather information, Renee. So please bear with me. Okay?"

"Sure, anything, Sheriff Bill, whatever it takes to get him," I said, knowing by the way the sheriff looked at me that he was on my side. I relaxed. I felt ready for whatever he wanted to ask me about Silver.

But he dropped the topic of Silver. "I need to ask you something that, from everything I'm coming across, I hate to ask you, Renee. But did you ever know a Gloria Jenkins? She used to go by Gloria Bridges when she was married to that man Josh Bridges, whose body those kids recently found out there at Florence Lake." He looked at me with empathy and kindness. And from the empathy and the kindness being tied up the way they were in how he asked the question, the edge of a knowing fell in on top of me. Not the full of it. No. Not at that moment. But enough to shake me into a realization that jerked me up inside to glimpse, unexpectedly, the possibility of a reality that I had never known to know existed, before.

I didn't speak. With the help of Mr. No-Wobbler, I rose and walked to the desk, reached into the cubbyhole, and pulled out Gloria's note. The aroma of it drifted around in the room again, and I got sick inside my heart. My hands were shaking. But the envelope gripped my hand. "Why did you ask me if I knew Gloria Jenkins, Sheriff Bill?"

He took stock of what I had done—reaching for the envelope—and said, like an adult might warn a child to be cautious crossing a street, "Renee, it's come direct to us that Samone and Gloria were very good friends."

My knees went weak, the red cane in one hand, the envelope in the other, and I said, "What do you mean 'very good friends'? How could Samone have a 'very good friend' that I didn't know?"

He left me to sit with the question. The deputy's face held compassion. I knew that my question had answered itself. The rest of the knowing tumbled in on top of me and swept me downstream.

The sheriff saw from the look on my face and how I had to sit down so suddenly to keep from falling that I had not known and did not know until then.

I stretched out my shaking hand to give him the envelope. He rose and walked over to me and took it. He stood silently, being with me in the taking of the envelope, like I was a valuable human being. I heard what he was saying to me without words.

He read Gloria's note. His face did not change. He passed the note to the deputy and waited for her to read it before he continued.

"Had you never met her, Renee?" he asked.

"No, and I did not know her or know anything about her. I got the note out of the mailbox the evening before I was raped. It didn't have a postmark. It had to have been dropped into my mailbox, Sheriff Bill, that day."

The deputy put the note back into the envelope and handed it to me. I did not want to touch it. But I found the strength to, and to get back up, and with the help of Mr. No-Wobbler, I walked over to the desk and put it back into the cubbyhole. They were very still and silent, the way people are who stand in front of a casket to view a dead body. I sat back down.

Gloria Jenkins had invaded my life while I didn't know it. I did not want her to have wanted anything from The Shoppe except the pretty things Samone kept on the shelves. But she had. And I had denied Samone the pretty things. Hadn't I? I had been a stupid fool.

Stray tears fell out onto my housecoat. I tried to hold back crying, though, to be strong. But suddenly, irrationally, I became angry at the sheriff for asking me about this woman when I had been raped by a man who was still running loose, a man whom the sheriff believed was still around Gargagun.

I raised my voice: "What in the world does any of that have to do with that maniac who raped me being at large, Sheriff Bill? What? What? What?"

I broke down. The deputy came to my side and kneeled at my chair and sat there with me. The sheriff didn't say anything. He let the deputy be with me. After I blew my nose and wiped my face, I lowered my voice and asked, again, "Sheriff Bill, tell me, what does this have to do with my rape?"

He said, "Renee, I don't know for sure, but it could be that this note and whatever is in that box might help us understand better how to connect the dots."

"What do you mean 'connect the dots,' Sheriff?" I stood up.

"I am not sure, Renee. Right now, we are looking at what appears to be three murders in the span of a year. All three people that were murdered knew each other, appear to have had relationships of some kind."

For the first time, I lifted my eyes higher than my living room and my rape and I heard, in a totally new way, Silver's words that night as he entered this room: that he'd come to pay my husband back for what he had done. I had not remembered to speak about that to the deputy the night of the rape, so I told the sheriff what he had said.

"Thank you, Renee," he said. "Interesting that he knew Samone. Wonder how he knew him." His words echoed around the room. There, that was the real question. I scratched Mr. No-Wobbler on the floor.

"In time, we'll get to the bottom of all of this, Renee," he said.

"Okay," I said. I am not sure I believed, though, that there was a bottom.

He continued, "As far as the safety deposit box, Renee, we could likely get a judge to issue an order to let us in this box immediately. The report from the fire marshall points to arson in Gloria Jenkins' death, and she dropped this off with you the day she died, and she knew Samone and was married to Josh Bridges—"

"Okay," I interrupted him.

"But," he continued, ignoring my interruption, "we could wait until the day after Labor Day and you go to the bank to follow Gloria Jenkins' request."

"I can't think straight, Sheriff Bill. Your coming here today has opened up a side of things I didn't know before."

I was thinking that all the while life is happening, a person thinks she's in it and she isn't; and all the while she's not in it, it is sucking her in and she's clueless.

He looked at the deputy and handed it off to her.

"Renee, it's your decision, of course," she said, "but if we go to court to get an order to open the box, it'll make the newspapers and you'll be in the spotlight. Who knows what that might do to Silver! It could possibly put you in greater danger, since he is still at large."

"It couldn't make him any meaner." I said, but I was afraid now, more than ever, entangled in a web I did not weave, which I'd believed, up until that very moment, had begun when I dropped the Cosmopolitan.

I had always thought that maybe, just maybe, if I had not done that, if I'd kept the magazine above my waist, none of this would have ever happened, the web, my being in it, my gifting Silver with the thread for the weaving. But those people sitting there in my living room that day had just given me information that Samone was having an affair with Gloria Jenkins; Silver knew Samone. The reality seemed to be that Silver found me. I did not begin the weaving of a web. I was an insignificant, curious fly who crawled upon the existing web, the willing feast, to be eaten alive.

The sheriff's voice brought me back into the room with them. He said, "If we wait, nothing is likely to occur in the next two weeks to negatively alter our investigation, and we can assign a plain clothes officer to go with you to the bank after Labor Day without any hullabaloo in the court or the newspapers."

I was trembling. Words like "court" and "plain clothes officer" and "in the spotlight" were for glitzy people in murder mysteries, not for me, a battered woman who'd turned into a hermit trying to heal. The fear in me said, "Let's wait the two weeks."

After they left, I called Charlie. "The sheriff and one of his deputies have been here, Charlie."

"Have they arrested him?"

"No."

"Are you okay?"

"No," I said, hardness in my voice.

I could hear him thinking. Like an air traffic controller directing a pilot, he said, "Sit still. I'll be right there."

I hurriedly dressed and combed my hair.

Charlie had a key to all the doors.

I heard him let himself inside. He called out as he opened the door, "I'm here, Renee; what's going on?" A fear was in his face that I had never seen before. "Are you okay?" he asked.

"I don't know," I said. I told him about the sheriff's visit and, in the telling, asked him, "Charlie, did you know anything about Samone's having some kind of relationship with Gloria Jenkins?"

He said, simply, "Yes."

'Oh my God, Charlie. You knew. If you slapped me, it wouldn't hurt me anymore. You have betrayed me, too?" I flung around, threw down Mr. No-Wobbler, and said, "Keep this thing, you conniving son of a bitch."

I hobbled to my bedroom, slammed the door, and locked it.

Charlie did not know what to do. He went to the kitchen and poured an iced tea and brought it on a tray to my bedroom door. Knocked. I made not a sound. Charlie propped Mr. No-Wobbler up against the wall by my door. He knocked, again. I did not speak. He pressed his ear against my door. I was silent. Lost again in that freezing in the heat of August, but I knew then that there was no coverlet anywhere for it.

And, even if there were, and Charlie were it, he, too, was in my mind like the rest of them. I could not trust him.

Charlie set the tray on a table in the hallway, wrote me a note, and laid it on the tray: "When you are ready to talk, Renee, I will explain to you what I knew and why I did not tell you. I am here. I am not going to leave you no matter how angry you are with anybody, particularly me. And, you have a right to be angry with me."

Charlie lay down on the sofa in the living room and he, the strong man that he'd become, began to weep. Eventually he fell asleep, recalling that last afternoon with Samone. And the potato chip bag. He felt like that potato chip bag.

38.

FIXING TO FIND OUT

Silver slept at the headquarters. Otherwise he roamed, rarely encountering Seth Maddox one on one.

"My words fell on deaf ears with Silver," Maddox said to himself, recollecting their talk and the great big kink Silver'd thrown into his relationship with Max Tribling. Everything everywhere was falling apart, with nobody left to listen to him. Gloria, his sounding board, was gone. Dead. "Gotta mend me some fences. I underestimated that Hough fella. Thought he was innocent a' everything except working for pittance at Max's refrigeration plant. Guess I'm gettin' mighty rusty in my old age," he said, continuing to talk to himself.

Maddox took a sip of coffee and dialed up Max Tribling. "Wanna get this right between us, Max. You wouldn't listen the other day when you called. Don't blame you. But hear me out now. You owe that to me, all we've been through together."

"Well, say what you gotta say."

"You think I'm stupid enough, Max, and dumb enough, to want to peeve you over something like this? You're too smart to even get close to believing that."

Tribling sighed and said, "I'm not very smart, Seth, to get taken on a business transaction, on over-storage, at that. What if the next 'un is ten times as much? Be like throwing good money away for nothing."

"Max, you know better'n that. We've gotta fix it. Can I come down that way tomorrow and settle up and take you to lunch out there at that catfish place? I'm as hungry for catfish as a baby for a bottle. And I'm hungrier than that to get you satisfied."

"I think the folding green would help my indigestion, Seth. Considerably. After we get that taken care of, I could probably be talked into eating a bite of them catfish, if they're fried up whole with the tail and fins still on 'em."

"That's it, then," Maddox said, relief in his voice. "I'll leave here in the morning."

About nine the next morning, he drove south to Cairo.

*****

The same day that Seth Maddox called Tribling, Cavenaugh Jones sat on his patio sipping a gin and tonic over ice, reasoning out loud about his nowhere-to-be-found client. The whole thing puzzled him. "Hough couldn't have escaped jail and vanished without some kind of help. But he didn't have a soul to call to help get him out of jail. He's innocent as I am. He was framed. He didn't drag a body to Florence Lake and then be stupid enough to sit out there with the dead man's coat in his truck."

Jones' mind shifted to Gloria, who had turned up dead the very night he'd tried to call her to set up a time to see her and bend her ear about her ex, Josh Bridges, to try to explore any relationship Bridges might have had with Hough. Gloria was not a friend, just an old classmate; they ran in different circles in high school, but when he was around her then, she always seemed to be a shy and tenderhearted, streetwise young woman. After high school, she found a job in a factory on the outskirts of town, where she had remained. Over time she had been promoted up the line to eventually become the manager's respected assistant. She was impeccably dressed. Refined. Too refined, for sure, to have married the hoodlum that they found dead out at Florence Lake. So, under the influence of the gin and tonic and the nagging incongruities scattered all over the Hough case, Jones decided he should travel to Cairo to snoop around, despite the absence of his client.

At about ten o'clock the next morning, Jones' old station wagon crept out around the corner toward the main highway south.

*****

216

The same morning that Maddox and Jones departed for Cairo, Ashley picked up Renee for her first outing since the rape: a picnic. Renee and Mr. No-Wobbler settled in the front seat, bringing with them the palpable weight of depression. Ashley had come to accept the heaviness in her sister. She just smiled and said, "So glad we are doing this, Renee. Charlie is right: you've been cooped up in that house too long. It's time for you to get back into living."

"I don't want to talk about Charlie. I don't believe a word he says," Renee replied, puffing out her lips that began to tremble.

Ashley stepped on the brakes and stopped dead still in Renee's driveway. "What in the world are you talking about? Charlie's a good friend to you and Janie. And to me."

"Don't be too sure. He deceived me."

"Deceived you? What do you mean, 'deceived you,' Renee?"

"He kept the truth from me," Renee said, burying her face in her hands.

Ashley turned toward her and touched her shoulder. "What kind of truth, sis, did he keep from you?"

"He misled me, Ashley."

"Misled you, sis? How?"

Renee blurted it out: "He knew that Samone was having an affair with Gloria Jenkins and he kept it from me. Charlie hid it from me."

Ashley took a deep breath. "Samone? Had an affair?"

"Yes."

"No, Renee!" Ashley sat there, her mouth open. "Samone adored you and Janie!"

"I don't know who Samone adored. I don't even know who Samone was," Renee said.

Ashley fiddled with her bracelet, trying to think through what she'd just heard.

"And Charlie knew all along. Never told me." Renee blew her nose.

Ashley turned off the ignition key, but kept her hand on it like somewhere in it was some kind of answer. She was thinking that no one had ever taught her what to do in that kind of situation. She said, "Renee, the Samone I knew didn't have affairs. Maybe you misunderstood Charlie. Have you talked with him, gotten any details?"

Renee did not answer. She sat there in the front seat of Ashley's car lost in the summer heat.

Finally, Ashley started the car again, turned the AC on high, and pulled out of the drive. The car's moving appeared to ignite a compulsion in Renee to answer her sister as rapidly as possible: "No, I don't need to talk with him about it. The sheriff broke the news to me. Said it right out that Samone and that woman were good friends, slanting the good friends. No other way he could have meant it. And afterwards, I asked Charlie if he had known. He didn't even take a breath. Said flat out, 'Yes.'"

Ashley let Renee's words sit and take hold. She said, "Renee, I know this is rough on you. Darn, it has to hurt. I am so very sorry. But, sis, Charlie didn't have an affair on you. He didn't force Samone to have an affair, if he had one. You need to talk with Charlie. You don't need any more problems right now, certainly not with him. Talk with him. Find out what he knew."

"That is impossible. I am never going to speak to him again. I will never trust him, ever again," Renee said.

As Ashley listened to Renee's angry outburst about Samone and Charlie, she stopped at the stop sign at the subdivision exit and entered the highway. A white van pulled out from a pine thicket onto the road behind them. It kept pace a safe distance back from them. Eventually, Ashley turned onto the Natchez Trace. She entered a picnic area with benches in a shade of trees overlooking a wide expanse of flat grass pasture. The van pulled off the road about a hundred yards back, out of sight. The guard at the entrance to the picnic area waved at the women.

Ashley waved back and said to Renee, "His mother works in our office; I knew we'd be safe here today. Let's get out and leave all this Charlie stuff in the car for a while; I picked up some deviled eggs and ham sandwiches from the Delish Deli."

"The Delish Deli? Where Charlie has been buying so much of our food since I've been home?"

"Yes."

"Well, then, I'm not hungry," Renee said.

"We are not spoiling this picnic, Renee. Shut it down until after we eat."

*****

Jones easily located the refrigeration plant: it covered several acres on the west side of town, but he realized that his gas tank was sitting on empty, so he pulled in to gas up at a service station nearby, handing the smiling female behind the counter a ten dollar bill. He said, "Looks like that's some kind of huge refrigeration company down the road. Been thinking about getting some help with killing a hog this year."

"Well, it's the right place," she said. "They ran a news article last year saying it was the biggest of its kind in the south. Got its own catch pen and slaughter house on one side and a whole ice plant on the other side: ship ice all over the United States from here."

"Is that right? Well, do you suppose they'd do business with a man with just one hog to kill?" Jones asked, waiting on his change.

"Oh, yeah, my uncle's got a little farm outside of town and he's been using 'em for years. They handle little or big, farmers in pickups or transfer trucks, whatever."

"Sure do thank you. Who'd I see down there at that place to set up something for this fall, do you know?" Jones asked the woman, who seemed to be enjoying advertising the plant.

"Oh, you just walk in the office down there and somebody'll tell you what you need to know. Course it's Mr. Max's place. He's rich from it. Lives in a mansion outside of town with its own servants' quarters, swimming pool, and tennis court, they say. His wife's into society."

"Well, I declare, into society?"

"Oh, he's not. Mr. Max's not into society. He's a regular guy."

Jones was amazed at how much a person could learn from a service station employee.

"It's his wife. She stays gone most of the time, off in a foreign country. But Mr. Max, nah, I don't guess he ever leaves town. He stays here and counts that money. Loves that money. Course, she spends a lot, I'd guess. He don't seem to care. He's a magnet for money." She laughed.

Jones laughed with her. "Sure wish I had that problem. Sure do thank you."

The attendant nodded, "Me, too, mister, me too. You are welcome. You come back, now."

Jones drove to the plant. The wide expanse of glass at the front entrance and the sparse landscaping around the building seemed cold. "Guess it should be cold," he said to himself. "It's a refrigeration plant."

A woman behind another glass enclosure inside smiled and listened to his questions about his getting a hog killed in the fall, handing him a glossy brochure with a price list and operating hours. "We can take care of your needs, sir. Will be glad to," she said.

"I appreciate that. I will definitely get back with you," Jones said and turned to leave. There, in clear view, Jones watched Seth Maddox exit a door about twenty-five yards off to the right. He was with a short, fat man whose stomach leaned out over his belt. The two men stepped into a side parking area, Maddox listening intently to the short, fat man who seemed to be doing all the talking. And frowning.

Jones turned back toward the receptionist in hopes of avoiding possible recognition by Maddox.

"What does Mr. Tribling look like, ma'am?" he asked.

"Like Santa Claus, without a beard or a red suit."

Then she, too, saw Tribling outside with Maddox. She pointed toward him. "There, that's Mr. Tribling, sir. Of course, you'd need to make an appointment to see him. But it couldn't be today. That's one of his very good friends who has come to take him to lunch. When those two get together, I never schedule him any other appointments for the rest of the day."

"Of course," Jones replied. "I'll come back—just stopping by on my way to a meeting. Sure do thank you." He remained inside studying the brochure he'd received, watching Maddox and Tribling walk step in step to the same vehicle. They got inside together. Maddox drove; they exited the parking lot, the short, fat man still talking, Maddox listening. Jones waited until their car topped the hill. He walked to his, started it, and headed north back to Gargagun.

*****

The ham sandwiches were delicious. They sat at the picnic table under a shade tree and drank lemonade and ate, mostly in silence. No talk of Samone or Charlie. As they gathered their leftovers and cleared the picnic table, the white van pulled into a parking space within view.

The driver appeared to be some kind of carpenter or plumber taking a lunch break, drinking a Coke. They paid him no mind, waved good-bye to the guard, and passed the van to return to Ashley's car. She drove them to Gargagun. The white van peeled off from behind them just outside the entrance to the subdivision.

At Renee's, the women hugged. Renee thanked Ashley for the picnic, but she didn't invite her inside. She took a valium and slept.

Ashley drove back to the office and called Charlie. He seemed relieved to hear her voice. "Renee's very upset, Charlie," she said.

"I know," Charlie said, calm resignation in his words. "She needs time, Ashley. It threw me, too, when Sam told me about it just before he died. Which made suicide so hard for me to take."

"He told you? So it's true, then: Samone was having an affair." Ashley's voice dropped at the end of her words, sadness replacing a question mark.

"Well, I'm still trying to figure it out, been trying to for a year now, Ashley. He said that he knew the woman, that she'd lit some kind of light in him."

"Some kind of light?"

"Yes. I did not tell Renee because I really did not know exactly what to tell her, and I did not want her hurt anymore."

"Thank you, Charlie," Ashley said, exhaling relief. "I hope Renee's anger won't drive you away. She's sure suffering right now."

"I am her friend, Ashley. I am not going anywhere."

*****

"Let me get this straight," the sheriff said, slurping his coffee. "You drove all the way to Cairo today to snoop around?"

"Didn't have anything better to do, Bill. I can't keep clients; they escape," Jones said.

"You have any idea how or where he escaped?" the sheriff asked. He pushed back his chair and stood, stretching, lifting his long arms high into the air, sighing.

Jones stood up, also, and said, "No, none, but I need to impose on you if you don't mind."

"How's that?"

"I need to talk with you, Bill. Can we take a walk?" Jones asked.

"Let me get my hat," the sheriff said. He set the Stetson on his head and told the dispatcher, "We are gonna go solve the world's problems. Be back after awhile. Contact me if you need me."

"I've got things covered here, Mr. Bill." she said, shooing them off with the push of her right hand—ancient, wrinkled, and strong, with nails painted bright red, the polish chipped.

The men stepped out onto the street. "I've walked about all I can walk this morning. Sittin'll help my brain. Mind if we ride in my car a ways and pick us a cool spot somewhere up under some trees? Would do me good, and we'd have privacy."

"Sounds like a plan to me, Bill," Jones said. "I just appreciate your time."

They settled in on a big flat rock in an oak grove alongside a frisky stream a few miles out from Gargagun. Jones cleared the rock of any critters. The sheriff stretched out on his back and propped his hat on his stomach. Jones sat facing the water, the gurgling sound methodical, relaxing.

"Good resting music, this stream, you know," the sheriff said.

"It is for sure. Don't you go to sleep on me now, Bill. I may have some real music for your ears," Jones said.

"I'm waiting."

Jones related what he'd seen and heard in Cairo, and, being a stickler for integrity, he was careful not to discuss his client, per se, or anything the client had ever told him.

Sheriff Bill listened without interrupting him. When Jones completed the story, the sheriff said, "Well, if that doesn't tie up some lose threads and create some new ones, in light of the two murders and the time difference between them and the forensics report."

"It was the forensics report triggered my trip, Bill."

"Yeah, and we've had a rape and an arson added to the mix, since the murders."

"Who was raped?"

"Samone's widow. She says Silver M. Conway did it."

"Samone's widow? You mean Samone Sims, the man you had just arrested my client Cal Hough for killing back a year ago?"

"Yeah."

"Samone's widow?" Jones said again. He shook his head. "Lord, she's gotten her share of trouble. From a good family, herself." He stood up.

"Isn't that Silver fellow one of Maddox's yahoos?" Jones asked, creases crumpling up his forehead.

"Yeah. And a great deal more than a yahoo," the sheriff said, rolling himself up into a sitting position, picking up a leafy twig lying by him, holding it up, and examining the veins in the leaves. Thinking.

"What ya mean, 'a great deal more than a yahoo,' Bill?" Jones felt a flush of adrenalin.

"I mean they are the same blood."

"How's that?"

"Silver's mama's husband was not Silver's daddy."

"The hell you say. How'd I miss that?"

"It's not common knowledge. I wouldn't have known except an aunt of mine, long dead, worked out at an orphanage where Silver lived for a time. She told me." The sheriff stood up and retrieved his hat: it had fallen off the side of the rock. He put it back on his head. "Guess we'd better make our way back to town. No way to thank you for this information. Sure interesting."

They began the walk back to the sheriff's car. As a courteous afterthought, the sheriff asked, "Don't guess you got any more on Maddox, have you? Other than what you saw today?"

"Well, yeah, and it's probably nothing."

"What?"

"My ex, who lives around the corner from where Gloria Jenkins lived, was babysitting a friend's little boy the day of the fire at Gloria's. Anyway, guess who pulled his pickup in on that street and parked it late that morning, all friendly, talking to the little boy, waving to my ex, as he walked in the direction of Gloria's house?"

"Maddox?" the sheriff asked, a revelation crossing his face.

"Bingo!" Jones replied.

*****

It was hardly any time after Cal Hough and his wife began Tennessee living that she told him, "I'm so lonesome I can't stand it."

"I know bound'a be hard, baby," he said and hugged her.

"It'd help me to go visit my sister Vorene for jist a spell," she begged him. "I won't stay long. Jist get a dose of talking. Maybe I can stand it here, then."

Cal was against it and told her so, but she began crying and said, "I'm leaving one way or tother; going back down there a see her with yore blessing or not. Ain't anything here fur me to do. Nothing. My rheumatize is a fighting these mountains and I'm tired a fighting."

They took the most of the week's check he'd picked up the day before from the logging business, where he was now working, and bought her a bus ticket on into Cairo. She left before sun up that morning carrying a paper bag with a sausage biscuit, an apple, and a Moon Pie. He bought her a Coca-Cola out of the machine before he saw her to the bus, kissed her hard on the lips, and told her, "Keep low, now, sweetheart, down there Cairo. This ain't over. You git seen or anything, the law'll know you're a straight shot back to me."

"Ain't no law out there in them woods where Vorene lives. You know that. They wouldn't know me no how. I'll be scarce." She smiled and took a seat on the bus just above him. He stood watching it pull out. She waved at him from the window. He waved back.

39.

THE SUNDAY BEFORE LABOR DAY

I argued out loud with myself, "Samone smelled your hair back there on the stoop of your parents' house and lied to you, deliberately. He tricked you. He must have been with her, even back there that day in the lantana bed."

Then I sided with him and said, "No, you pushed him off into her arms, Renee; it was you. You peeled onions and ignored him. Left him alone when you were together."

But I got so tired from all of the grasping to understand who we had been and so frightened that I would never know the truth and I missed him so. I was broken. And confused about what Samone had done to unleash that monster Silver on me. And how Charlie had cornered up with Samone. Charlie, my first glimmer of light, he'd tricked me, too: he had known full well that I didn't have a marriage, and he had kept it from me.

He quit coming over. Oh, he tried a few times. I wouldn't let him. I asked him for my house keys back. He looked at me with sad eyes and said, "I understand, Renee."

"Understand? What in hell do you understand, Charlie? How stupid I was, not knowing that Samone was cheating on me, but you did?"

He kept his lips tight and held a look of helplessness on his face. And he said, "Take care of yourself, Renee. I'm here when you need me."

So he doesn't come around anymore, and I couldn't trust him if he did. I'd been double cheated.

Janie went to my parents until time for school to start, a week after Labor Day. And Ashley as much as left me. After the picnic, she said, "Renee, I know all of this news about Samone has been hard on you. It has been hard on all of us. Mother's been crying. Daddy's been cursing a blue streak, threatening Samone."

"Threatening Samone, Ashley? He is dead."

"Well, I know that, Renee," she yelled at me like I had caused Daddy to go into his rage. She said, "I told him, I said, 'Daddy, the man is dead and gone. You can't do any more to him.' Daddy snapped back at me, said, 'I wish to almighty hell I could.'"

Somehow, hearing that, I felt responsible and ashamed. I blurted out, "I guess we are all going crazy, Ashley. But, at least Daddy gets it."

She just stood there looking at me like, yes, I was the whole problem, and she'd like to throw something at me. "We all get it, Renee!"

I started crying. It fell out. I wanted her to help me with it. I said, "And now, on top of everything, I'm sure that Charlie had to have been in on it." I knew when I said it I shouldn't have.

Ashley's eyes got wide. She steadied herself with her hand on the top of the chest near the front door. "In on what, Renee?"

"That woman."

She shook her head, lowered her voice almost to a whisper, and said, "Samone is one thing. I know you are hurting so bad from losing him and getting the news a year later that how he died was not even what you were told. And then learning that he was having an affair with some woman."

"You've got that right," I said sarcastically, thinking: How dare you say all of that to me just now?

She refused to let it alone. "Renee, Charlie hasn't had an affair with that woman. None of Samone's doings were Charlie's fault. You are simply off base blaming him for only trying to protect you from any more pain."

"Humph!" I whirled.

"You're making Charlie the fall guy, Renee."

"The fall guy? How could I make Charlie the fall guy? I don't know what he knew, and I've discovered I can't trust who he is. I didn't even know Samone, my own husband, though Charlie certainly did. I have no idea who I am anymore. I guess I never did."

She stared at me like she didn't understand a word I said. "I am going for a grocery run," she said. She slammed the door behind her. About an hour later, she returned and put away the groceries, unnecessarily banging cabinet doors, as I stood in the kitchen, watching, knowing not to speak. She folded the last paper bag, stuffed it in the bag holder, and brushed her hands together. "There!" she said. She grabbed her purse and keys and opened the front door.

Mr. No-Wobbler and I followed her. "What have I done to you now, Ashley?"

With a smile nowhere near her face and anchored in a weighty calmness like a coastline holds at some point before a hurricane arrives, she proclaimed, "Your cabinets are stocked. Your fridge is full. You have a phone. You've got a lot on your mind. I think you need some time to do some thinking. Alone. Keep your doors locked and don't let anyone in. Call me if you need me."

"Well you need not worry about me. Everything's bolted down."

"Good."

"Anyway," I astonished myself in saying it, "that cowardly monster is not gonna do anything to get his tail caught. I signed the papers against him; they've issued a warrant for his arrest. He's bound to be a million miles away."

"Okay." That was all she said, "Okay." She left.

Of course, answering the door had not been a problem. No one came by. Not even her. They'd all deserted me, like I had some kind of disease they might catch. Anyway, I was mad at 'em, every one of 'em. They didn't understand me, and I was not going to beg them to try.

"I'm losing my mind," I told my counselor.

She smiled. "Renee, there would be something wrong with you if you weren't a bit irrational." That's the way she put it, irrational. I guess that's nice talk for it being okay for me to be insane. I was so blue I wanted to lie on the floor and fade into it.

Nobody in my life made any sense. Except, strangely enough, Mrs. Mabel. She called every day. She had not come over, just called. Listened to me. I think if I had told her I was about to sell my house, put Janie up for adoption, and become a pole dancer, she would've said, "Well now, Renee, if that is what you think you should do."

She insisted, however, that I go with her to The Corral, a general store on the outskirts of Gargagun, for its Third Annual Pre-Labor Day Sunday Sale on, of all things, art and BBQ.

"Oh, it's a mecca, Renee, for artists and craftspeople. Everybody shows off work. But it's the BBQ that is the big draw. Everything in the store is on sale. Didn't you see the flyer in the middle of Friday's newspaper?"

"Well, I'm not sure, honestly, I'm not much in the mood to get out—"

She barely took a breath and continued her persuasion: "It would be fun, Renee; no need to buy anything; just get out into people; have some fun."

"I know . . ."

"Anyway, their famous BBQ is buy a pound, get a pound free. Limit ten pounds."

"Sure sounds like a bargain . . ."

"Oh, it is, and it's the best you will ever eat; so many people shop that they hire extra help just to work the butcher department."

"Okay, Mrs. Mabel, maybe we could buy a couple of pounds of the BBQ and split it?" I suggested, dreading the thought of doing anything other than crawling back into the sheets and sleeping the entire day.

"Oh, good. Wear something comfortable, Renee. And don't forget to bring Mr. No-Wobbler. We may need him to clear us a path through the store." She chuckled.

We arrived at The Corral, an old concrete building out in the middle of a dusty nowhere, to find it the center of Gargagun's universe and, though not a place for wearing Sunday clothes, it was a virtual anthill of folks who'd just come from church, dressed in their finest, weaving in and out, carrying paper bags of BBQ back to dusty cars and trucks squeezed in a too-full dirty parking lot

"Isn't it remarkable?" Mrs. Mabel said, blushing like a midwife who had just helped birth a baby.

"Why, yes, it's incredible," I said, taking it in.

"I would never have guessed shopping for art and BBQ would be so popular on Sunday," I said, shaking my head, thinking how the whole scene looked like a cartoon from The New Yorker.

"Oh, Renee, the Sunday before Labor Day has become a tradition here at The Corral. They say that there are reporters here from newspapers as far away as Birmingham and Nashville," she said, grinning wide.

She drove at the speed of a turtle through the parking lot, twice, hunting a parking place. I silently congratulated myself on having worn sneakers for the walk with Mr. No-Wobbler from what I envisioned would be out along the highway. But, on her second drive through, something from on high must have looked down on us and had compassion for us: a teenager backed a sports car out of a parking place directly in front of the entrance to The Corral.

Mrs. Mabel, unsurprised, blew the teen a kiss and pulled into the parking space. "There," she said, as if she had arranged the entire thing, "maybe parking here will make it easier on you and Mr. No-Wobbler, dear." She removed the keys from the ignition and sat with them in her lap, pondering something.

"Are you okay, Mrs. Mabel?" I asked.

"Oh, yes, dear, I was just wondering if it would be impolite of me to ask you to go on in, alone, and start checking things out while I run next door to the seed store right quick to pick up some turnip green seeds. I know just where they'll be; I won't be planting them for a few more weeks, but it will save me another trip. It won't take a minute. Then, I'll meet you inside The Corral at the butcher shop."

"Absolutely. That will be fine. Get your seeds. I am slow, anyway. I won't have to rush. I can take my time. Meet you at the butcher shop."

She seemed relieved. "Thank you, Renee."

After she helped Mr. No-Wobbler and me out of the car, she hung her enormous black patent leather pocketbook over her left arm and proceeded toward the end of the same building in which The Corral was housed and through a door atop which hung a rusty red sign: Key's Garden and Seeds. On one side of the door, dirty glass windows dimmed the geometry of haphazard stacks of large sacks of fertilizer and garden soil; on the other side of the door, skinny metal seed racks cradled tiny seed packages, their rainbow of colors dimmed by the dirty windows.

Mr. No-Wobbler and I stepped into The Corral, a vast dark trap packed with people, its narrow aisles alive with hyped-up shoppers who exuded the expectancy of cruise ship travelers about to depart the harbor. The general store's high ceilings were sparsely dotted with fluorescent fixtures, many of them blown out, and its windows were blurred with old dirt, like those at Key's Garden and Seeds, all of which successfully conspired to foreclose even the existence of the sun. The dimness was off putting, but it reminded me that one of the lamps in Janie's room had blown a bulb and I needed a replacement. I lifted my eyes above the crowd. They fell on a lightbulb display to the right of the butcher shop.

Good, I said to myself. Perfect. That's where I'm to meet Mrs. Mabel, anyway. I'm destined to find light in here for Janie.

So I zigzagged along the right side of the building through the crowd viewing the art on the dusty pea-green faded shelves that ran the length of the building. In a previous life, they probably held cans of baked beans and potted meat and Spam and sweet potatoes. Now, they held wide easels displaying the art of nursing home patients, crayon drawings of grade school children, and watercolor pieces scotch-taped to the rims of the shelves, all a kind of budding out of life in the darkness. Strewn among the display were hand-whittled wooden statues of various sizes. Propped up along the bottom shelf were oil paintings, some awkward, some thick with paint, heavy, like the room, primitive, dark in color and theme, full of foreboding. I shivered and felt oddly repulsed by the display.

The beehive of shoppers exerted every effort to thwart my eventual arrival at the lightbulb display, but I succeeded, amazed to discover that from that vantage point I had a clear view of the seven or eight rows of salivating humanity, stretched the full width of the twenty-foot white butcher display case. They were waiting in lines ten and twelve deep to buy BBQ from a team of employees in starched white coats behind the case, methodically taking and filling orders. I peered around the row of shoppers nearest me to try to view the inside of the butcher case. It brimmed with juicy, crisp BBQ ribs the color of red wine, and pulled pork, piled high, steam rising up off of it. Maybe Mrs. Mabel and I should buy four pounds instead of two, I thought.

It was in that instant, when the juices flowed into my mouth and I hungered for the sweet tartness of the BBQ, that I saw him, a workman in dirty coveralls, well-groomed, with thick brown hair, not Silver's hair. He had a perfectly trimmed matching brown mustache. Nothing about the outside of the man looked like Silver. Not even his shoes, dirty, thick-soled black work shoes, laced around prongs sticking up along each side of the center seam, the laces mismatched, the bows tied at different heights on each shoe. I saw only the side of the man, for he was in line, looking toward the butcher case, waiting his turn to give his order to one of the salespeople. But his coverall sleeve was pushed back—I guess for relief from the oppressive heat—and his left arm below the pushed-up sleeve was covered in that red fuzz. The man could have had blue hair and been wearing angel's wings. With that red arm fuzz, he was Silver.

I stopped dead still and found myself back up against the wall in my living room. Sweating. And then I smelled him. Ivory soap. They could have poured an entire store full of warm BBQ sauce over all of us weaving around in that store, but it could not have covered the stink of that Ivory soap on that man. There he was, right before my very eyes. But I did not panic. I was grounded in something bigger than me.

Silver had no idea that I was watching him. And he probably would not have cared for me or anyone to have been watching him, believing that we couldn't see him in those coveralls, wearing that expensive hair and mustache and those shoes, smudged with that dirt. He was wrong. Seeing him flipped a knowing on in me: I would do whatever was necessary to rid myself of that monster. In the knowing, I felt Samone standing there with me, just like he had been that night in the bathroom, but he had morphed into an anger inside me now.

My stomach rumbled. I did not want my stomach rumbling to get his attention, so I moved toward the front door, as fast as a woman with a red cane could move. I stumbled. I used Mr. No-Wobbler to part the sea of people, trying to think of a way to get word to the sheriff. My heart was beating all over my body.

At the checkout area, I fell headlong into Mrs. Mabel. "Mrs. Mabel, he's in there, right now. He's in there," I tried to whisper loudly so only she would take notice. But I didn't have to worry. The people around me weren't interested in what I was saying. They were shuffling in to get to the art and BBQ and shuffling back past us to get out of the store with their purchases, smiling and floating in the smell of BBQ and the glorious commerce of it all.

"Who, Renee? Who?" She stuffed the tiny paper sack of turnip green seeds into her purse.

"Silver, Mrs. Mabel. He was standing in front of the butcher case dressed like a workman in coveralls, wearing a brown wig and a false mustache." I was sweating down my arms inside my blouse. I was weeping.

Without blinking an eye, Mrs. Mabel said as calmly as if she were offering me a piece of pie, "Guess what, Renee? There's the sheriff sitting out front in his car, parked right next to mine."

He was. I ran to him—Mr. No-Wobbler and I did. He saw my face. It took only a few words before he was in the store, past me, his deputy with him. "Come behind me, Renee," he said. "Don't make a scene. Just quietly point him out."

At the exact moment that I raised my arm to show the sheriff the man who was not who he was dressed to be, Silver turned and faced us head on. The sheriff recognized him, too.

Silver pushed a woman down in front of him and scaled the butcher case like he had wings. The sheriff and the deputy scaled the butcher case in pursuit. People screamed. The Corral became a madhouse of confused shoppers dropping packages, uncertain what to do, where to flee. The woman Silver had thrown to the floor lost her little boy in the assault. She screamed his name, "David! David!" A toddler, dressed in a short seersucker jumper, was up against the butcher case crying, his thumb in his mouth, his nose running. His mother scrambled to her feet. Grabbed him. Pulled him over to hide with her behind a bin of apples rather than try to fight the mob rolling toward the front door.

I just stood there. Stone cold. Engraved in the space. Waiting. Out of the corner of my eyes, I saw Mrs. Mabel about ten feet behind me, inching in toward me against the flow of the shoppers trying to escape.

Suddenly, like a boogeyman, Silver jumped back across the case and directly on top of me. Miraculously, Mr. No-Wobbler and I did not fall. But Silver circled me with his left arm and set me in front, between him and the butcher case. He poked the butcher knife he'd grabbed from the chopping block behind the case under my chin and jabbed the tip of it against my jawbone. Blood began dripping down onto my shoulder. I could hear the drops plopping on my white blouse, but I could not feel the knife in my skin.

The sheriff rose up from behind the case and lunged back across it, toward us. People behind the counter scurried around, grabbing towels to tend the deputy, who was down, bleeding.

"Leave that woman be, Silver," Sheriff Bill said. "Leave her be. She's not well and the last thing you need right now is any more charges on you. You just assaulted my deputy. Pray he makes it."

Despite being held with a knife in my neck by a man who knew I was the only thing standing between him and freedom, I became focused intently on Sheriff Bill and how he had a way about him that I had seen in my house that day: he could tell you the hard truth and not make you mad. Which seemed to actually calm Silver down some, though I still felt his body shaking against my back, the knife moving in my throat.

"I'll stab her, Sheriff," he said. "If you come at me, I'll cut her throat out. Let us leave and I'll drop her off at the front."

I knew that he wouldn't leave me anywhere in any way that I could ever talk.

So I said, "Shoot him, Sheriff Bill. Shoot him!" Though it was probably Samone telling me what to say.

"Don't pull your gun, Sheriff," Silver said. "You do and she's dead. Would work best that way, I think, anyway."

I didn't care if he killed me. I'd turned loose inside, the way I'd turned loose the night of the rape, but in The Corral, it was to Silver's disadvantage.

Silver pulled me with him, inching us back toward the door. I couldn't see where we were going. I kept holding on to Mr. No-Wobbler, trying not to fall. But I still was not afraid. I was livid at being dragged through the store, people having to dodge and hide. I realized that I needed to resist Silver's pull or he would get us out of the store. I demanded, "Don't let him get away, Sheriff Bill."

Silver slapped me. "Shut your face up, you whore," he said through gritted teeth. I could feel his eyes on the sheriff, who was moving in on us now, very slowly, continuing to talk soft, deliberate directions to Silver.

"Easy, Silver, this woman's bad injured. Let her loose. We can get this worked out. Take it easy now, son. Throw down that knife . . ."

As we passed the produce department and that table of apples behind which that woman and her son David were hunkered down, Mrs. Mabel stepped out in front of Silver's back. Like a traffic cop at an intersection, she blocked the aisle. He stumbled. The knife popped out of his hand. It rocketed off across the aisle up toward the cereal section. I heard it clang as it hit the floor. The interruption completely surprised him. He tried to stop falling over Mrs. Mabel, though he had no idea what he'd encountered. He just kept rocking around, grappling to hold onto me.

Mrs. Mabel rolled out from under him and landed on her stomach. She rose up on her knees on the floor like a phoenix, reared back, and bashed him about the face and shoulders with that big black patent leather handbag.

It startled him. He, reflexively, raised his arms to catch the blows. He dropped his hold on me. I reeled away from him. He remained sprawled across the floor, not yet horizontal but not upright, hesitating in midair for a split second. Then he plopped across the aisle, twisting his head around behind him, trying to find what to hit.

I don't know how I knew to do it, but seeing his legs spread wide in front of me, I grabbed Mr. No-Wobbler with both of my hands and punctured him directly in the center of the space between his two legs. It hit home. He screamed and cursed and rolled over on his side, grabbing himself like a baby.

I smiled. I hit him again and again across his back, and Mrs. Mabel continued her assault on him with the black patent leather purse, blow after blow, across his head. I believe she would have simply beaten him to death, but Sheriff Bill and several bystanders relieved us.

The sheriff handcuffed him. The bystanders helped the sheriff confine Silver behind the wire mesh divider in the sheriff's car. Two more vehicles from the Sheriff's Office arrived.

The paper headlines the next day read: "Alleged Rapist No Match For Patent Leather Purse."

*****

I sat shaking in Mrs. Mabel's car watching the sheriff's car depart.

"Are you up to driving to the jail, Renee?" she asked, fumbling to find her keys, her blouse out of her waistband, her hair looking as if it had experienced a strong wind, and her purse handle torn loose, dangling. Before I could answer, she continued, "Sure hope I didn't lose my keys hitting that man in the head, Renee, or break 'em, even." She laughed a nervous laugh.

"Yes, I am up to anything," I said, not knowing if I had the energy to breathe.

Inside the jail, from down the length of the cellblock hallway, we heard the mumble of voices. I experienced relief knowing that Silver's was among them. It struck me that he and those other prisoners in there were only locked up in a jail. I had been locked up inside. For years. And Samone couldn't get to me. So he had ended up dead. And I had gotten raped. But, I was, despite all of this, finally feeling free. Inside.

The female deputy behind the desk recognized me. "You are Renee Sims, aren't you?"

"Yes ma'am. I'm the one that man raped."

She pushed her chair back and walked into the area where Silver was being booked.

Sheriff Bill walked out into the waiting area. He hugged me and shook Mrs. Mabel's hand. "Thank you, ladies. Are you okay, Renee?"

"Yes, yes, I am fine."

"Mrs. Mabel," he said, "it is good to see you again. If you ever need a job, call, I'll get you on the force."

Disheveled and giddy, she said, "Sheriff Bill, I thank you for your confidence, sir; I can't think of any better way to spend my time, but I suppose I will have to stick to my flowers."

He grinned. "You were very brave, Renee," he said. "You know, this thing is just starting. Are you up to it?"

"Yes. I'm up to whatever I have to do to put that man away, Sheriff Bill."

"Would you be willing to go on record here, now, identifying him as the man that raped you, Renee?"

"Yes, sir."

We waited. They lined up some men under a light. Silver was one of them. I sat in a place where he could not see me. I looked him in the eyes and pointed him out. A woman took things down in shorthand and I signed some papers.

Afterwards, the sheriff said, "Thank you, Renee. One of our deputies will drive you and Mrs. Mabel home." He took me aside and whispered, "Please go home and rest. We have more work to do day after tomorrow at the bank. I'm hoping it might put a lid on the jar."

During the ride home in the sheriff's vehicle, Mrs. Mabel and I held onto each other. "I sure wish Samone could have seen the look of fear on Silver's face today, Mrs. Mabel," I told her. "It must have been how

I looked that night he bent me over the commode in my own house and raped me."

"Yes, dear," she said. She gripped my hand tighter and cleared her throat.

When I got home, I called Ashley. Within fifteen minutes, Charlie was standing at my front door. I let him in.

*****

Mrs. Mabel poured herself a double sherry in the finest piece of cut glass she owned and purposely sat down on the lowered commode lid in her bathroom, intending to run her tub bath.

"Salute," she said, lifting the stemware. She wept. She never got around to turning on the faucet in the tub, what with trips to refill her glass four times during the reliving of the afternoon.

"I'll have to get that handbag to the shoe shop this week and get it repaired," she said to herself. "It's still got lots of life left in it."

At some point she stumbled to the bedroom and crawled into her bed without cleaning her face—which she had not done in years. She slept in her housecoat. She dreamed that she was an angel and was flying down into deep pits and gathering up lost people and helping them get home.

40.

RECOLLECTIONS

Just at dusk the Sunday before Labor Day, Vorene leaned against the red Coca-Cola flip-top icebox under the Hardwick Service Station awning, where the Greyhound always took on and dropped off passengers at its last stop before New Orleans. As Sarah stepped off the bus, Vorene hugged her and said, "I've been worrieder than anything about you, Sarah. You okay?"

Sarah blushed. "Oh, I'm good, Vorene, shore am. Sure 'preciate yore pickin' me up. I knew I just hadta talk to somebody fur a spell, Vorene, and Cal ain't no use for that."

Vorene patted her arm. She held onto her.

Sarah said, "You ain't changed a bit, not even with the worrying, Vorene. Naw. Did it when we wuz kids out chasin' them lightnin' bugs: you'd say, 'Don't you git yoreself out there in that grass, now, Sarah, just ain't no tellin' the snakes in it.'"

Vorene laughed. "I did say somethin' like that. I remember it, Sarah, like it were yesterday. Sorta is, you comin' this fer piece to see me. So proud you did."

Sarah opened the passenger door of Vorene's looked-just-bought pickup to face a brown bench seat that appeared to have been assaulted with a pickax; she wrapped her thin flowered chintz skirt tight around her thighs, so as not to snag it, and set her paper bag holding her things into the gaping hole in the middle of the seat. "There now," she said, pleased, her tiny hands pressing outward across her skirt, her back settling in, a queen who had mounted her carriage and awaited departure.

"The seat does look bad, don't it," Vorene said, "but it sure runs good. Belonged new to one of Marty's poker buddies, a mechanic.

About a week after he bought it, he left his pet monkeys in it one night while he was gambling. Came back to this. We got it for hardly nothing. I generally keep a jug of good ole spring water in that hole there where you just set your things."

"The water hole is a pur-tee good idea, Vorene," Sarah said, grinning.

"Yeah, it makes the best of it, don't it," Vorene said.

Vorene always made the best of it, had to over the years to survive with a ninth grade education, two kids who ran her in circles from can to can't, and Marty, as good a man as you'd want to find, who simply loved gambling more than anything and almost always lost more than he won, after which he'd hug her up tight and whisper in her ear, "I shore do love you, hun."

Vorene drove. Sarah talked. At first, Vorene let Sarah's words happen around her, as they bounced along the dirt road back down into the holler toward home, and later that evening, too, as she squeezed the dough in the wooden bowl into biscuits to bake while the pork fried up crisp in the iron skillet. But somewhere in the listening to Sarah's bemoaning her Cal's being framed and arrested while delivering a side of beef up to Gargagun, Vorene decided that she oughta go over to the refrigeration plant where she worked and take a look at the delivery ticket on that beef. Wouldn't likely help anything, but it couldn't hurt.

It being a holiday weekend, the plant was closed, but years ago she'd been issued a key to the door near her work counter, so she and Sarah would have it to themselves for the looking. No one would be in the area except the security guard, who played poker regularly with Marty.

So, before the sun even thought about rising on Labor Day, Vorene slipped out of the bed and made the coffee and more biscuits. She left the biscuits setting on the back of the stove with a bowl of scrambled eggs for Marty and the kids. She tapped Sarah on the shoulder and said, "You're sure sleeping like an angel, but get up, Sarah. I've been thinking 'bout this thing on Cal. Got us some checking on stuff to get done today at the plant. I've got ya a biscuit and egg sandwich here in this paper bag and a cup of coffee jist like ya like it in this fruit jar. C'mon, now, get yourself dressed."

The security guard waved 'em in. "How's that old man, Vorene?" he asked her.

"He's fat and sassy," she said and waved back.

Vorene quickly found the invoice for the beef Cal had delivered to Gargagun. She read it over twice to make sure she had not misread it, for it was irregular in every respect: it was in pencil; delivery originated from "telephone call"; Tribling's initials were by the delivery entry, also in pencil; and the delivery designation was "Gargagun," without specific pricing or delivery address. The number of the intake ticket was written in the "Notes" section, along with the words "delivery by Hough, only." Tribling's personal secretary had completed and initialed the "Notes" section. Vorene copied the invoice and folded it up neatly, tucking it into her Sears and Roebuck shopping bag purse, asking herself how it could have been that she had never before seen that invoice until then.

She muttered to Sarah, "Every beef ticket and invoice comes through me, every one of 'em, but this invoice I ain't never seen 'til today. Mr. Tribling's personal secretary worked it, looks like, and she musta come in here and filed it herself, too. Which don't make no sense to me, what with all she has to do and it being my job."

Sarah had a blank look on her face. She didn't even understand what an invoice was.

"Let's go, Sarah," Vorene said, annoyed and confused. At the door out of the plant, Vorene saw the stack of newspapers, already delivered, even on Labor Day, so she picked one up; the plant always kept them alongside every entrance, free for employees and customers. There, as big as life, on the front page of the newspaper was a photograph of Silver M. Conway, a man she'd done paperwork for on a side of beef after he'd delivered it to the cooler, back about a year ago. His good looks had struck her that day, as had his habit of flipping back a strand of his red hair up off his eye, over and over, which, she told a coworker, "would worry a person to death if he weren't so good looking."

"Wait, Sarah, if ya don't mind, I wanna see why this fellar's got the front page." She saw the headline under his picture, "Alleged Rapist Captured During Failed Attempt to Kidnap Victim." She grabbed at her throat. "Good Lord in heaven, Sarah," she said, waving the front page in front of her sister, "this man was right here in this place last year and I did the intake ticket for him on some beef he delivered back to the cooler for keeping."

Something about the sum and substance of it all tugged at her gut and compelled her to pull the Silver M. Conway intake ticket. Low and behold, its number matched the cross-reference on the Hough delivery invoice. Cross-references between numbers on intake tickets and delivery invoices were a strict requirement by the plant, never to be omitted under any circumstances. She simply had to sit down and catch her breath.

She said to Sarah, "Something's plain crazy 'bout this. The invoice for the delivery what got Cal framed joins up with the ticket number on the side of beef that Silver M. Conway—this man here in the paper—brought in last year: they smack dab match." Vorene scratched her head. She wrinkled her face. "Why would Mr. Tribling be all up in regular stuff like delivering beef to a man the paper says is a rapist?"

Sarah grabbed the newspaper out of Vorene's hands, pointed to Silver's photo, and asked, "You mean the beef brought in by this man who raped that woman was what my Cal delivered up there that got him arrested?"

"Yeah, it's right here in the paperwork we keep, Sarah! They make us cross-reference every intake and delivery, have to, or Mr. Max says, 'IRS'll get us.' Lawdy, he'd rather take a beating than have IRS folks snooping around. When they come into the plant, he has to take tranquilizers." Vorene copied the Silver M. Conway intake ticket and clipped it to the delivery invoice inside her purse.

Ordinarily, at this point, she would have said, "Sarah, let's get out of here," but with what she had learned being so strange and there being so many questions rambling around in her head, she did something she hardly ever did: she sat down and read a complete article in the newspaper, the one about Silver M. Conway, to learn all she could about him.

Sarah picked up a paper, too, and began reading, albeit very slowly, moving her mouth with her words. Reading was not something she ever did very much.

When Vorene finished the article on the rape, she saw another article down at the bottom of the front page about the recent murders in Gargagun—no big headlines, old news. It mentioned her brother-in-law's arrest for having the dead man's coat in his truck and his whacking the guard in the head, escaping jail, vanishing into thin air.

"Look, Sarah, look, here's news about Cal and all."

In order to finish the article on the murders, Vorene turned the newspaper over to the back and there, to her astonishment, was a picture of a coat that she had actually seen herself in the cab of Silver M. Conway's truck the day he brought the beef in. The picture took up a fourth of the back page of the paper. At first, she became elated. Then, though, she realized the significance of what she was seeing. She blurted out, "How'd a suppose-to-be rapist have a dead man's coat spread out on the seat by him, back a year ago when he brought in that side of beef, and it be the coat what was in Cal's pickup a year later that got him arrested? I seen that coat, that very one, with my own eyes, 'cause I had to catch him to hand him his copy of the intake ticket that he had accidentally left on the counter."

"If that don't beat all!" Sarah replied, with as much a lack of understanding in her statement as amazement. But, thinking started going on in her eyes.

"Sure as anything, I reached right in through the passenger's window and handed him the pink copy of the delivery ticket right over that stinky coat. It smelled like something gone bad— not him, the coat: he hadn't stunk when he was in the office earlier. Plus, with it stinking, I was thinking who had so little sense to be carrying a stinking coat in the hot summertime when nobody with any sense would be wearing a coat, and it was not even his size, little, and he's big and tall. Wouldn't have fit him. Couldn't have stretched it on him."

Sarah's mouth fell open. She just sat there taking it in and said, trance-like, "The raper had the coat fore Cal ever thought about workin' fer this place?"

"Hell's bells, Sarah, I'd swear on a stack of Bibles that man they say raped that woman drove out of here that day a year ago with that exact same coat in his truck."

Sarah pointed to the coat on the back of the paper and asked, "And that there's the coat whut got Cal locked up?"

"Yep. Sure looks to be."

Mystification spread all over Sarah's childlike face. She said, "Well, Vorene, that don't make no sense a'tall, no it don't; how'd it get from Mr. Conway's truck to Cal's pickup? It can't jump."

Something about her words made it funny for a split second, and they both burst out laughing at the idea of a coat from a year before jumping into Cal's pickup. But the laughing gave Vorene an unexpected understanding. Her truth radar hit something. Being in the mix of that with her sister and her brother-in-law hiding off up in the state of Tennessee, though all new to her, had suddenly turned, with the information she'd just discovered, into an obsession to figure the thing out. She was good at figuring things out, simple things in order to survive, like how to make a roasted chicken last a week or how to cut a worn out sheet down the middle and turn the edges in and sew them together to give it another year of use. This was not much different, just more rested on it.

She folded the newspaper, put it also in her purse, and said, "Sarah, tell ya what let's me and you do. Let's take these papers home with us and read 'em again, good, and think this through and talk it over with Marty. Maybe we oughta do something."

Sarah scratched her temple. "What can we do, Vorene? We ain't nothing but little people down here, me, in fact, sorta hiding out. I shore can't do nothing a'tall to get Cal caught."

*****

In the late afternoon, when Marty came in, he looked at all the articles and the invoices and listened to Vorene's story. He said, "Honey, didn't yo papa know that man up there that's the sheriff in Gargagun? Why don't you call him?"

That night at about ten p.m., Sheriff Bill drove into Vorene's yard.

He told Anna after supper, "I hate to leave so late, but when that woman called me and told me she had 'seen that coat what got a man arrested,' as she put it, I knew I'd drive to the Pacific Ocean, if need be, to talk to her tonight, no matter how tired I am."

He knocked on the door. Vorene was alone in the front room, with Sarah hiding in the back bedroom and Marty out at the river playing poker.

"Thank you, Sheriff, for coming all this way so late, and all," Vorene said. "I sure hope I ain't making no big thing outta nothing but I knowed I had to tell somebody and I trust you. Iz why I called you. My papa used to live up there in Gargagun. Thought the world of you. Here. Look at his picture. You know him?"

She held up a faded photograph. There, staring Sheriff Bill in the face, was a snapshot of the old man who used to sit on the front steps of the courthouse, day after day, whittling. About a year before he ran for sheriff, Bill Trailor was bogged down in the ifs, ands, and buts of such a step. He stopped one day and sat down by the old man; they began talking.

The old man let Bill talk his doubts out of his system, and then he told him, "Bill Trailor, you get a nudging to do something, better do it. Don't, it'll come get ya when ya ain't a lookin'.'"

Sheriff Bill told Vorene about that day and said, "Your papa's words meant a lot to me. You could say they helped direct my life. He was a good man, Vorene. I'm glad you called me."

"Well, I know something bad's done happened to that woman up there, Sheriff, from what the paper sez, and I know you'll do right by it like I know you'll do right by my brother-in-law who escaped and that there coat and all, which I'm not sayin' iz anyway connected, no, not that, but what I am saying is I can't figure why that man suppose to be a rapist had the very coat of a dead man and, later, it jumped into Cal Hough's truck without him a knowing it and got him arrested."

She laid out the paperwork she'd retrieved from the plant earlier that day, explaining the significance of it to her. And, she explained what happened the day Silver delivered the beef for storage to the plant.

"You've done exactly the right thing, Vorene. Exactly. Can I take this paperwork with me?" the sheriff asked.

"Oh, sure, Sheriff. Like I say, I know you will do right by it." Relief crept across her face when she handed it to him.

"I'll try to do right by everybody, Vorene, but that may mean that you will need to come to Gargagun and go before a grand jury pretty soon. Will you do it?"

"If'n the truth will help Sarah's huzban, who wouldn't harm anybody, won't even set a rat trap at their house, I sure will, Mr. Bill. You'n count on me."

"Thank you, Vorene. I wish your papa was still alive to know what a good thing you did today."

"Aw, he knows, he knows, just can't whittle with uz no more."

*****

When he arrived back in Gargagun, Sheriff Bill called the district attorney. "Hate like everything to wake you, but could you please come by first thing in the morning? I got some paperwork from a woman down south of Cairo tonight. She works at that refrigeration plant. The paperwork and what she told me will have you chomping at the bit, added to that stuff that Jones happened upon."

"Bears it out?" the DA asked, sitting up in his bed.

"Does, and answers the coat question. Looks like this could be the piece of the puzzle to give us the real man with the coat, the man we just jailed on that rape."

"Well, I do declare. Interesting. Interesting." The DA stroked his jaw. His eyes got big. "I'll see you bright and early tomorrow for certain. Put everything in your safe, okay?"

"Already sealed up there. Sure hate I had to wake you," the sheriff said, settling his feet on the floor in his office, stretching.

"Bill, I'll stay awake all night to get this kind of news. Thanks."

"Me, too," the sheriff said, thinking, as he hung up the phone, what if I'd never known Vorene's papa and sat down that day to talk with him?

*****

Silver's first phone call out of the jail on Sunday night was of no use. Seth didn't answer. So Silver reasoned that he was out somewhere. It didn't matter; everything was closed down, anyway. He'd make the best of it. Truth was, he dreaded facing Seth's wrath over his getting in such a fix. Silver spread out on the cot in the jail cell. It wasn't too uncomfortable. He'd have time to figure out how to handle everything with Seth. Plus, he knew Seth would get this off his back. He always got everything taken care of. And, it was just a woman, anyway. What difference could his having sex with a woman have to do with anything? He fell asleep.

The next morning, Labor Day, as the coffee in the jail was brewing, Silver coaxed the deputy to let him make another call.

"Hullo," Seth said into the receiver.

"Hey, we got us a problem," Silver said.

"What kind of problem? I noticed you never paid my advice no mind and have been out somewhere whooping it up over the weekend."

"Naw, I'm in jail."

"In jail? What they got you in there for?" Seth asked.

"Said I raped a woman."

"Put Bill Trailor on."

"Hello, Seth," the sheriff said as he watched the deputies return Silver to his cell.

"What'n hell you doing, Bill, holding that boy?" Seth asked.

"Doing my job, Seth." The sheriff stood up and shifted the receiver to his other ear. "He 'bout killed me and one of my deputies and the woman who says he raped her."

"What you mean, Bill?" Seth's voice rattled.

"I mean he attacked me, stuck a knife in my deputy, tried to kidnap the woman that says he raped her. Haven't you seen the morning paper?"

"No, Bill, I haven't seen the morning paper, but no matter what is in the morning paper, I am gonna have my way and get that boy out of there, final. Do you hear me?"

The sheriff could hear fear hanging on Seth's words.

"It's no different than high school, Bill Trailor. Not a dang thing has changed between us. You still gonna end up saying how high when I say jump."

The sheriff let lots of air get inside the space between his lips and the phone receiver. He thought through what he was going to say before he said it and spoke with a calm. "Seth, you know damn well I am going to abide by the law and treat Silver right, whatever that is. But your son's neck's in a noose, Seth. And your just wanting him out won't get him out."

Bill Trailor's confidence had always annoyed Seth. It did, again, that morning.

Seth's voice rose as he said, "You will be letting him out. You are not running the show."

"Seth, you are right that some things have not changed. You still try to bully folks when you can. But you can't bully me or this office." Bill Trailor took a deep breath, thinking how good it felt, saying that. "The court will determine the bond situation Tuesday, Seth."

"My lawyer'll be on this," Seth said, and he slammed down the phone. He picked it up again and called Pickens and Slim, Attorneys at Law, up in Memphis.

41.

THE BOX

Tuesday after Labor Day spread out under a postcard blue sky, adrift in rays of mellow autumn sunshine, which danced into Renee's bedroom windows and woke her from a dream. Samone was in the dream, but she could not see him, though she was sitting on his lap in their living room, which was a place she'd never been before. He spoke to her, "It's okay. Do what you need to do. Let Charlie help you." Like magic, the words became musical notes that tumbled in and around boxes in a long tunnel, opening them, one after another, revealing them all to be empty, until the music snapped open the top of the largest box at the far end, which Renee knew held something important. So she stretched over into the box, anxious to know its contents, but the sunshine woke her before she could ever see what was inside. Frustrated, she rubbed the sleep out of her eyes and remembered: Today's the day I open the safe-deposit box at Caleon Bank.

*****

Deputy James arrived wearing street clothes and driving an unmarked car to escort Renee to the bank. She declined Renee's offer of coffee. "Thanks, I'm coffeed up," she said, smiling. "How are you feeling today, Renee, about all of this?"

"The truth is I wish I could just leave it alone and go on not knowing what is in the box, but I can't; it wouldn't be fair. The box may hold more than information about Samone and that woman Gloria."

"Yes, I expect you're right," Deputy James said, warmness in her words.

"I've been in the dark for such a long time, Deputy James, about so much and not even known I was in the dark. I've denied recognizing things that didn't suit me to see. That's a sorry way to live. I've been stupid, but I'm not stupid, and I can't stay stupid anymore," Renee said, feeling a rush of adrenalin, coaxing her to stand. She reached for Mr. No-Wobbler.

The profundity of what Renee had just spoken hit Deputy James. She nodded. Remained silent.

"But, it's scary," Renee pled, leaning in on Mr. No-Wobbler.

"Yes, Renee, it's scary to find out things that we don't want to know. Very scary."

Renee's eyes watered up.

"And that may happen today, but remember, Renee, that bank box does not hold the secret to you. No. It may hold the secrets of other lives that have touched yours, which is why it is going to take courage for you to do this today. But, you have that courage. And, you are not alone."

"Thanks. I know I'm not alone." She pulled a tissue from her purse and began dabbing at her eyes. Sniffling. "Thank you for being with me."

"No problem whatsoever. It's my job and I like doing it."

"And, Charlie's with me," Renee said, looking up like she'd just realized that. "He definitely gives me courage. Oh, I almost forgot to mention: can he go with us to the bank today?"

"Absolutely. Shall we go over and pick him up?"

"No, he wants to meet us there. Says he'll bring me home afterwards," Renee said, her shoulders relaxing in the realization he'd be present. Then she tightened up, held her jaw firm, and said, "The truth is, Deputy James, Charlie and I have been on the outs. It's been my fault, every bit of it; I've been low and grouchy, but he's about as patient a person as I've ever known, and he's good to me. He's just a good person. I need him."

Deputy James smiled. "Come on. Let's get this done," she said.

As they approached the car parked in the driveway, Mrs. Mabel teetered across her yard toward them, waving with one hand and raising her skirt with the other, like she was crossing a creek and didn't want to get her skirt wet. "Morning, Renee. I'll be thinking about you today. Just wanted you to know that."

"Thanks, Mrs. Mabel. I need it. I've got butterflies."

"That's a good thing. Let those butterflies help you walk," Mrs. Mabel said.

The deputy nodded at her. "Good to see you, Mrs. Mabel; I hear the sheriff thinks you ought to come to work with us. Is my job in danger?"

"May be, Deputy James." She winked at the deputy, smiled from ear to ear, slapped her thighs, and said, "Got 'em you need caught, Renee and I can bring 'em in."

The deputy chuckled. "I hope you know there's not enough repayment for your bravery on Sunday. Sure appreciate you and all you did and are doing."

"No repayment needed and I sure appreciate you, Deputy James," Mrs. Mabel said. "Please take good care of this young lady today."

Renee grinned, hugged Mrs. Mabel, and settled in the car with Mr. No-Wobbler.

Mrs. Mabel stepped onto the grass and cupped her hands to her mouth to megaphone her words: "I was delighted to have the chance to bash that fellow in the face and I'll do it again if you need any bashing after today, Renee. I keep my purse on a hook by the door all the time. Just call me."

All three women laughed out loud.

*****

Deputy James had known Carl Rather, the Caleon Bank president, for years, and had worked with him before on various matters. The day that she and Sheriff Trailor had broken the news to Renee about Samone and Gloria, the deputy returned to Rather the safe-deposit box signature card that was taped to the key in Gloria's note. In addition, as a courtesy and to assure a smooth process unlocking the box, she had also called him a few days prior to their visit to inform him that she was escorting Renee in to unlock box #506.

She said, "Mr. Rather, if we need to get a court order to get in the box, the sheriff says we can likely get one."

"Hold on," he said, "let me look." He pulled the info on box #506 and picked up the phone receiver. "You don't need anything more, Deputy; Gloria Jenkins listed Renee Sims on #506 as a co-user of the box from the outset. You brought the signature card in yourself. Everything is up to snuff on this box."

"Okay, thanks, Carl. Did Gloria Jenkins have another box the sheriff's office needs to know about with the arson investigation ongoing?"

"Yes, she opened another one the same day she opened this one, but although she took a signature card out to get another signature on it for additional access by another person, she never returned it."

"Okay, I'll tell the sheriff. Thanks, Carl. By the way, Renee Sims is using a cane and hasn't been out much since the rape. Where's the best place for us to park for her to get into the bank easily and her visit be as inconspicuous as possible?"

"I'd say come in on Grey Street that runs behind the bank and pull into one of our reserved parking places out back of the bank. There's a ramp to the door on that side. I'll tell the security guard to hold a parking place for you."

"Thanks so much," Deputy James replied.

*****

As they neared the bank, Renee's face reddened.

"My heart is beating so fast, Deputy James; there's so much happening so quickly; I feel like I am on a runaway train."

"You won't fall off the rails, Renee," Deputy James said, "I'm holding your arm."

Carl Rather welcomed them. They sat across from him. He picked up the paperwork from his credenza, obtained Renee's signature to enter the box, and took her key.

"Does it seem hot in here to you?" Renee asked.

"It does. I'll get you a glass of water," Deputy James said.

When she walked to the water cooler in the cashier's cage, she looked up to see Seth Maddox and two men enter the bank and seat themselves across from the senior VP for loans.

Back in Carl Rather's office, she handed Renee the glass of water and said, "Mr. Rather, I'd be more comfortable if we could walk back into the safe-deposit box vault, rather than sit here any longer. Can Renee take her water with her?"

"Of course; here, I'll carry it for you, Renee," he said. They proceeded like three soldiers into the vault, and Rather situated the women in a private room at the far end of it.

As he turned to go get box #506, Charlie walked in. Renee rushed to him, shaking. He held onto her.

"Mr. Rather, can Charlie stay with us to open the box?" she asked.

"Sure, it's your decision, Renee, who you want with you."

Deputy James closed the door to give the three of them complete privacy. She sat in one of the chairs along the wall, remaining to herself, observing, leaving Charlie and Renee together across the room, waiting, talking low with each other.

Mr. Rather brought in #506, an enormous green metal box. He set it on a bare table in the center of the room. "I'll be out at my desk if you need anything; just let me know if I can help you in any way." He departed.

They all stared at box #506. "Charlie, will you please open it?" Renee asked. Sweat popped out across her top lip.

"Of course," he said, standing over it, slipping aside the latch, and lifting its lid, which was only half as long as the full length of the box.

Renee did exactly what she'd done in the dream. She leaned over and looked inside. It was empty.

"I can't see anything, Charlie," she remarked, disgusted. "You mean we've come all this way to open an empty box?" She covered her face with her hands.

"There's bound to be something in the box, Renee. Why else would we be here? Let me see."

Renee stepped back, and he put his hand inside, stretching his arm back into the darkness in the far end of the box. "It's not empty. Something is in here, Renee." He pulled out a couple of thin manila envelopes, atop which sat a reel-to-reel tape sealed in a round metal canister. Attached to the canister was a typewritten transcript of the tape's contents, labeled: "Gloria Jenkins Speaks. 31.5 minutes."

Charlie pushed box #506 aside, opened the transcript, and laid it out on the table. The two women stood on either side of him. They all began silently reading it.

In the transcript Gloria introduced herself and Clark Milloy, Milloy Tapes, Inc., Gargagun, who was taping her and who had provided the tape transcript. She identified the date as August 1, 1967, which was only a little over a month prior.

She explained that there would be three copies of the tape and transcript: one in lock box #506, Caleon Bank; one in a sealed envelope in trust with her attorney Lomax Day, with instructions to him to deliver the sealed package containing a tape and transcript, unopened and intact, on September 15, 1967, at 9 a.m., to the sheriff of Gargagun, regardless of any circumstances of any kind whatsoever; and one in lock box #507, Caleon Bank, to which Clark Milloy would be provided a key. He was under similar instructions, except that his delivery was to be to the editor of the Gargagun Post on September 15, 1967, but not before 2 p.m. on that date.

The transcript continued:

"Nobody's forcing me to do any of this. I'm doing it because I saw Silver M. Conway kill two men in cold blood. He told me last week he was going to 'put me where I could not sing.' I believe he's gonna kill me. I don't want to die and people not know the truth.

"And, the truth is that Samone Sims and I were friends for months and happened to be together up at Miller's Barn, Florence Lake, August 1, 1966, when Silver M. Conway walked in on us and held us at gunpoint, forcing Samone outside.

"I begged him not to, but Silver M. Conway shot Samone in the head right in front of me. And within minutes, Josh Bridges drove up and paid Silver money for killing Samone. Then, as Josh Bridges walked toward the barn, Silver M. Conway shot him in the head and killed him, too.

"Silver'd thought it all out, because he pressed the gun into Samone's hand, squeezing his fingers around it, then threw it down on the ground to make it look like Samone had shot himself, which Samone would never do. He loved his family too much for that. They need to know that. That he loved them. Yes, he and I were friends, but he loved Renee and Janie."

Renee began to sob. Tears were dropping out of Charlie's eyes.

The deputy reached over them and turned the page for them to continue the reading of the transcript.

"Silver took Bridges' coat off of him and wrapped his body in a plastic bag and put it on dry ice which he had stored beforehand in the barn. Silver forced me, in a state of shock, to drive my car out and follow him—he drove Bridges' truck to a farmhouse where Seth Maddox was waiting. Other than Samone's vehicle, I never saw any others around Miller's Barn, so I guess Silver had walked there from somewhere.

"Seth Maddox paid Silver for killing Bridges. They laughed about it. I hated Josh Bridges, but I didn't want him or anybody murdered.

"I never wanted my being Samone's friend to bring him harm. But, it did. That's why Bridges hired Silver to kill Samone, because of me. I know that had to be the reason. And it has about driven me crazy.

"Seth kept me like a prisoner with him for what seemed an eternity, trying to get me to calm down and believe everything was all right. I have been in shock and constantly afraid of Silver killing me, too, when he got the chance to do it and get away with it. He's mean, but not a regular mean. I don't think he has a conscience.

"Finally, after Seth thought I was all right and could make it on my own, he took me home, though Silver didn't want him to and argued with him about it.

"Silver has kept badgering me and taunting me. I know he will kill me. It's just a matter of time. Lately, he drives the block by my house, over and over, and he calls and speaks just enough for me to recognize his voice and then he hangs up. It's happening more and more.

"Seth likes me and I think he would protect me if he could, but he will never cross Silver, because Seth Maddox is Silver's daddy. The birth proof is out at Vern Orphanage.

"So, I finally reached my limit, and unbeknownst to anybody, to try to save myself, I went to Lomax Day. To help make this legal, he had his secretary type up the papers for a person to sign who might tape me.

"I'm not afraid that Lomax Day will tell Seth or Silver anything, because Seth's men set fire to Lomax Day's barn full of prize horses about three years ago, to get back at him for representing one of Seth's enemies.

"Oh, Seth had enemies, but none ever got the goods on him and if they had, that other sheriff wouldn't have done much. He was scared of mixing it up with Seth Maddox and his Raleigh Mafia, which, I'm ashamed to say, I've worked in and been a part of, now, for almost thirty-five years. But, I grew up in it; it's all I've ever known, 'til Samone, and then his murder, which has shook me into not doing anything anymore except trying to stay alive from Silver."

"Well. There it is in black and white," Deputy James said, shaking her head. She cleared her throat, turned the page, and they read in some detail about the Raleigh Mafia and Max Tribling's complicity in it and Gloria's long friendship with Seth Maddox and her reliance on him, over the years, for her livelihood.

Toward the end of the tape, Gloria said, "I wouldn't have ever thought I'd be telling on Seth, for he's been like a brother to me all my life, but what I know makes me too dangerous for Silver to leave alone. He will never let me live. It's all I can think about night and day, that, and that I have spent my entire life messing up other people's lives. It's all I ever did and I thought it was normal. I've been lost.

"And, if Silver doesn't kill me, I'll end up in jail, anyway, after Lomax Day and Clark Milloy get this to the law and the news, like I've instructed them, but it doesn't matter. I'm already in jail, and the only way I can get free, whether I live a day or a hundred, is to tell about Samone's killing in a way that the law can take notice and arrest Seth and Silver.

"As far as Josh Bridges, I didn't want him being murdered, but he was a son of a bitch. We were never married. It was just a front for the business.

"You're gonna say why didn't I just go tell the law all about this. I guess the truth is I am a coward to do this any other way, 'cause if I hadn't been, I'd have already left this whole thing a long time ago and lived right. But I couldn't get out. Seth would have never let me."

At the bottom of the transcript was an acknowledgement that met with statutory requirements. It was typed up on Lomax Day's letterhead, executed by Clark Milloy, Milloy Tapes, Inc., and notarized by a notary in Milloy's office where the taping occurred. It said, in part, that at the request and direction of Gloria Jenkins, Milloy had taped and transcribed the contents of the tape and that he did not have personal knowledge of any of the statements made by Gloria Jenkins in the tape/transcript or know the truth or veracity of the information in the Gloria Jenkins tape/transcript, but he had personally made the tape and transcribed it and each was a true and accurate depiction of what Gloria Jenkins had said and he would release the tape and transcript pursuant to Gloria Jenkins' directions, for justice to be done.

*****

Though it was not evident from the transcript, Gloria had been sobbing at the end of the tape.

And, though neither the tape nor the transcript reflected it, Clark Milloy's eye twitch, which always kicked in when he was nervous, was overly active during the taping. After he completed the taping, he confronted Gloria, whom he'd never met before until she hired him for the work. "Ma'am, I can't sit on this. It's life or death stuff."

She nodded in agreement. "Yes sir, it is; that's why I've requested you release the tape and transcript to the news on September 15. But, if you release any information of any kind prior to then, Seth will kill me, himself; plus, nobody will believe you on your word alone, and, even though I will need you to sign this signature card for the safe-deposit box where a copy of the tape and transcript will be available to you, I will not drop the signature card off at the bank until closing time on September 14, so prior to the fifteenth it'll only be your word, no proof, and Seth Maddox'll kill you, too."

Gloria patiently waited on him to sign the card and type the transcript, the speed of his eye twitch increasing. She personally delivered all the packages to the bank boxes she'd already rented and to Lomax Day, with her instructions to him.

*****

Unexpectedly, that evening, Milloy told his wife, "I'm worn out from working. You and me need to take us a vacation this fall, after September 15. I have some important business that day, but I'd like to be packed and us go on over to my brother's cabin on the Coosa River in Alabama for a spell. Whatcha think about that?"

She asked Milloy if he was okay. He was a workaholic and they had not taken a vacation since they'd been married. Also, though Milloy never drank that much, he began keeping a beer in one hand all the time.

His wife remarked to him later that week, "Sweetheart, you've got to see a doctor about that eye twitch. I've never seen it this bad."

"It'll be fine," he said.

*****

In addition to the tape and transcript, there were two manila envelopes in box #506. Envelope #1 contained photos: Samone Sims sitting on Gloria's deck and one with her right arm around him, her left out holding the camera on them; Josh Bridges and Gloria Jenkins sitting together on a swing in a park during the time they were married; and Seth Maddox and Silver M. Conway at a kitchen table.

On the back of each of the photographs, penned in the same handwriting that Renee had seen on the pink note and red envelope left in her mailbox, were the descriptions of the persons in them and the occasions.

Envelope #2 was bulky. It contained a thousand $100 bills. On the outside of the envelope, written in the same handwriting Renee had seen on the pink notecard and the red envelope were the words, "My gift to Renee and Janie. Not enough, but all lawful money."

Renee fainted. Charlie moved her to the sofa in Carl Rather's private office.

Deputy James grabbed the contents of box #506 and carried the treasure trove to the sheriff, waiting behind the bank. He took custody of it.

"I don't know what of this a court will let the DA use in a trial, Sheriff Trailor, but there's probable cause in here for a grand jury," Deputy James said.

"I'm headed to the DA right now, Deputy James."

Deputy James returned to Carl Rather's office to find Renee, pale and sitting up. Eventually, with Charlie's and Mr. No-Wobbler's help, she stood.

"You all right, Renee?" Deputy James asked.

"I am. In one way, it's no more than I expected. But, now that I know it, I realize that thinking it is one thing and knowing it is another. But, I'm okay, and though it sounds crazy, somehow, I feel a load lifted," she said.

"I took the contents of the box to Sheriff Trailor, Renee. He has custody now. And, as he left, he told me he was carrying everything directly to the District Attorney's Office."

Renee nodded and began to cry. "It's gonna have Samone spread around everywhere, isn't it, Deputy Jones? And us, Janie and me? In the papers. On the radio. In the news."

Deputy James did not respond. Neither did Charlie.

Renee took a deep breath and remembered last night's dream and Samone's instructions to her in the dream: "It's okay. Do what you need to do. Let Charlie help you."

She sat down again, a far away look in her eyes. "A year ago, I was just the widow of a man who had committed suicide."

Charlie put his arm around her.

"I guess a person's world has to completely collapse before they understand the value of it," she said.

The deputy looked at her. "You can get through this," she said.

Charlie kept holding her up.

Carl Rather stepped into the room and asked, "Can I be of any help?"

"Yes, Mr. Rather, thank you," Deputy James replied. "Please keep it in confidence that we were all here today. I think the law will be able to get its job done easier that way."

"No problem whatsoever," Rather replied. He showed them out the side door of his office.

*****

Charlie sat with Renee that afternoon and let her cry. He listened to her say whatever she wanted to say.

She wiped her nose. "You are a good friend, Charlie. I hate to ask you to do this, but would you please sit here and let me sleep? I don't want to be alone this afternoon."

"I will, Renee."

She went to her bedroom and closed the door and got into her bed and slept through supper and on into late morning the next day.

Charlie made Janie's supper and got her to bed and found a sheet to make his own bed on the sofa again, but his sleeping there was different that time. And he dreamed of Sam carrying a big red shoebox. Sam smiled at him and patted him on the back, as a great horse-drawn carriage appeared carrying a potato chip bag, which was holding the reins of several horses. Sam lifted the potato chip bag from the carriage and handed it to Charlie. It was announced through a loudspeaker that the potato chip bag was an important medicine to cure the world's ills. Sam departed, and, as he stepped over mountains toward the ocean, he waved to Charlie. "It is in your hands. Take care of everything, Charlie." They closed their school lockers and walked down the hall together. Renee appeared carrying Clem and joined them, and Janie popped up in front of the foursome, smiling.

Charlie woke.

*****

After Vorene testified before the grand jury, Sheriff Bill walked her to her truck. She stood there awkwardly, like she wanted to say something. She reached up quick and hugged his neck, grinning a lovely toothless grin.

"My papa was right, Sheriff Trailor. Wish he coulda seen me today going in there and telling what helped my sister."

"Aw, he saw, Vorene, and he's somewhere whittling and grinning about it," Sheriff Bill said. He looked her straight in the eyes and said, "Vorene, I want you to get on out of Gargagun and go straight home. Keep this quiet. Some of my folks are going to follow you to make sure you get there okay. But you need to be careful. Then, there'll be trials ahead. I don't expect any guilty pleas. Are you up to all of that?"

Her eyes twinkled with courage, and the gap in her teeth looked beautiful. "Sheriff, you can count on me long as the Lord lets me breathe."

"Well, I want you breathing for a long time."

Water trickled down her face. She reached in her bosom and pulled out a pink flowered handkerchief and began wiping her face.

The sheriff dropped his head to give her some privacy, thinking how the Lord sure did a good day's work creating Vorene.

She cranked the pickup.

He said, "Vorene, tell your brother-in-law that the charges have been dropped against him. That he and his wife can come and go wherever and however they please. Won't anybody in Gargagun be bothering 'em."

"Thank you, Sheriff Trailor." She tucked the pink flowered handkerchief back inside her bosom, pushed the straight shift up into reverse, and rolled the pickup out of the parking space into the street, the sheriff motioning her when the street was clear. She steered her pickup south back to Cairo.

As an unmarked sheriff's vehicle pulled out behind Vorene, Clark Milloy edged his way down the courthouse steps to his car. "Whew, never thought I'd be glad to get a subpoena to testify in a court, but it sure feels good. Course, I can't say nothing about what I said there, to you, sweetheart," he told his wife, at his side.

"Clark," she said, tugging at his sleeve, "your eyes have stopped twitching."

*****

Silver had remained in jail without bond on the charges for rape, resisting arrest, attempted kidnapping, and assault of a public officer.

Aside from those charges, the grand jury indicted him for the murders of Josh Bridges, Samone Sims, and Gloria Jenkins, and the kidnapping of Gloria Jenkins.

The grand jury indicted Seth Maddox for the murders of Josh Bridges, Gloria Jenkins, and arson of a dwelling.

The feds opened an investigation of Seth Maddox's business operations and Max Tribling.

42.

THE CYCLE OF LIFE

"You'd be proud of me, Sam; I won't need to pull up my khakis tonight," Charlie said to the mirror. He was in a high-end men's clothing store on the corner across from Mac's Coffee Shop, where he'd come to buy new clothes, even a tie.

Mrs. Spear, the saleslady there, who'd known him since he was born, was amazed when he walked in and asked her for help. "Charlie, are you going somewhere to need new clothes?" she asked.

"Yes'm, I think I am," he replied. "Mrs. Spear, how many good shirts does a man need to stay looking decent?"

She laughed. "Well, Charlie, now that depends. Will you be able to wash clothes regularly on this trip?"

She believes I am actually taking a trip, he thought, realizing that he actually was leaving the world he'd lived in for over thirty years to travel a long distance into a way of life he wanted, but had not much knowledge about. "Yes'm, I'll be able to wash," he told her.

Mrs. Spear gave the matter some thought and said, "Well, Charlie, wherever you are going, you need to look good. I'll help you."

"Okay," he said, "but, suppose I was just staying put here in Gargagun, for a man like me, working at his art every day, and going out around town here, what do I need to look well dressed?"

"You need the pants you're trying on that I am going to alter for you and about half a dozen more and some good shirts. Find your size and tell me what you don't like, color wise, and I'll pick out the shirts for you. Can you come by later and pick everything up?" she asked, the measuring tape dangling around her neck, swishing back and forth as she talked and pulled on his pants legs to assure they hit his foot at the right length. She pinned the pants up. "Give this a look in the mirror, Charlie, if you will," she said, standing back, her head cocked to one side.

"Perfect," he said. "I like the pants and the length."

"Good. I do, too."

"Mrs. Spear, I need an outfit to wear tonight. Can I pick these pants and a shirt up in an hour or so?"

"You sure can, baby," she said. "About three o'clock."

She smiled like she was in on a secret as Charlie departed, and before his feet hit the sidewalk outside, she called Mrs. Mabel and spent a considerable part of the time that it took her to hemstitch the pants cuffs praising her for bringing Renee and Charlie together.

*****

When Renee answered the door, she looked like a peach.

"My God, you look beautiful, Renee," Charlie said. He got all flustered, but he did manage to say, "Here are the cookies and the bread and the wine. I'm not much into wine; I don't know what is what. The man at the store said you'd like this."

"It will be delicious," Renee said.

She could not believe her eyes. This man was not the bedraggled Charlie that she'd always known. His pants fit perfectly. They were creased like the steel blade of a knife. His shirt was pressed, and his new belt looked made to match what he was wearing.

"I hope you are not going to be angry with me," she said. "Ashley insisted on taking Janie tonight. Mother hasn't seen her in a while and Ashley wanted to let her spend the night there."

"The brownies will hold for her, Renee. I'm glad we will be able to sit and talk. How has Janie done after learning the truth about Sam's not coming back?"

"She's taking it well, Charlie. Thank you for helping me talk with her. She told me last night that she had decided, anyway, even before we told her, that he was being very slow about coming home and she figured he'd likely gone on to heaven, since her friend's uncle didn't come back and that's where they said he was."

Charlie smiled.

Renee continued, "Before I could explain, she said, 'That's good. I love him there or here. Do you think, though, Mommy, that he still loves me?'"

"What did you tell her, Renee, about Sam's loving her?"

"I told her that he would never stop loving her or being with her no matter where he was. Janie said back to me, 'I know, Mommy, he visits me sometimes.'"

Charlie felt a shiver. Renee saw it and handed him the bottle of wine and a corkscrew. Charlie uncorked the wine and poured them each a glass. When he handed Renee her glass, he said, "I know what Janie means; he visits me sometimes, too, Renee. I feel him around."

"I know. He's stayed with us through this." And then, what had always bothered her about what Samone had said years ago about Charlie popped out: "Charlie, did you really suggest to Samone that he take Sharon to the homecoming dance?"

"What?" he asked and sat up on the edge of his seat. "What are you talking about, Renee?"

"That's the only thing I've ever held against you, Charlie," she said, and then she paused and her smile faded, "except, of course, your keeping the Gloria Jenkins thing from me."

Charlie knew that was bound to come and they had to wade through it. He said, "Renee, I knew next to nothing about Gloria Jenkins, and I only learned about her the day before we lost Sam. I never had a chance to get enough information from him to even begin to understand what the truth was, myself. So, I surely was not about to hurt you by bringing up something so serious about which I really had no actual knowledge. I would never hurt you like that." His eyebrows dropped. And he sat silent, vulnerable, beautifully open.

The realization of Charlie's kindness slapped her and she said, "I'm sorry, Charlie; I was mean to you." She was ashamed.

"No, you weren't mean. You were hurt. And afraid."

"We'll get through this, Charlie."

"We will get through this, Renee. That you can count on."

But Renee couldn't leave the Sharon matter alone. She said, "Well, you should know, Charlie, that Samone said that you told him that he should take Sharon to the homecoming dance. Did you?"

"Heavens no, Renee. Sam made up Sharon. I would never have suggested he take her around the block, much less to the homecoming dance."

"So, he made that up?"

"Yeah, he made it up to try to seem worldly, so you'd go with him to the dance."

They both laughed.

Charlie had never expected to laugh about anything with Renee that night. He grabbed the good fortune, lifted his wine glass, and said, "Cheers! To Sam and his not taking Sharon to the dance and to us."

"Cheers back, Charlie." Renee felt understood. It was exactly the opposite of how she'd felt back there years ago chopping onions and feeling left out. How had she changed that much? She said, "You have a new outfit, don't you, Charlie? I like it a lot. Pants look nice."

Charlie could never remember anyone in his entire life telling him his clothes looked nice. "Thank you, Renee. Mrs. Spear helped me pick out some things; I've let myself go for so long. You've made me realize that."

"What do you mean, Charlie?" she asked, truthfully not knowing.

Charlie set the wine glass on the coffee table and decided it was time to start coming to terms with what had been and what was and do his best to do it all without screwing up. "Being with you, Renee, has made me realize how alone I've been and that I—we—need companionship."

Renee just looked at him, startled. Her face felt hot. He wasn't telling her anything she didn't know. She had just been afraid to know it until he said it to her in words. Somehow, all the commas in the world that she had ever lived behind were, in his speaking those simple words, erased.

Charlie continued, "Oh, I get companionship with my cartoons, the Clem character, and all the other characters I draw and write about every day, Renee, but I've been cloistered all my life, just dawdling around."

"Dawdling around! I don't think so, Charlie. You certainly have not dawdled around the past several months. I couldn't have made it without you."

"Thank you, Renee."

*****

After supper, Charlie did the dishes.

Renee insisted that he wear an apron. "You can't mess up those wonderful new slacks with dishwater," she told him. He smiled.

Renee and Mr. No-Wobbler sat in the kitchen with him; Charlie and Renee talked nonstop. The last dish dried and in the cabinet, Charlie hung the apron on the cabinet knob and hugged her neck. "You're a good cook, Renee. Sure enjoyed supper, the food, but the company was the best I've ever had. Get you some sleep. I will check on you tomorrow."

She hugged his neck at the front door and told him, "You are a smart, kind man, Charlie. Thank you for everything. I do not know what I would do without you."

She sat in the living room and listened to Charlie back his sedan out of the drive, thinking how he seemed to be doing it that night with more precision than ever before. She crawled into bed and fell into a deep, satisfying sleep. She dreamed of Charlie. It was a dream that she could not see. There was no action. It was a feeling. A feeling that simply comforted her.

*****

Charlie lay awake listening to the stillness. "Sam," he said out loud, "you surely picked a wonderful woman to be your wife; she's stealing my heart."

*****

Early morning came on a streaking of light that crept up into the grime inside the tiny jail, like it was ferreting out something in the old building.

The jail keeper was slow getting breakfast to the prisoners, pushing the food cart into the hallway, yelling back to Pete, the young man who helped her, "Come on in and let's get these folks fed. We can't take all day."

Pete walked past the cart with the keys and began passing out the trays. At the next to the last cell, he stopped. Stood there. Frozen. Mute.

"What's the matter, Pete?" the jail keeper asked.

"He's dead. Hung himself with his own pants. That Silver man is dead."

*****

They let Seth Maddox out in chains for the funeral. Nobody showed, except him and a preacher, but over beyond the boxwoods stood a woman and a man watching the emptiness of it. The woman held onto a red cane. The man held onto the woman.

After the preacher read the Twenty-Third Psalm out into the space of the place, Seth, unaware of what had been read or of how they'd ended up there with somebody reading a Bible over Silver, clanged toward the patrol car for the ride back to his cell. He asked the deputy who'd brought him to the burial site if he knew who those two strangers were, standing over there watching Silver's pine box being lowered into the soil.

"Looks to me like that woman said he raped her. And some man that was a friend of her husband."

Seth Maddox stopped hobbling toward the patrol car and stood and looked at them from the distance, though, with his cataracts, he could barely make out their faces. He said to the deputy, "If Silver hadn't had him no desires 'bout that woman, there, I guess he'd still be alive and free and me a free man, too. He wouldn't ever listen."

Charlie and Renee watched the patrol car creep down the gravel road out of the graveyard. The man in the backseat was crying.

"Renee, Silver will never harm you anymore. That is over. Now, we are going to learn to live with its having happened and live past it." He knew they didn't yet understand what all that meant. But that was okay. They had the rest of their lives to learn to understand it.

When Charlie dropped Renee off, Janie came running to the door, Ashley trailing behind her.

"Look what I found. Look what I found," Janie said. She held out an enormous warty bullfrog.

"Is that Clem, Renee?" Charlie asked, his heart racing, remembering his own words to Sam that day: "Ain't it the biggest bullfrog you've ever seen, Sam? Wartiest, too. What you talkin' about warty. Com'ere, help me trap him, Sam."

Renee looked in closer at the throbbing frog.

But before she could answer, Janie asked, "Can I keep him, please?"

"Yes, Charlie," Renee said. "If it's not Clem, it's his kin."

"Does that mean I can keep him?" Janie asked, again. "I can keep him?"

"Yes, Janie, you can keep him," Renee said.

Charlie bent down and patted the bullfrog and said to Janie, "I have the perfect red shoebox for him to live in."

"A red shoebox? Oh, yippee," Janie said, jumping up and down.

Charlie winked at Renee.

Renee smiled.

The bullfrog croaked.

CPSIA information can be obtained
at www.ICGtesting.com
Printed in the USA
LVOW12s1034211216
518204LV00001B/41/P